the first nove

"Heartfelt. . . . Readers will eagerly await the next novel in Fox's series after reading this poignant romance."
—*Booklist*

"A fun, sassy, well-written, hysterical, heartfelt, and entertaining book." —Fiction Vixen Book Reviews

"Refreshing. . . . This was a great book that had me laughing out loud." —Night Owl Reviews

"A cute, funny, fast-paced romantic novel filled with humor [and] heartwarming moments . . . a great read on a cold night in front of a warm fire."
—Manic Readers

"Addison Fox charmed the heck out of me with her first Alaskan Nights novel. I cannot wait to return to the wonderful town of Indigo, Alaska."
—Romance Junkies

"Steamy encounters . . . keep the blood pumping all the way to a sweet ending." —*Publishers Weekly*

"[A] fun, sexy story." —The Romance Dish

"Fox does a fantastic job. . . . The characters are dynamic and interesting." —*Romantic Times*

continued . . .

"An exciting series."   —Risqué Reviews

"[A] superb . . . urban romantic fantasy."
                                   —Genre Go Round Reviews

Warrior Ascended

"[A] powerful romance."   —*Publishers Weekly*

"[A] blast to read . . . kept me turning the pages until I finished it."   —Errant Dreams Reviews

"Fox debuts with a strong start to the Warriors of the Zodiac series . . . [a] powerful romance."
                                        —*Publishers Weekly*

"This new series puts a delightful twist to the Greek gods and the myths surrounding them. Each character has [his or her] own depth and talents that will keep you turning the pages and begging for more. A great start to a promising paranormal series!"—Fresh Fiction

"Promise[s] plenty of action, treachery, and romance!"
                                        —*Romantic Times*

Also by Addison Fox

Come Fly With Me

An Alaskan Nights Novel

Addison Fox

A SIGNET ECLIPSE BOOK

SIGNET ECLIPSE
Published by New American Library, a division of
Penguin Group (USA) Inc., 375 Hudson Street,
New York, New York 10014, USA
Penguin Group (Canada), 90 Eglinton Avenue East, Suite 700, Toronto,
Ontario M4P 2Y3, Canada (a division of Pearson Penguin Canada Inc.)
Penguin Books Ltd., 80 Strand, London WC2R 0RL, England
Penguin Ireland, 25 St. Stephen's Green, Dublin 2,
Ireland (a division of Penguin Books Ltd.)
Penguin Group (Australia), 250 Camberwell Road, Camberwell, Victoria 3124,
Australia (a division of Pearson Australia Group Pty. Ltd.)
Penguin Books India Pvt. Ltd., 11 Community Centre, Panchsheel Park,
New Delhi - 110 017, India
Penguin Group (NZ), 67 Apollo Drive, Rosedale, Auckland 0632,
New Zealand (a division of Pearson New Zealand Ltd.)
Penguin Books (South Africa) (Pty.) Ltd., 24 Sturdee Avenue,
Rosebank, Johannesburg 2196, South Africa

Penguin Books Ltd., Registered Offices:
80 Strand, London WC2R 0RL, England

First published by Signet Eclipse, an imprint of New American Library,
a division of Penguin Group (USA) Inc.

First Printing, November 2012
10 9 8 7 6 5 4 3 2 1

PUBLISHER'S NOTE
This is a work of fiction. Names, characters, places, and incidents either are the
product of the author's imagination or are used fictitiously, and any resemblance to actual persons, living or dead, business establishments, events, or
locales is entirely coincidental.
    The publisher does not have any control over and does not assume any re-
sponsibility for author or third-party Web sites or their content.

ALWAYS LEARNING   **PEARSON**

For Audrey
You smile and the world is brighter.

Chapter One

Grier Thompson lined up the champagne flutes in neat, even rows. Her CPA's heart gloried in the precise organization and order to be found in the close attention to detail. By her calculation, it would take about three and a half bottles of bubbly to fill all the flutes to properly ring in the new year.

The sounds of her mother's annual New Year's Eve bash swelled from the other side of the swinging kitchen door as she poured glass after glass, but the happy laughter only pushed her further into her own gloomy thoughts. She'd believed coming home for the holidays would be just the thing to shake her out of the doldrums, but unlike her accurate champagne estimate, she'd sorely miscalculated this trip.

Without warning, a barrage of images from the previous New Year's Eve assailed her. She'd attended the same party and smiled and laughed with all the people she'd known for years, a bright diamond sparkling on her left hand and a smart, handsome fiancé by her side.

God, so much had changed in the ensuing twelve months.

The fiancé she'd looked forward to marrying was no longer a part of her life.

The accounting firm where she'd excelled had abandoned her without so much as a good-bye.

And the father who'd ignored her for her entire life had come calling in the form of a contested inheritance in the far-flung reaches of Alaska.

"And now you've got an annoying case of self-pity to boot," she mumbled to herself as she reached for a glass. "Which is about as appealing as an infection."

"What did you say, darling?" The door swung open to reveal her mother's oldest and dearest friend, Monica, as she floated into the kitchen, a surprisingly bright swath of feathers adorning the crown of her head. "I heard you talking about an unpleasant matter?"

Grier almost choked on her sip of champagne as she glanced quickly around the kitchen. "Oh, it's nothing." Her eyes alighted on one of the bottles. "Just muttering about that last cork. What a beast it was."

"Of course, darling." Monica's bright blue gaze was sharp and radiated understanding, but she said nothing more as she reached for a large tray stacked on the far counter. "I thought you could use some help with the champagne. The natives are getting restless out there."

Grier glanced at the clock and saw she had less than ten minutes to go until the new year.

An unexpected wave of anticipation swamped her, even as she knew her life was so far from figured out, she might as well have been standing on Fifth Avenue, naked and wearing a sign: WILL WORK FOR ANSWERS.

Yet that stubborn spark of hope persisted.

Last year she thought she had it all figured out, and through the ensuing months she'd come to realize she understood almost nothing.

But she did understand *herself* a hell of a lot better and that had to count for something.

Monica handed Grier one of the two trays set aside for champagne and busied herself arranging glasses. "Your mother said your friend Sloan was up in Alaska with you."

A memory of her best friend bundled head to toe in a quilted coat made Grier smile. "It was nice to have her there for a few weeks."

"And she's getting married?" Although Monica's voice was casual, Grier sensed something she couldn't quite put her finger on hovering beneath the question. "To the town lawyer, right?"

"Yes, to Walker Montgomery."

"Isn't he your lawyer, too?"

Grier busied herself with her own tray, forcing Monica to ask the questions. "He is."

"How's that all going? You know your mother—she doesn't say much. I swear, she's been rattling on about this party for a month and there just hasn't been room to talk about anything else. I've never been so glad to ring in a new year."

Do I ever know my mother, Grier thought to herself. Patrice Thompson was a piece of work. One of New York's most well-established blue bloods—"Patty-cakes" to all who knew and loved her—she wouldn't deign to discuss anything that delved deeper than surface matters. Or involved complicated emotions. Or even remotely indicated she and her daughter had a family secret. No, she would never touch such a potential scandal—even if it left her at odds with her only daughter.

"It's moving slowly."

Monica's smile was comforting when she spoke. "A side product of all that cold weather?"

The champagne flutes sat in tidy rows on her tray, but Grier still fiddled with them to make the rows perfect. "More like a half sister who doesn't want me there and who's contesting the will."

"Grier." Monica's concerned tone boiled over to something unmistakably possessive as she pulled her into a hug. "I had no idea."

Grier couldn't ignore the warmth—or the comfort—of the embrace that enveloped her even through the cool sequins of Monica's dress. "Of course not. It's not like Mom to share that sort of thing."

"Your mother is reserved, darling. You know that."

It was an oft-repeated phrase throughout her childhood and Grier couldn't help but hear it as a cop-out. "Reserved" was an excuse, a way of interacting with people that allowed a person to skip over the hard parts of life with a stoic demeanor and an unwillingness to acknowledge anything was wrong.

A loud ding broke the moment as the buzzer on her phone sounded. She and Monica turned at the same time to look at where it lay on the counter.

Suddenly Grier was swamped by a new emotion as

she read the text that had appeared on the smooth screen.

WISHING YOU A HAPPY NEW YEAR. WHEN YOU GET BACK TO INDIGO WE NEED TO PICK UP WHERE WE LEFT OFF. I'M NOT WALKING AWAY, GRIER.

A sly smile lit Monica's face and Grier knew she'd seen the message. "That's a rather bold way to wish someone a happy new year."

Grier reached for the phone and turned it facedown on the counter. "It's nothing."

Monica's smile only grew broader. "You sure about that? Because that sounds like unfinished business to me. And I've found in my lengthy observations of the males of our species that unfinished business is a rather enjoyable pastime."

"It's really nothing."

"Actually, my dear"—Monica reached over and ran a hand down her back—"that blush riding high on your cheeks suggests otherwise. But I also understand the need to keep a secret or two."

When Grier didn't say anything, Monica added, "It also seems like a lovely way to ring in a new year. Text messages full of promise and, if I'm not mistaken, perhaps passion and determination."

With that, Monica picked up her tray of champagne and headed through the swinging doors and into the party. Grier reached for the phone, intent on putting it into her pocket before grabbing the tray, but couldn't resist one more glance at the message.

I'M NOT WALKING AWAY, GRIER.

Mick.

On a soft sigh, Grier followed Monica's path through the swinging doors. She couldn't quite muster up the same degree of revelry as the other partygoers, but she had to admit that her spirits were higher than when she'd walked into the kitchen to pour the champagne.

After the year she'd had, she barely thought herself capable of feeling anything. Yet just the thought of him—all six feet two inches of rugged Alaskan male—made her body quiver as something close to anticipation hummed in her veins.

He was the one thing she missed from her stay in Indigo, and even after time away and the distance between them, her powerful response to him had her body growing warm and her breath catching in her chest.

A loud burst of laughter interrupted her thoughts and she lifted her champagne flute to match the other partygoers.

If she touched the phone in her pocket as the entire room screamed, "Happy New Year!" well, that would be her little secret.

That stubborn little spark of hope lit once more.

Perhaps the new year could hold something worth looking forward to—something more than the heartache of sorting through the mess her father had left for her in Indigo.

Maybe it was time Grier Thompson, New York blue blood, acted on a bit of her reckless Alaskan roots.

*   *   *

The first thing Grier saw as she stepped off the elevator the following morning was Sloan. She was perpetually stunning, with a long, lean, willowy frame and blond hair that artfully fell around her shoulders. Grier knew if she didn't love her so much, she'd hate her on sight.

Just on principle.

Fortunately, she not only loved Sloan McKinley to pieces, but she was exceedingly happy to see that her friend's normally ethereal beauty had morphed into something even lovelier.

She held the beauty of a woman in love.

The object of her best friend's affection, Walker Montgomery, moved up behind Sloan to reach for Grier's bags. "Happy New Year, Grier." He bussed her cheek with a quick kiss before eyeing the roll-aboard suitcase and oversized tote.

"This is all you have?"

"Yep." She squeezed Sloan's hand before dropping it to turn toward Walker. "Let me guess. There are at least four pieces of luggage in that car out there"—she pointed toward the front door of her mother's apartment building—"as well as her full carry-on allotment."

"Are you actually siding with him?" Sloan crossed her arms. "What happened to the unbreakable bonds of sisterhood? Besides, I had to bring some stuff back for the move."

"Because Armani is so incredibly necessary in the middle of Alaska," Walker muttered in a whispered voice that no one missed.

"Exactly," Sloan hollered at his retreating back before turning toward Grier with a big smile. "If he weren't so mind-numbingly hot, I know I'd have a better comeback than that."

Grier wrapped an arm around Sloan's waist as they started for the door. "Your brains are just scrambled."

"I'm not that far gone." Sloan squeezed back before dropping her arm to walk through the door the doorman held wide.

"Oh, I don't know—your lipstick is awfully smudged, suggesting an arduous kissing session on the car ride over here."

Sloan's gasp only made the high five Grier shared with her doorman, Bart, that much sweeter as he followed them both out onto the sidewalk.

Bart helped Walker deal with the luggage and within moments they were headed for the airport.

"Your mom didn't come down. Is everything all right?"

The complete absence of any attempt to couch her question in a casual offering was appreciated and Grier led with a small sigh. "We said our good-byes this morning. She's been seeing someone and he invited her up to Vermont for a few days of skiing."

"How charming."

"Sloan." Walker nudged her knee.

"Don't worry about it, Walker." Grier waved a hand. "Sloan's tone always smacks of judgment and derision when she talks about my mother. And since she's the only person I know who will actually be honest about it, I can't quite fault her for it."

"It's not judgment and derision," Sloan said, jumping in. "It's just annoyed puzzlement. And it's not like my mother's a giant picnic, either. I just think Pattycakes could be a wee bit more sympathetic to your plight at the moment."

Grier didn't miss Walker's narrowed eyes, but he kept his mouth firmly shut. "But if she were sympathetic, it would mean acknowledging she had sex with an Alaskan pipeline worker and I was the result."

"Has she even talked about it?"

"Nope." Grier played with the small fringe on the border of her sweater. "You'd think I was immaculately conceived."

"So for the last eight days you've gotten nothing out of her?"

"She's locked up tighter than a drum and that's after several sessions of beating around the bush and two very pointed requests for information."

Since she'd been tired of talking about her mother for the majority of her adult life, Grier leaped on the topic that would most assuredly switch the tone of the conversation.

"Did you set the date?"

Sloan's adoring glance toward Walker gave away the answer before either of them spoke. "We ultimately settled on two dates. There's no way half of Scarsdale's headed to Alaska for a wedding. Besides, I like the residents of Indigo far too much to ask them to house the equivalent of rich aliens for a week. So we're doing it here. Labor Day weekend."

"What no one here knows, however"—Walker

leaned forward on a conspiratorial whisper—"is that the real ceremony will take place in Indigo over the Fourth of July."

"Your mother knows this?"

"Hell no." Sloan flopped back against the seat in mock horror. "She thinks she and my father are coming up for Walker's annual family reunion."

"I like it. Sneaky yet full of sweet and romantic overtones."

"Walker and I get the wedding we want and my mother gets the wedding she wants."

"It's terrifyingly brilliant." Grier smiled as Walker wrapped his arm around her friend and pressed a light kiss to her temple.

The confines of the car suddenly felt a bit too small and Grier found herself staring out the window as the driver took them across the bridge toward Queens. Her mind drifted to Mick—a situation that happened all too often—and she wondered what it would be like to see him again.

They'd barely spoken since early December, both keeping their distance since the night he caught her outside her father's house, attempting to break in.

Unbidden, her thoughts filled with the powerful sensations she had felt that night. The feel of his large body boxing her in against the door and the understanding embedded deep in those clear blue eyes of his.

Her father's house was off-limits to both her and her half sister, Kate, until their joined inheritance was sorted out, but she'd thought to sneak in a private moment and look around. Even without her saying anything, Mick had understood.

He'd also stopped her from actually breaking and entering, but he hadn't been able to stop the frustrated tears that had her running from her father's house.

And from Mick.

In the ensuing weeks, they'd seen each other at a town hall meeting as well as at Walker's grandmother's holiday tree trimming, and Grier had thought maybe they could put what had happened behind them and move on. Just because they'd seen each other naked one night didn't mean they couldn't be cordial and pleasant to each other.

And then he'd gone and sent that text on New Year's Eve and all her plans for easygoing and casual flew out the window.

Because no matter what she said and no matter how hard she tried to tell herself a relationship with Mick O'Shaughnessy was a bad idea, she hadn't been able to stop herself from rereading that text message several times a day.

And she also hadn't been quite able to dismiss the thought that a relationship with Mick O'Shaughnessy was a very, very good idea.

Mick walked through his preflight routine, checking things off on his clipboard and making notes. He saw the slightest beginnings of wear on a few parts and wanted to get them ordered and installed before slight wear became a big problem in the middle of winter.

And he also scratched a reminder to put the fuel order in since Jack never managed to remember that one.

As if he'd conjured him up, Jack's large frame came into view as he rounded the side of the plane. "You put the fuel order in?" Mick asked.

A few shades of pink crept through Jack's five o'clock shadow. "No."

Mick waved his clipboard. "That's why I just made a note of it. I swear, you have our taxes in a fucking month early, but you can't remember that we actually need fuel to fly the planes."

"Yeah, well, Uncle Sam won't take too kindly to our ferrying passengers if we don't pay our taxes, so I suppose that makes us even."

Mick couldn't hold back the good-natured smile. "So long as you remember there's nothing to tax if we can't get the plane off the ground."

"I suppose that's why we're a good team."

"That we are. The best." Mick crossed the hangar toward a desk he kept in the corner and bent down toward the small fridge next to it. "You want anything?"

"Coke."

Mick grabbed two and crossed toward an old sofa that had seen about twenty Alaska winters and dropped down on a worn cushion. "I've got about a half hour until I need to leave, and you look like you've got something on your mind."

Mick had known the man for a long time. Jack had about eight years on him, but from the first summer Mick had worked for him in high school, they'd been like brothers. He'd seen Jack through his marriage to

Molly, standing up for him in the ceremony. They'd built a business together, and Mick had been there when Jack's world came crumbling down with Molly's cancer diagnosis and subsequent losing battle with the disease.

And now he had had the great good fortune of seeing his friend smile again since he started officially seeing Jessica McFarland.

"You're a crafty bastard, O'Shaughnessy. You don't miss a thing."

Mick took a long drag on his Coke. "So, what's up?"

"I've been doing a lot of thinking and I've talked to Jess about it a bit."

Mick simply waited and took another sip.

"And I'd like to spend more time with her. I was so busy building the business when Molly and I were first starting out that I missed out on a lot. And I don't want that to happen again, you know?"

Mick did know. He also knew that Jack had tirelessly taken on a substantial workload to expand their clientele, followed by an even more grueling one to buffer the loneliness after his wife died.

The man deserved a break. And it was time to start thinking about ways to expand their business that didn't take the two of them killing themselves.

"Funny you should mention it since I've been thinking similar things."

"You're not mad?"

"Are you telling me you're never getting into a plane again?"

"Hell no." Mick almost laughed at the affronted look

on his friend's face, but he also knew that shadow of horror in Jack's clenched jaw was the proof he needed that all would be well.

Once a pilot, always a pilot.

The love of flying got to a man—it gripped the gut like a living thing and refused to let go. He'd had it his whole life, so he knew the symptoms.

"All I'm saying is I'd like to slow down a bit. Maybe bring in another pilot or two. Or one pilot and someone to handle the books."

"Seriously, lover boy, you're preaching to the choir. I'm sick of being the one ordering fuel." Mick pointed to the clipboard he'd laid on the counter when he'd gotten the Cokes earlier. "And I'd love nothing more than to make a list of what I need and have an office manager who ordered them instead of making the calls myself."

Jack took the ribbing in stride. "I'm not the only one around here who's got a woman on the brain. It's not a very large secret that you're leaving in a few minutes to pick up Grier."

Mick shrugged. Although he knew as well as the next person small towns thrived on gossip, the endless chatter had grown abrasive over the holidays. "Walker and Sloan are on the plane, too."

"A minor detail no one's interested in."

"Funny how quickly the town's favorite son is old news."

Jack stood and pulled out a large pair of heavy work gloves. "You're a favorite son, too, Mick. It's amazing how often you choose to ignore that fact."

Mick didn't move until he heard the hangar door slam shut on a gust of wind. Only then did he stand and cross to the recycle bin and drop his empty can.

Getting all riled up about the fuel that kept Indigo running through the winter—and spring, summer and fall, for that matter—was useless. If his neighbors wanted to gossip about his interest in Grier, he couldn't stop them. Besides, he had far bigger things on his mind.

Like the woman who waited for him at the end of his next flight.

Grier stared out her window at the bright lights of Anchorage as the plane did a hard bank to the right. After miles of darkness, the lights were a welcoming beacon.

She was home.

Or at least what passed for home for another month. Six weeks, tops.

That had been Walker's latest estimate of how much longer it would take to clear up Jonas Winston's last will and testament.

Walker had been kind enough to give her an out the week before, suggesting she could stay in New York and allow him to handle the majority of the proceedings, with her presence necessary only once everything was finalized, but she had refused.

It was bad enough her half sister, Kate, had been the recipient of their father's love and affection for the first twenty-six years of her life. She'd be damned if she'd let the woman have easy access to Jonas's things while Grier sat four thousand miles away waiting for news.

The funny thing was, she acknowledged to herself

as she reached beneath her seat for her tote, it wasn't even Jonas's possessions she really cared about. She had a home; she certainly didn't need his.

What she did need were answers.

And some small piece of him she could keep.

Sloan smiled a groggy half grin from across the aisle. "You ready?"

"As I'll ever be."

Walker helped her collect her suitcase from the overhead and, as if time were on fast-forward, before she could blink she was filing out of the plane's side door.

The jet bridge was a short walk, but her gaze caught on one of the many tourism posters framed along the corrugated walls: INDIGO TRAVEL AND TRANSPORT.

Mick's company.

As if to simply reinforce the connection, the photo showed Mick and his partner, Jack, bookending the front propeller of one of their planes, broad smiles on their faces. Each sported shoulders like a football player, but where Jack had the heavier build of a grizzly bear, Mick was lean and rangy.

Not for the first time, Grier tried to grasp exactly what it was that made the men up here quite so appealing. It had struck her from the first moments she entered the small town of Indigo, Alaska. She'd assumed the men of Alaska would be hale and hearty. She hadn't counted on their being quite so lovable.

A couple of women behind her giggled and Grier tuned in to their conversation, pulling her attention from the poster as she continued moving down the jet bridge.

"Rachel said the men up here were good-looking."

"She didn't say they looked like Greek gods." Another giggle floated up. "I think we need to kick off our visit by supporting the local economy."

"Indigo Travel and Transport," her friend replied, and Grier didn't miss the light slap of a high five.

Sloan turned from where she walked a few paces ahead and reached for her hand.

"Come on," she whispered on a tight squeeze. "It'll be fine."

Grier took comfort in the support her friend always seemed to share with such simple, effortless ease.

And then the jet bridge ended and Grier suddenly realized she had a far bigger problem than misplaced jealousy over giggling singletons.

Mick O'Shaughnessy was waiting for her.

Mick fought the wave of nerves that dive-bombed his stomach as he waited for Grier to come out of the door to gate seven. He'd played the conversation in his head about fifty different ways since walking into the airport an hour ago and hadn't settled on anything.

"Hi." Yeah, a real smooth opener.

"Good to see you." What was he, a talk show host?

"Happy New Year." Only if he were Dick Fucking Clark.

And then there were no words, save one, as Grier walked through the door with Sloan and Walker.

Wow.

Mick lifted his hand in a wave to catch her attention and the rest of the airport faded away.

How had this happened?

He loved women. He loved their perspective and the way their take on the world around them was just . . . different from his. And unlike a lot of men he knew, he loved their company in bed or out.

But Grier Thompson was different.

She was . . . *so much more*, somehow. More interesting. More enticing. More compelling than anyone he'd ever met.

"Hi."

"Hi." He leaned down before he could stop himself and pressed a quick kiss on her cheek. The light scent of her filled his nose and the nerves flooding his stomach shifted into something a great deal more interesting.

Need. Desire. *And hunger*.

Walker slapped him on the shoulder and reached for his hand, the moment shattered in the wake of his friend's exuberance. Mick didn't miss the frustration that crossed Sloan's gorgeous cheekbones, and it was that slight acknowledgment that had him smiling and slapping Walker on the back as they embraced.

Damn, but he'd missed his friend—even if he was about as subtle as a freight train.

He reached for Sloan next, not surprised to hear the lightly whispered "sorry" as she hugged him.

"Good flight?"

A round of murmured "yes's" and they were off.

Mick reached for the handle of Grier's suitcase and pointed toward the herd of people heading down the corridor. "Baggage claim's that way."

"This is all I have."

Mick glanced down at the small roll-aboard in his grip and the large bag that sat on top of it. "But you were gone more than a week."

"I packed light."

"Oh."

The first smile he'd seen lit up her face. "You were expecting six pieces of matched Louis Vuitton?"

He couldn't hold back the grin, the last vestiges of nervous energy fading in the bright light of her smile. "Maybe only four."

Grier's smile brightened even further as something suspiciously like mischief alighted in the depths of her gray gaze. "Ask Sloan how many bags she brought."

Mick had spent far too many years with Walker and their other best friend, Roman, to ask a question so deliberately posed. With a broad smile for Sloan, he pointed in the direction of the claim area.

"I'm sure every piece is full of well-needed items."

"Ass kisser," Grier muttered as Sloan gifted him with a broad smile.

"Nope." Feeling lighter than he had in days, he draped a casual arm around Grier's shoulders and leaned down to whisper in her ear. "I'm just very, very smart."

Chapter Two

Grier tamped down on the rush of joy that assaulted her in waves from the base of her neck straight down her spine the moment Mick wrapped his arm around her. Although he had dropped his arm when they'd arrived in the baggage area, she could still feel the heavy weight of where his body had rested against hers. She could still smell his delicious scent—a mix of leather and fresh air that had her body reacting in needy hunger.

"That's quite a welcome," Sloan whispered as the men moved off to grab her bags. "And I'm suddenly quite pleased I packed half my apartment since it gives us a few extra minutes to talk."

"Oh please." Grier waved a hand. "That's not even half your closet."

"Shhh—that's our secret."

"And now you're just a liar as I know damn well Walker has actually seen your apartment."

"The apartment, yes. I won't let him within ten feet of my closet. And you're stalling."

"And you're making too much of this. Whatever else Mick O'Shaughnessy is to me, he is my friend."

"That man had his arm wrapped around you in a rather possessive grasp. It was way more than friendly. And those women from the plane who ogled his photo on the jet bridge"—Sloan pointed at them standing at the far side of the claim area—"haven't stopped giving you the evil eye. Even they can see there's something between you."

"He's a toucher."

"Not to me."

"Walker would beat him senseless."

"Grier, you know what I mean."

"I'm actually trying to ignore what you mean."

Sloan moved so Grier was forced to look at her and not the slow-moving baggage belt. "Why are you being so stubborn about this?"

"Hello, pot?"

"Grier, I'm serious."

"I'm serious, too, Sloan. I appreciate the concern, but there's nothing between Mick and me." Before her friend could object or call her on her bullshit, Grier clarified. "Nothing that can be acted on."

The men had Sloan's luggage and were headed back in their direction. "Now let's go collect your treasure trove of clothing and get going."

Before she could drag her own bag behind her, Sloan laid a hand on her arm. "Please, wait a sec. Look. I'll cut out the pushy shit if you'll promise me one thing."

"What's that?"

"Give him a chance. The two of you might surprise yourselves."

"Maybe it just looks like we fit on the surface."

"Or maybe it's real."

She'd never been very good at keeping things from Sloan and she was getting tired of defending a position she knew was rather flimsy, so Grier opted for the truth. "What if it's just a matter of history repeating itself?"

"He's not like Jason. He's nothing like him."

"Actually, I was talking about my mother and father."

The light that dawned brightly in Sloan's blue eyes let Grier know she'd finally gotten through.

"Some things just aren't meant to be, Sloan. And I'm living proof of that reality."

The flight to Indigo was short, and before Mick knew it, he was helping Walker drag Sloan's bags to the house while the women stayed in the warmth of his SUV.

"She wanted to bring six," Walker said on a heavy huff of air as he dropped one of the largest suitcases at his front door before digging in his pockets for his keys.

"Six suitcases? No shit?"

"Scout's honor." The keys jingled from the tip of Walker's fingers as he got the key in the lock. "You sure you don't want to come with us tonight? My grandmother said the more, the merrier."

"You guys enjoy. I know Sophie's eager to see you."

"You're practically her second grandson and you're definitely her favorite. Truth be told, I think she likes you more than she likes me."

Mick was surprised by how closely Walker's words matched Jack's earlier.

"Favorite son."

Brushing it off along with the painful reminder that his own father certainly didn't see him that way, Mick lifted his two bags and followed Walker into the entranceway. "Of course she does—she's got outstanding taste. But seeing as how my grandmother did her typical feast for Christmas and how Maggie out at the airstrip cooked her New Year's Day spread, all I can say is that it's your turn, buddy."

"Traitor," Walker muttered as he flipped a light switch.

"No, I'm a dutiful grandson who's already paid his holiday dues."

They headed back to the SUV and Mick wanted to laugh at the sight of Sloan struggling with her oversized carry-on tote. The besotted, sloppy smile that crossed his best friend's face was proof positive Walker's bitching about the suitcases was all for show as he stepped up to help her.

They all said a round of good-byes, cut short by the biting cold, and Grier turned on a wave to open the door to the passenger seat. Even in heavy layers of winter padding, she captivated him, her dark hair flowing down her back out of the wool hat that sat slightly askew on her head.

God, he had it bad.

There were about a million things he loved about his home, but winter attire wasn't one of them. Nevertheless, he'd accepted long ago that the women up here spent a good portion of the year dressed up like the Michelin Man, with sizable acres of wool and plaid to add color.

So how did she manage to make that heavy padding look sexy and adorable, all in one fell swoop?

Grier lifted a booted foot to step on the running panel beneath the door and the hard-packed snow caking her foot was slippery, catching her off-balance. He was already moving toward her to help her up into the car when her footing went out from under her and she tumbled back against him.

His chest took the impact of her fall and his arms wrapped around her to steady her. Unwilling to miss the fortuitous opportunity, Mick tightened his hold and leaned in toward her ear. "You okay?"

"Y-y-yeah. Sure."

He fought the overwhelming urge to bend down and kiss the exposed swath of skin at the base of her neck visible where her scarf parted, but he held himself back, whispering instead. "Positive?"

He saw heavy puffs rise into the air as her breathing turned shallow and felt his own ramp up in response.

"I'm fine. Really."

Shifting his hold to her elbow, he took her at her word and took a step back. "Let me help you up into the car."

"Thanks."

Mick crossed to his own side and climbed in. He could see the Indigo Blue from Walker's front door, which meant their time together was about to come to an end.

"Did you have a nice holiday?" The breathy overtones that had filled her voice only moments before were gone, floating away on the cold night air.

"It was good. My grandmother cooked a feast on Christmas that produced a week of excellent leftovers."

He got a small laugh at that, but she didn't say anything else as she stared out the window. "What about you?"

The lightest of sighs escaped her lips before she spoke. "The holidays were the usual—quiet and dignified. Except, of course, for my mother's annual New Year's Eve bash. It's quite the crush."

The image of Grier mixing it up with New York's blue bloods had his fingers tightening on the steering wheel. "Your mother likes to entertain?"

"She likes being the center of society's attention. Which is quite the opposite end of the spectrum from entertaining, truth be told."

"I can imagine." He couldn't, but Mick had pieced together a few comments from Walker and Avery along with his own observations. Although he really didn't know much about Grier's background, what he did know was that the bright and interesting woman sitting next to him had built those attributes pretty much all on her own merits.

"You didn't enjoy the party?"

"I never enjoy the party."

The words were out before he could stop them. "So why go?"

"I was home for eight days. It was a lot easier than

picking a fight. Besides, I didn't have any plans this year."

"Sloan and Walker were in the city."

Grier glanced up at him, a half smile filling her face. "And they were incredibly sweet to invite me to their evening of take-out food and wine, but they're so wrapped up in each other—as they should be—that I didn't want to intrude."

"That I can understand. Jack and Jessica spent the holiday slobbering all over each other. It would have been gross if it hadn't been so sweet." The porte co-chere came into view as Mick swung into the parking lot of the hotel.

"Is that a note of jealousy I detect?"

"About Jack and Jess?" At her nod, he kept going. "Not in the least. I'm happy for them. I just don't want to see it."

Grier did laugh at that, the light, breezy sound echoing through the car. "Point taken. Love is in the air."

His hand tightened on the handle of her roll-aboard. "Is it?"

"It certainly seems to be."

Grier winced at her overly bright tone, but refused to let the moment become heavy with innuendo. She couldn't overanalyze every word that came out of her mouth to Mick, no matter how nervous he made her.

And she certainly couldn't sit and analyze those crazy moments she'd spent in his arms when all she'd wanted to do was turn her head ever so slightly so she could capture his lips with hers. Or the strong, steady feel of his back pressed to hers that had her standing in the circle of his arms just a few moments more than necessary. They had shared one night together weeks ago, and she needed to get past it.

The real rub of it all, Grier knew, was that when she got right down to it, the man made her jumpy. Off-balance. Uncentered.

And she loved it.

Before she could dwell on it further, Mick pulled up to the hotel and turned to face her. His searching blue gaze softened as crinkles wrapped around the corners of his eyes, pulling her from her memories. "The grand-mothers are in their glory. Not only have Walker and Sloan and Jack and Jess hooked up, but they're taking credit for two more successful matches from the dinner dance at the end of the year."

Grier couldn't stop the bubble of laughter as the image of the town grandmothers took root. "Why do I have visions of them rubbing their hands together like a group of villainesses in a bad silent movie?"

"Don't think I haven't wondered over the years if the three grandmothers had formed a coven and were practicing witchcraft outside the Indigo city limits during a full moon."

An image of a sweet, gray-haired woman with bright blue eyes filled her mind's eye. "Your cute, incredibly charming grandmother doesn't strike me as the type."

"Oh, don't let that pleasant demeanor fool you. Mary O'Shaughnessy may be small, but she'd give a grizzly a run for its money. Add to it she's extra ornery when under the influence of Sophie and Julia, and I wouldn't bet against her. Those three take matchmaking very seriously."

Grier couldn't stop laughing as she unbuckled her seat belt. How was it possible that he made her deeply uneasy yet he was so easy to be with?

It was a question with no simple answers.

The hotel lobby glowed brightly as she stared out the windows. "It's nice to be back."

"Do you really feel that way?"

Grier turned back to face him. "Well, yeah."

"The town wasn't all that friendly to you when you arrived. That's saying something if you still like Indigo anyway."

"The town's incredibly charming. And no, people weren't all that friendly," she acknowledged, unable to lie. Those first few weeks had been more disorienting— and deeply disappointing—than she even wanted to admit to herself. "But everyone came around after Sloan showed up."

"Does that bother you?"

His curious tone stopped her up short. "Do you really care about this?"

"Yeah, actually. I do. I didn't think your initial reception in town was very fair. Still don't, but I am glad folks came around."

"It's a lot to ask of people. They've known Kate forever and I was the interloper."

His gaze drifted back to her. "You're Jonas Winston's daughter, not an interloper."

"Illegitimate daughter."

"You're his *daughter*, Grier. Don't let anyone diminish that, least of all yourself."

The earnest tone and hard set of his jaw lit a small spark of something she couldn't quite define. His conviction—his absolute belief in her—was heady. And it was something she'd never experienced from anyone other than Sloan.

As if he sensed the moment had gotten too tense, a broad smile cracked his face as his blue eyes found hers. "You're a keeper, Grier Thompson, and I'm damn glad you're here."

"Mick—" She broke off, not sure what to say, because she *was* glad to be here. With him.

And she didn't quite know what to do about it.

"Go ahead on in. I'll take care of your bags."

"Grier!" Avery's shriek echoed around the lobby of the Indigo Blue as she ran from behind the check-in desk to greet Grier, grabbing her in a huge bear hug. Mick stood off to the side, unable to hide his amusement at Avery's enthusiastic response to their arrival.

Grier took in the warm hug and squeezed back just as hard.

Oh, how she'd missed Avery Marks.

They'd known each other for only a short time—not even six weeks—but the woman had become as essential to her life as Sloan was.

A quick nip of gratitude filled her memories as she thought about her first month in Indigo. The chilly reception, with no support from anyone save Walker and his legal advice, had nearly done her in.

And now she was hugging her new friend as if they'd known each other for years, more at home with her than anyone she'd grown up with or knew in New York.

Avery turned to buss Mick's cheek with a quick kiss before dragging them both toward the hotel's large bar area. "Drinks are on me. I've missed you."

"You saw me yesterday," Mick teased her as they moved up toward the dark wood of the bar.

"Oh yeah, that's right. I had to use you as a stand-in so I could gossip with someone."

"Ooh. You've got juicies? Who's riding the gossip train now?" Grier smiled as she slid onto one of the heavy leather-covered stools that rimmed the edge of the bar, then reached for a handful of pretzels from a small silver dish. "I want to hear all about it."

Mick pointed toward the far side of the bar as Avery pulled on the tap for his beer. "That's my cue to go. I see Doc Cloud just came in, so why don't you pour me one for him, too? I think I'll engage in some gossip of my own."

Avery reached for another glass and deftly began curling it in her hands as it filled with bright amber liquid. "Discussing—oh, excuse me, *betting*—on this week's bowl games does not constitute gossip."

"Nah, but it's a hell of a lot more fun." Mick grabbed the two foaming beers off the counter, then leaned down to press a quick kiss on Grier's lips.

Grier felt her mouth drop into a small, shocked *O* of surprise as he pulled away. Once again, his rich, warm scent surrounded her and she could still feel the hard imprint of his lips against hers.

He deliberately didn't look back as he crossed the lobby to where Doc Cloud settled himself in a chair and she fought to close her mouth so she didn't look like a gaping fish.

"Do I even need to ask the question or is there a gigantic bubble above my head with words in it?" A wicked grin spread across Avery's face as she twisted the corkscrew in a bottle of Cabernet that Grier had become particularly fond of.

"First, you sound just like Sloan. And second, I had no idea he was going to do that."

"It didn't stop you from enjoying it."

Grier refused to respond for fear of digging a hole for herself she'd not be able to climb back out of.

She *had* enjoyed it.

That brief, possessive touch of his lips and the merry twinkle in his bright blue eyes had sent a shot of heat to her core that she'd likely be reliving long into the night.

"He's still crazy about you, you know," Avery added as she poured the rich red wine.

"Yeah."

"And . . . ?"

"And what, Avery? Nothing's changed."

"You mean you haven't turned over a new leaf for the new year?"

"And what new leaf would that be? The one that says I'll indiscriminately knock boots with the hot bush pilot until I go home again in four to six weeks? I don't think so."

"It's not indiscriminate if it's only one hot bush pilot."

"It doesn't change the four-to-six-weeks part." Grier reached for her wine. "Walker thinks it'll all be wrapped up by then."

"And then you're going to leave?"

Grier swirled the wine in her glass. "I've got a phone interview for a job tomorrow."

"Is it something you want?"

The question struck Grier with swift clarity and in that moment, all the reasons she and Sloan had come to care for Avery so quickly were clear.

"You're not upset?"

Avery laid a hand over hers, the show of solidarity and silent support a beacon Grier wanted to cling to.

"Of course not. I'm disappointed at the idea I won't see you all that often, but I want what's best for you. You're my friend and I want you to be happy."

"It's at a very well-respected accounting firm. It's not quite what I was doing before and it's nowhere near the partner track I was on, but it's something. Seeing as how my name's not exactly golden among the New York firms right now, I'm grateful for the opportunity."

Avery lifted her own wine and swirled it in the light, her actions casual and her voice low enough so the few patrons assembled around the bar wouldn't hear. "Why should your name be mud? From the little you've said, it was your ex's fault you were dismissed."

"Doesn't matter. I'm the reason his behavior was exposed. I'm damaged goods."

"You look pretty saucy from here."

"It's that fresh Alaska air."

Avery flashed another wicked grin. "I think it's the fresh Alaska men."

Grier risked a glance over her shoulder to where Mick and Doc Cloud sat in overstuffed chairs, engaged in comfortable conversation. She couldn't argue with Avery's point, no matter how many times she told herself she couldn't—or shouldn't—partake of the locals. There was *something* about this one particular man.

Mick had shed his leather jacket and she could see the heavy flannel shirt that covered his broad shoulders. Even when he was sitting, his coiled, rangy strength drew her attention so that she could barely see anything but him.

Uncomfortable with the renewed wave of heat that had her thick wool sweater suddenly feeling much too heavy, Grier shifted her gaze toward Doc Cloud. Despite his age, which she estimated to be about seventy-five, he had a hale and hearty attractiveness that was unusual this late in life. The doctor had an incredibly appealing competence and underlying strength.

Maybe there really was something in the Alaska air.

Or, she acknowledged to herself, maybe it was that people had different priorities than she was used to.

In Indigo, friendships didn't depend on how much money you made or who your friends were or whether you kept your mouth shut after watching your fiancé humiliate you.

Grier took a thoughtful sip of her wine as she allowed her gaze to continue to roam around the room. People she recognized—townsfolk she'd gotten to know over the last few months—sat in small conversation areas while a waitress worked the room, taking care of everyone.

She'd nearly turned back in her seat—more than ready to hear all of Avery's good gossip—when the front door of the Indigo Blue opened.

And her half sister, Kate, walked through the door.

Chapter Three

Kate Winston tugged at the neckline of her heavy sweater as she walked into the warm lobby of the Indigo Blue. She hadn't wanted to come out tonight, but Trina had insisted she make some attempt to be social. The holidays had been about as interesting as a root canal—and about as painful, too—and she hadn't done much socializing.

She certainly hadn't *felt* very social. Her father was gone and the holidays had been just as difficult as she'd known they would be.

But at least she'd made it through the first Christmas without him.

That now made Halloween, Thanksgiving and Christmas she'd passed, not to mention New Year's Day. If she took out the birthdays to come in January—hers and her father's—she could almost believe she was halfway through the first year of grieving.

Almost.

"Oh shit." Kate heard Trina's not so lightly whispered curse. "I didn't know."

Kate didn't need to look across the room to know

what had brought on the sudden wash of silence that had hushed every patron in the bar.

Her half sister, Grier, was back in town.

On a soft sigh, Kate crossed the room toward an empty set of chairs that formed a small conversation area. "Come on, Trina. Let's grab a seat."

She'd be damned if she'd run away. This was *her* home.

"We can leave if you want and go to Maguire's."

Kate didn't miss Grier's gaze as it caught her from across the room before the woman turned back around on her barstool. A quick spark fired in her blood as the low hum of conversation started up again. "No."

"Look at her over there," Trina added, warming up to the subtle battle of wills. "Thick as thieves. You'd think Avery would have more respect for the locals instead of taking the side of an interloper."

"Are we really going to have this conversation again?"

"Yes, because you refuse to have it for the first time, let alone again. Why won't you talk about this?"

Kate knew exactly why she wasn't talking about it— because whatever she said would not only be quoted across town faster than she could walk the four blocks home, but it would be twisted beyond all recognition as it traveled. She knew not everyone thought of Grier in the same way Trina did.

As an interloper.

In fact, she knew a lot of people were starting to think Grier had a rather decent claim to a place in town. And they had also begun to think of Grier Thompson as their own.

Just like her father had.

"What can I get for you?" Avery's smile was broad and her warm brown gaze was tinged with sympathy.

"Chardonnay." Kate heard the clipped notes of her own voice but wasn't all that inclined to hide them. The friendly smile she could take.

The sympathy was off-limits.

"Strawberry margarita," Trina added. "And some of that bar mix you have."

"Be right back."

Trina fluffed her hair as she leaned forward to whisper across the small table that separated their chairs. "Look at her over there. She's a barmaid, for Christ's sake, and she's run right back to her friend to gossip about you. I know it."

Kate let her gaze roam back to the bar, but since she heard the distinct words "Super Bowl contenders," "Giants" and "Packers," rise from Avery's direction, she was hard-pressed to believe the conversation had anything to do with her.

Trina's phone went off and her friend leaped up like a cat that'd just been doused with water. "It's that guy I met on New Year's Eve. I'll be right back."

As Trina hot-footed it across the bar, her voice echoing for anyone to hear, Kate returned to her morose thoughts. Avery wasn't gossiping about her. And she hadn't been anything but kind when she'd come to take their drink order.

So why was she struggling so hard to accept the kindness?

"May I sit down?"

Kate looked up quickly to see Grier standing in front of her, pointing to an empty seat, a glass of white wine in her hands.

"Sure."

"Here's your wine. Avery had to go hunt up strawberry margarita mix."

"Thanks." Gray eyes so like her own bored into her as Kate accepted the drink.

"Did you have a nice holiday?"

"No. You?"

"Not particularly."

"I thought New York was paradise at Christmas." The words were out before she could stop them. It wasn't like she was keeping up with Grier's actions or anything.

And hey, Indigo was a small town and gossip was the engine that kept it warm in the winter. Everyone knew Grier had gone home.

It was a simple enough question.

"Well then, I guess paradise is overrated."

Kate didn't miss Grier's gaze drifting toward Mick O'Shaughnessy as she said the words.

Before she could respond, Grier's focus quickly swung back to her. "How did you do? You know, with the fact that this was the first holiday without our father."

The words struck a painful chord somewhere in the middle of her chest and her throat felt suddenly choked with unshed tears. Fighting for composure, Kate focused on the small flame of annoyance at the "our father" term.

"Christmas was his favorite time of the year, you know."

"No, I didn't." Grier's voice tightened on the words as her familiar gray eyes grew overbright.

It was petty and small and Kate hated herself for doing it, but the tears cleared from her throat as the silly and unfounded anger sparked to life in her belly. "Oh yes. This was his absolute favorite time of the year. He decorated to the hilt and his house always had the best lights. He started doing that when I was a small kid because I loved it so much."

The words hit their mark, as the high pink of Grier's cheeks faded away.

"I'm sure it was spectacular."

Kate reached for her wine and took a delicate sip, her gaze focused somewhere around the middle of Grier's neck. "It was. Memories I'll have forever."

"Of course." Grier focused on her own glass of wine as an unpleasant—*awkward*—quiet filled the space between them.

The real person inside—the one Kate had always taken pride in being—wanted to say something soothing, but that awful ache that had descended in the center of her chest the day she realized her father wasn't going to get better refused to lift.

Trina flounced back across the lobby, her smile not nearly as broad as when she left. Kate could only assume New Year's Eve guy wasn't quite as enthusiastic about a repeat evening as Trina was.

"Where's my margarita?"

"Avery's getting the mix," Grier said quietly.

Trina sighed heavily. "I knew we should have gone to Maguire's. They've always got what I like."

Grier stood. "Well, I'll let you two enjoy the rest of your evening. I just wanted to say hello."

"Tell Avery I changed my mind," Trina called after Grier's departing back. "Come on, Kate. Let's get out of here."

The little demon that had ridden in on her shoulder reared up and Kate refused to hold back in the name of friendship. "Bad call?"

"He wanted me to come down to Anchorage next weekend."

"That was quick." Kate reached for her purse and quickly fumbled around the bottom for her wallet.

"I said I'd rather he came up here for an afternoon and I'd show him around."

"And?"

"He's not interested. Said it was me coming to Anchorage or nothing." Trina flipped her hair behind her as she reached for her coat. "Who knows. Maybe I'll go."

"Trina—" Kate broke off, knowing it was fruitless.

"Oh, don't give me that look. I'm sick of this place and I'm sick of how boring it is and I'm sick of the fact that nothing ever changes. Maybe a little fun is just what I need."

"Yeah, but he's clearly not interested in getting to know you."

"Maybe all that's overrated anyway." Trina ran a hand through her vivid red hair before nodding toward the door. "Come on. Let's change the scenery. This place is dead."

Kate shook her head as she threw a ten on the small table, then stood to follow Trina out. The bad mood she'd walked in with had gone from bad to worse.

And she knew a change of scenery wasn't going to lift her spirits.

"I'm going up to my room. It's been a long day." Grier pushed her half-drunk glass of wine across the bar toward Avery. "I'll come down in the morning and we'll catch up."

"You okay?" Confusion stamped itself across Avery's features as she stowed a bottle of bright red margarita mix under the bar. "Did I miss something?"

"Just an ill-timed attempt at making amends."

"Grier—" Avery broke off. "What happened? Where are Kate and Trina?"

"I think I heard something about walking over to Maguire's."

"Are you okay?"

"I'm fine. Really, I'm fine. It's been an incredibly long day and I just need to crawl into bed. I promise I'll be more fun tomorrow." Grier stood, forcing an overly bright smile on her face. "We'll catch up then."

Avery looked about to argue and Grier could see the moment when she decided against it, her head bobbing in a slight nod. "Your bags were brought up when you came in, so go on up and relax. And I'm holding you to the catch-up session."

"Absolutely."

"One thing."

Grier looked up from where she gathered her coat and purse. "What's that?"

"If you change your mind about company, holler at me. I'll bring the cookies."

"Thanks."

Grier shot a quick glance at Mick and Doc Cloud. The urge to take the coward's way out was strong, but she'd already tried to be the bigger person once this evening. She might as well stick to it and keep up her new year's streak. Crossing to the two men, she didn't miss their smiles as she approached.

"It's been a long day, so I'm going to head up."

"You sure?" Mick's gaze was steady as understanding shone from the deep blue pools of his eyes.

"Yep. I left New York at six this morning and I'm beat."

Doc Cloud stood first and leaned forward to give her a soft kiss on the cheek. "Sleep well and welcome home, Grier."

Home.

The word struck her hard and fast and she fought past the sudden lack of air in her lungs. "Thanks, Dr. Cloud."

"Mick. Thanks for the ride." She saw him step off to move closer and she shifted back, then turned on her heel.

She had to get out of here.

Now.

The soft, muted lights of the bar blurred as she crossed the room, blinking back tears. She would not cry.

Would. Not. Cry.

Doc Cloud had only been being nice. And although Kate had been anything but, it didn't bear worrying about.

She wasn't home.

And she wasn't going to find a way to make amends with her sister.

And she wasn't ever going to have memories of Christmas or anything else with her father.

On a heavy sigh, she shoved her hair behind her ear with one hand and stabbed at the elevator button with the other.

She was just tired. That was all. This sadness would pass.

The elevator door slid open and Grier stepped in, grateful when the doors slid closed again and she was cocooned in the privacy of the elevator. Life had been a bit overwhelming, but she'd be fine. She always was. Things would straighten out with her father's estate and she'd get her life back and go home.

To New York.

The only home she'd ever known.

The doors slid open and she reached for her key card. Avery and Susan, the Indigo's owner, had been kind enough to leave her things intact at the hotel, the holidays being one of their slower times. It was one of the most charming things about Indigo. They'd done it, not because they had to, but simply out of kindness.

The room wasn't being used for any other purpose, so they were more than happy to do her a favor.

Such a simple gesture. Warm. Friendly.

"Are you okay?"

Grier nearly dropped her key card as Mick's voice enveloped her from behind. Whirling, she didn't miss the concern etched on his face in light lines or the frown that creased his forehead.

"Yeah. Sure. Like I said downstairs, I'm just tired."

"You practically ran out of the lobby."

"And here you are, following me."

"I wanted to make sure you were okay."

The jumpy feeling that fired her blood every time she even thought about him sparked to life as her gaze drank in his broad shoulders and large frame.

"How'd you get up here?"

"The stairs."

"How'd you know I was . . ." She trailed off as memories of their one night together filled her mind and fired more warmth to her already-sensitized nerve endings. "Never mind."

The concern that bracketed the corners of his mouth quirked into a lazy grin and Grier knew he remembered *exactly* which room was hers.

And from the desire that darkened his baby blues, she knew he also remembered every detail as clearly as she did.

"Look, Mick, I appreciate the concern. Really, I do. But I'm fi—"

She swallowed her words as he moved in, whip-fast, his mouth taking immediate possession of hers. Her back pressed against the door of her room and her thick coat bunched between them, but it all faded to nothingness at the joy of being in his arms again.

His hands sprawled on either side of her head as he used his body to press her against the door. While the feeling should have been claustrophobic, Grier only wanted more as the desperate urge to take everything he could give beat through her.

Heat curled through her belly—warm and welcome—when his large, capable hands shifted from the door to cover her hips. Mick pulled her against him and the unmistakable proof of his arousal where it pressed against her stomach only heightened the moment. Brilliant sparks of pure, feminine appreciation lit her up.

She dropped her coat and purse between them as she reached to wrap her arms around his neck. His pulse beat heavy under her hands and the hair at his nape was soft as her fingers threaded through the longish strands.

A light moan rose up in her throat as he continued the relentless sensual assault, as his lips plundered hers with an urgent, restless need. With unerring precision, his tongue tangled with hers over and over, dragging one erotic sensation after another from their joining.

No matter how much she argued with herself to stay away from him, this *thing* between them—a desperate, urgent need that clawed and grabbed and *demanded*—simply would not be sated. One single night with him had not been enough.

Mick lifted his head as that wicked smile once again returned to his lips. The fact that his eyes were a bright, glazed blue gave her some solace that he was as affected as she was by what burned between them.

"So you're fine?"

"I'm fine." The words were soft and breathy and slightly strangled, completely belying her quick assurance.

He took another step back. "I can see that."

"Really, Mick, I am." Her words gained strength and it was only the evidence that she'd regained some of her equilibrium that kept her from pulling him right back against her.

He took one more step back as his smile faded. "I meant every word of that text I sent you on New Year's Eve. I'm not walking away from what's between us. I will, however"—he leaned in and pressed one hard, quick kiss to her lips—"let you get some sleep."

Long after he'd disappeared back through the stairwell, Grier stood there, her back still pressed to the door with her coat and purse at her feet. She knew Mick wasn't walking away.

But what would happen when she eventually did?

Chapter Four

Grier hit mile two of her run as Jon Bon Jovi's luscious voice came through her earbuds. Although she wasn't so sure he was accurate about being able to go home, she'd never argue the fact that he was sweet accompaniment to her daily torture routine.

With Jon's voice keeping her pace at a fast clip, she allowed her gaze to roam the room. The Indigo Blue boasted an impressive workout facility, practically putting her gym back in New York to shame. Even if all of it was likely another gift from Roman, the hotel owner's absent son and current high-scoring forward of the NHL, she had to admire the gleaming rows of well-kept machines and ruthlessly organized weight racks.

The strains of Bon Jovi gave way to some Donna Summer, followed by Pink as Grier cranked up the incline.

If you're gonna sweat, you might as well make it worthwhile, the annoying voice in her head whispered, pushing her on. She'd had the same workout routine for more than a decade and it never failed to piss her off that she'd yet to find a song combination that made the incline portion of her run palatable.

But God bless Pink for almost getting her there.

The strains of Trouble floated over her consciousness as she sweated toward mile three and with the music came thoughts of Mick.

The man was trouble, all right. Two point eight seconds in his company and she was ready to drool. Five more seconds and she was wrapped in his arms, her brains leaching out of her head.

How did that happen?

And why did it have to happen at the worst possible moment in her life?

The waving of a hand caught her up short and Grier almost fumbled on the machine as Sloan's eyes grew wide.

"I'm sorry!"

Grier waved back as she righted her footing and reached for her earbuds. "What are you doing here?"

"Nearly killing you on your run, apparently. I'm sorry."

"You just snuck up on me, that's all." Grier lowered the treadmill's incline, then the speed, until she was moving at a brisk walk.

"How is it possible you're here at six thirty in the morning? After flying all day yesterday?"

"I could say the same for you."

"You're a machine."

"No, I'm just awfully fond of pancakes."

Sloan's gaze perked up in carb-inspired anticipation. "Does that mean you'll go to the diner and get some with me?"

"Sure, just so long as you get your lazy ass on that treadmill over there."

"Hey." Sloan's eyes widened in mock offense. "My lazy ass has already been up and active this morning."

"Sex doesn't count."

"It burns calories."

Grier pointed to the machine. "That burns more and you've got a wedding dress to fit into. Hop to it, fuck bunny."

"As always, you're far too astute for your own good."

"That's what you get for having an anal mathematician for a best friend. I can calculate calories from twenty paces."

The two of them fell into companionable silence as Sloan started her workout. Grier appreciated the time together. Although they'd been apart for only a little more than a week, she'd missed her friend.

And knew it was only the beginning, as Sloan would be moving to Indigo permanently now that she was marrying Walker.

"You all right?"

Grier glanced up from the neon face of her machine. "Yeah, why?"

"I don't know. You just looked really sad all of a sudden."

"I'm fine, really."

The moments ticked by, punctuated by the heavy *thwapping* of the running belts of both treadmills, before Sloan spoke again. "You looked a little uncomfortable last night. I mean, when you got over being really happy to see Mick and all."

Grier heard the thread of concern through Sloan's

teasing tone and wondered if she was that obvious. "I'm not going to ignore the man."

"Oh no? It seemed you were doing a pretty good job of it over the past few weeks."

"It was the holidays. I'm sure it's a busy time for him, with delivering packages and stuff. And then I was out of town."

"And you were avoiding him," Sloan said, contributing to the litany of excuses.

"I was not."

Sloan hit the speed on her machine with a heavy laugh. "Since delivering packages was the best you could come up with on short notice, I'm calling your bluff. You may be an awesome mathematician, but you're a lousy liar."

"All I meant was that he was busy."

Sloan nodded her head as her breathing grew heavier with the effects of her run. Despite the increased effort, it couldn't counterbalance the wicked gleam in her blue gaze. "And I'm in awe of your thoughtful understanding."

Grier hopped off the treadmill as her machine registered four miles, then crossed the room toward the weight rack. Although she usually followed the treadmill with the elliptical, the heavy weights would be a pleasant diversion from the hot seat.

"He's interested in you," Sloan added in a reasonable voice.

"Did you and Avery practice this?"

"And you're interested in him."

Grier reached for matched ten-pound weights and

began a slow repetition of biceps curls. "I'd also skip a workout every day if it didn't mean an ass the size of Washington. Just because I want something doesn't mean I can have it."

"So why are you making this so hard?"

"Because it is hard, Sloan. It's really hard. And my life's not going to wrap up in a nice neat bow, smack in the middle of Indigo, like yours is."

As soon as the words were out, Grier wished she could pull them back.

Wanted to pull them back.

Even though she was sort of relieved they were out.

She could only thank a decade and a half of friendship that instead of causing a rift, Sloan saw straight through to what was underneath the biting remark. With quick movements, she stopped her machine and was across the room. She took the weights and settled them back on the rack before turning around, her gaze full of understanding.

"You want to tell me what this is really all about?"

"We're talking about Mick and me."

"Yes, but what else? You and Mick have nothing to do with me."

The slight sense of relief she'd felt was rapidly beginning to feel petty and small, but she owed it to Sloan to see her words through.

"It's just slowly dawning on me that you're staying here. And I'm happy for you. So happy." Grier slashed a hand at her cheeks, irritated that not only was she making an ass of herself, but she was crying, too.

"We'll still be friends."

"Of course we will be. I'll hunt you down and hurt you if we aren't. But I'm not going to see you all the time and that fact is just beginning to register."

Sloan beckoned her over to sit on a nearby weight bench. "You're the sister of my heart, Grier. Nothing will change that. Not Walker. Not Alaska. Nothing."

"I know." A heavy sob escaped her as she nodded her head. "I do know that."

Sloan wrapped an arm around her. "And I'm sorry that you're in pain right now. That life is just so freaking shitty sometimes."

She laid her head on her friend's shoulder, the acceptance and understanding going a long way toward making the pain just a little more palatable. "Thanks."

"Especially when mine's so not shitty," Sloan whispered.

At that, Grier lifted her head. "Oh, Sloan. I'm happy for you. So very happy for you. Don't think for a single minute I'd take that away from you."

A matched set of tears lit her oldest friend's eyes as Sloan dashed them away. "I just see how sad you've been and it makes *me* sad. I want to take it away and I want something better for you. Especially when I see that something better standing right in front of you, interested in getting to know you."

"Don't you see? That's why it's the wrong time. How can I possibly start something with a person when my life is so fouled up?"

"Maybe it's exactly the right time."

Grier took a large sniff and couldn't hold back the small smile. "You're stubborn."

A lone eyebrow lifted above a watery blue iris. "You're seriously saying that to me?"

"If the Manolo fits . . ."

Sloan grabbed her in a tight hug. "I love you. I really, really love you."

"I love you back," Grier whispered, her grip equally fierce.

"All right then. I think we can say good-bye to the torture devices and hello to pancakes."

Grier dropped her arms and pointed toward the now-abandoned treadmills. "Just so long as you remember why I'm allowed to have bacon with mine and you're not."

"Hey. I exercised."

"You did, like, a half mile on that thing. And we all know what happens to girls who slack on their gym time."

Sloan wrapped an arm around her waist and pulled them determinedly toward the door. "What's that?"

"Their wedding dresses have to be let out."

"You are so evil, Grier Thompson."

Even if she hadn't found the right music to help her through those damn running inclines, Grier couldn't argue with their benefits.

And there was one benefit that sat pretty high on the list: the pure, unadulterated satisfaction that came from a large stack of fluffy pancakes loaded with melted butter and syrup.

"I think there are men at that back booth who would propose to you based on that breakfast alone." Sloan pointed a fork at her.

Grier turned to see a good number of the town's bachelors filling the booths along the back wall of the diner. She offered a little wave and smiled when several hale and hearty shouts returned the greeting.

"They're completely adorable."

Sloan gave the back wall another quick look before returning her focus back to her own stack. "Yeah, they really are."

"I heard several guys made love matches at the grandmothers' competition last month."

"A few. I've got interviews scheduled with the two that seem to still be going strong."

"There are three still going strong."

The voice floated over their booth with all the precision of a general's command and Grier looked up to see Sophie, Mary and Julia standing in a line next to their booth.

"Mrs. Montgomery." Sloan quickly stood and gave her future grandmother-in-law a quick kiss. "Won't you all join us?"

"We'd love to."

Grier fought the internal eye roll at the quick agreement. While she loved the grandmothers, their not-so-subtle insistence on getting their grandsons married off made them a bit scary when all assembled as a coordinated trio.

Which they clearly were this morning.

Grier jumped up quickly to allow Julia and Mary into her side of the booth and grabbed a chair from a nearby four-top to flank the end of their table. Once they were settled, fresh steaming mugs of coffee all around, the questions began. Grier was grateful she'd already eaten the majority of her breakfast or the inquisition would have ruined her appetite.

"How were your flights, girls?"

Grier took round one. "Fine, Mrs. O'Shaughnessy. Long, but uneventful."

"My, my." Julia patted Mary's arm. "To be that young and unaffected. It now takes me a week to recover from a flight."

"Unless it's Mick's flying. My grandson flies as smooth as the melted butter I'm going to have on my pancakes."

Grier saw Sloan's eyebrows rise slightly but kept her voice level. "He's an excellent pilot, Mrs. O'Shaughnessy."

"What do you girls have planned for today?"

Grier was grateful she didn't have to voice the reality of her plans for the day—absolutely nothing—when Sloan jumped in. "Not much. I've got a few things to catch up with on my articles, but other than that, just shaking off a bit of lingering jet lag."

"Well then, you can finish up your work and both of you can join us later at the meeting center."

"For what?" Even as she asked the words, Grier cursed the innate curiosity that had the words spilling out.

"We're prepping decorations for the upcoming Valentine's dance," Julia piped in proudly.

The damn curiosity—the curse of her life—kept pressing. "But February fourteenth is still several weeks away."

Mary patted her arm. "Oh, dear, we cut out more

than ten thousand hearts. It's never too early to get started on that."

"Ten thousand?" Her voice sounded strangled, even to her. "How many have you done?"

"About three. Hundred."

"Which means we'd love another few pairs of hands," Sophie jumped in quickly. "Avery's already coming and has volunteered to bring the wine."

"Hearts and wine sound perfect. How can we say no?" Sloan smiled sweetly.

Sophie took a large bite of pancake, her grin decidedly calculating. "You can't."

"Michael Patrick!"

Mick's grandmother's voice came loud and clear through his headphones as he flew over the south face of Denali. Why they let her take charge over at the airstrip he'd never know, especially since Maggie was fiercely protective of her radio waves, but somehow Mary O'Shaughnessy knew how to get around any obstacle that stood in her way.

He rubbed the back of his neck and let out a small sigh before flipping on his microphone. "What did I do?"

"You didn't do anything," Mary's voice came back, tart as a ripe lemon.

"So, what's with the Michael Patrick routine?"

"I need you to pick up some things for me on your run to Anchorage."

"Of course. I'm always happy to do that."

"I've got an order in at the art store. They're messengering it to the airport. You just need to get it for me."

"I thought I just picked up a load last week. As I re-call, there was about a ton of red construction paper."

"We needed more."

He didn't miss the prim voice or the slight quaver underneath that was the only tell he'd ever known her to have.

Was she lying?

"And I need you to bring it straight over to the town hall when you get back."

"Yes, ma'am."

"There's no need to be cheeky."

"I thought I was being polite."

"And there you go again. Cheeky."

He couldn't hold back the smile. "I'll see you later."

"Bring the supplies straight over."

"All right, already. I promise."

"See that you do."

As his grandmother's voice winked off his ear-phones, he could only shake his head at the strange set of orders. He knew she was up to something, but for the life of him, he had no idea what it was.

Thirty-five years of his grandmother's quirks en-sured he'd learn what she was up to soon enough, so he shifted his thoughts to the mountain. He'd nearly cleared the face as he headed south toward Anchorage, Denali's bright peaks gleaming in the morning sun-light, but it was a different flight that filled his mind's eye.

The injured researchers he'd pulled off the mountain in early December hadn't been far from his thoughts in the ensuing weeks. Although he knew it was natural for an experience as sharp as that one to linger for a while, he hadn't expected the restless nights or the unpleasant memories the trip had churned up.

Doc Cloud had prescribed a few tranquilizers for the really bad nights, but he'd yet to take one. Something about the medicine didn't sit well with him and he couldn't bring himself to sleep the problem off.

Unfortunately, he had to face the root of the problem—his past—head-on.

Even if there wasn't any way to fix it.

Jason Shriver woke with a start, his neck screaming painfully where he'd slouched asleep for the night in a leather chair in his father's study. An empty glass still smelling of the scotch he'd drunk the night before sat on the small table next to him, curling his stomach with its pungent odor.

It had been a shitty new year and clearly day three of it was starting with a bang. He glanced again at the glass, its empty contents mocking him as his father's harsh words pounded through his brain as if on a loop.

"What the hell were you thinking, Jason? You don't fuck around before the wedding. It's not only poor taste, but it gives the woman far too much time to think."

The words had changed slightly over the past two months, pending on the point his father was trying to emphasize, but the root of it remained the same. He'd screwed everything up by messing around in the office six weeks before his wedding and it reflected poorly on all of them.

"A real man knows how to be discreet, for Christ's sake. The office, in the middle of the afternoon?"

What had surprised him more than the lectures was the side of his father he'd never really acknowledged before. Did the old man think like that? Did he actually see the world in such antiquated ways?

Jason had known for years Thomas Shriver, distinguished lion of Wall Street, didn't know how to keep it in his pants. Oh, his father was discreet, but no one could go after that much ass and not get caught every now and again.

But he'd always thought the old man at least had some sense of responsibility for his actions. Instead, every word out of his father's mouth was like some business truism he needed in order to prove he was a success.

Twenty percent profit margin? Check.

Summerhouse in the Hamptons? Check.

Mistress? Check.

The problem was, Jason reflected as he reached for the glass of water one of the maids must have been kind enough to leave next to him, he'd never fully understood the impact of his father's actions on his mother.

How had she felt, all these years? Had his father hurt her? Or had she simply ignored it, thinking it was her duty to keep her mouth shut and smile?

Images of his mother's smooth smile and shielded gaze shifted to a new image.

Grier.

His small pixie with the quick smile and bright gray

eyes. He'd been attracted to her from the start, seeking her out after the first meeting they'd sat in together. He'd been in the firm's LA office for the first fifteen years of his career, only to come back to New York to begin the grooming process to take the old man's place.

His father had made it known that a wife was the natural next step in the progression to senior partner and ultimate head of the firm and he'd better get serious about it once he got back home.

He'd just never expected it to happen so fast.

Grier Thompson had made it incredibly easy to do his duty. She knew his world, both professionally and socially, and they had fallen into a relationship that was simple and uncomplicated.

So why had he screwed it up so badly?

He'd never considered himself a cheater. In fact, he'd never understood the guys who couldn't stay monogamous in a relationship. If you wanted to play it fast and loose, stay that way. Don't drag another person into it.

So what had happened?

Leaning forward, he scrubbed his hands over his cheeks, the weight of his actions like a boulder on his back. No matter how many times he asked himself, he couldn't come up with any other answer save one.

Simple and uncomplicated scared the almighty shit out of him.

Chapter Five

Since her evening summons to town hall meant she still had roughly ten hours to fill, Grier bundled up after breakfast with Sloan and decided to explore town. Although she'd been to most of the places on Main Street at some point since arriving in Indigo, she hadn't really spent any length of time anywhere beyond the diner and the hotel.

It was time to change that.

Her gaze settled on the Jitters, but any more coffee this morning and she'd actually have a nervous disorder, so she kept up her trek down the sidewalk. She passed Betsy's clothing shop and almost stopped in for a little retail therapy, but even that didn't quite suit her mood, so she kept on.

As she glanced across the street, Tasty's Bait and Tackle caught her attention. Tasty had been kind enough to give her, Sloan and Avery free hats the month before during an impromptu snowball fight on the square and she had a soft spot for the grizzled old proprietor. Since rumor had it he spent much of the winter ice fishing, she was surprised to see his bearded face peeking back at her through his shop window as he waved.

Grier waved back and knew where she'd stop next.

The nonexistent traffic on Main meant she didn't have to cross at the light and within moments she was stamping snow off her boots in the front of his store.

"Well, if it isn't Miz Grier." Tasty smiled at her from behind the counter. "You looked lost out there. I'm glad you came to pay me a visit."

She stopped midstomp as she worked to kick the last bit of snow off her boots. "Lost?"

"Lost in thought."

"I'll give you that."

"Speaking of giving, where's the hat I gave you?"

Since gray winter beanie caps were about as fashionable as a pair of granny panties, Grier had left the cap at the very bottom of her suitcase, but from the look on his eager face, she could hardly tell him that. "It's in my laundry basket."

"No worries." Tasty shook a hand. "I've got another one you can have."

Her lightly whispered "Thanks" was lost as he moved behind the long wooden counter that ran along the front half of his store. As he puttered off, her gaze alighted on a book that lay in front of his seat, its pastel-colored spine cracked. Curious, she moved closer, surprised to see it was a Regency romance by an author she had on auto-buy.

Tasty was back all too soon with the cap, his smile proud as he handed the gray monstrosity to her.

"You're a big reader?"

"Oh yeah. I love those Regencies. Ballrooms get me every time."

She took the cap he extended toward her with a smile. "That's romantic of you."

"I carry 'em in the bookstore I keep in the back. Fat lot of good it's done me, though."

"What do you mean?"

"I didn't get bid on again." At the puzzled look she gave him, he added in a forlorn tone, "At the auction."

"Oh."

Grier had heard about the bachelor auction that was part of the grandmothers' annual shenanigans to get their grandsons married off, but she'd missed the actual event as she'd tried to break in to her father's house while the festivities were going on. Her first and only attempt at breaking and entering had been a dismal failure, but it had put her smack-dab in Mick's arms once more.

Until she ran away like a frightened mouse who didn't know her head from her ass.

Tasty's words pulled her from the slightly embarrassing memory.

"Chooch says I need to stop looking so scary."

Although the woman had a point, Grier thought there might be a slightly less abrasive way to tell him. "Have you thought about shaving the beard?"

The look of horror that filled the man's eyes had her leaning forward. "I'm sorry. That didn't come out as I meant it. You need to be you, but maybe you could trim it a bit?"

"It is a little full."

"Exactly. Let the ladies see a bit more of your face."

"Hmmm." He ran a hand over his cheeks, the motion

so deliberate and thoughtful, Grier had the strangest urge to hug him. "You know, that Mick O'Shaughnessy is one lucky man."

"Mick doesn't have a beard."

"Hee hee." Tasty slapped his hand on the counter. "I was talking about you."

"Me?"

"You're a sweet girl, Grier. And you're a good person, sitting here shooting the shit with me. He's one lucky man."

"I'm not dating Mick."

"Sure you are."

"No, really, I'm not."

The smile fell from his face as her protests finally registered. "Well, why the hell not?"

The outburst wasn't what she'd expected—especially not after their bonding moment over personal grooming. "I'm sorry, Tasty, but I'm only here for a bit and then I'm headed home. Once I get things figured out with my father's estate."

"That's not right. You're one of us, now. You need to settle down right here just like your daddy always wanted."

"If that's what he wanted, he had an awfully funny way of showing it."

"I won't argue with you there. I told Jonas more than once he needed to get off his ass and call you. And then the cancer spread on 'em and he didn't do what was right." Tasty leaned forward. "Please don't hold it against him."

Something hard settled in the pit of her stomach and

she was caught off guard. Grier wanted to offer some mild-mannered, lovely retort—more than thirty years of having manners drilled into her almost had her offering up some nice platitude—but something held her back at the last minute.

She would have liked to have known her father. Would have liked to have known that she had a home somewhere in the world where someone wanted her.

But Jonas Winston hadn't been able to give that to her.

"Even if you do have a right to be madder than a rattler at him."

Tasty's words penetrated the dour moment and she smiled in spite of the roiling emotions she couldn't quite get under control. "They have rattlesnakes in Alaska?"

"Nah, it's too cold here for reptiles to survive. But I haven't spent my whole life in Alaska. I'm originally from Arizona."

"How'd you end up here?"

He shrugged. "Pipeline, same as so many others. Place sort of grew on me, so I stayed."

"I see."

He eyed the winter hat she'd rolled up into a tight ball in her hands. "You sure you want that?"

"What? Oh—" Grier looked down at her hands. "Of course I do."

Tasty's expression was a mixture of relief and dawning horror. "I just gotta figure out how to put that freebie into my accounting of my inventory."

"It's not too hard. Just count it as an expense against the business."

"That's usually where I get messed up." He pointed at an old computer sitting on a small desk behind him. "I'm not great with the numbers."

"Would you like some help?"

Whatever tense moments the two might have shared over her lack of commitment to Mick or Jonas's lackluster parenting skills evaporated as he extended a hand to unlock the small half-wall that separated his area from the customers. "Would you?"

"Sure. I haven't quite gone rusty on my accounting skills in the last six weeks."

"I'm sure glad you stopped in."

As Grier pulled up an old Quicken program on Tasty's computer—one that had matching floppy disks he proudly produced a few minutes later—she let out an inward sigh.

At least she wouldn't be bored this afternoon.

"Oxygen. Stat."

Grier came to a halt next to Avery where she shoveled off the front parking area of the hotel.

Avery's smile was broad as she stopped and looked up. "Tasty?"

"How'd you guess?"

"Word travels faster than the speed of sound in this town. Haven't you figured that out yet?"

Grier reached for another shovel sitting against the wall and took a patch a few feet away. "Yes, but how could anyone know? No one came into his store the whole time I was there."

Avery's eyebrows rose as she went back to her

freshly dug path. "Didn't you see all the people passing by outside the windows, checking out what you were doing in there?"

"I guess I missed them. I spent the afternoon helping him with his accounting. It took every ounce of focus I possess."

Avery let out a long, low laugh. "You sure your hair's not on fire?"

Grier tapped her shovel against a thick snowbank, admiring her neat, even row of now-clean asphalt. "No, but I will cop to popping a few antacids around the start of hour three. The man sells worms, chewing tobacco and a few other fishing items. He can't have more than one hundred SKUs in his total inventory. How'd he manage to mess them up so badly?"

"A few too many years with the wacky tobaccy will do it to most."

"Oh no, this was a special brand of madness even a drug-induced haze couldn't cause."

"Let's just say Tasty's talents lie in his people skills, not his math skills."

Grier positioned her shovel to begin a new, fresh row, debating her next words before simply letting them loose. "He mentioned my father."

"Tasty was good friends with your dad." Avery stamped her shovel with her foot, securing another wall of snow at the edge of the lot.

Grier began to push her shovel, suddenly glad for the listening ear. Sloan was wonderful and had done an incredible job of being a supportive listener, but she hadn't known Jonas.

And it was that perspective, Grier realized, she craved.

"You knew my father?"

"Everyone here knows one another." Avery paused a moment, indecision flashing in her dark brown eyes like a neon sign. And then the storm clouds cleared as if to say she'd made her decision. "But yeah, I knew your dad. He helped me out a few times with my mom."

"Helped you out? What do you mean?"

"My mom was an alcoholic. She died about a year and a half ago."

"Oh, Avery, I'm sorry."

"I'm not. And before you say anything," she rushed on, "I just mean that I'm not sorry she's not living a miserable existence anymore."

"Of course." Although she'd have taken Avery's side regardless, the pain she saw in her friend's gaze hit with the force of a battering ram.

Grier suddenly realized she wasn't the only one in turmoil.

And she wasn't the only one who suffered from the poor choices of a parent.

Whatever support she'd expected when she'd decided to open up, Grier appreciated that she'd gained so much more in befriending Avery Marks.

"My mother is a story for another day." It didn't escape Grier's notice Avery had momentarily stopped shoveling, even though her breathing was steady and even. "But your dad, on the other hand. He was a good man. I grew up in a house a few doors down from him and he kept a lookout for us. My mother was known for the occasional bender and Jonas had a way of sensing when I needed an extra hand."

Grier hazarded a guess. "Small-town grapevine again?"

Avery tapped her nose in the age-old gesture for "spot -on." "Yep. Maguire could see a bad night coming from a mile away. He'd send Jonas down to check on us."

"And your dad?"

"Was a very not-involved pipeline worker who ultimately went back to his other family when his time on the line was over."

"Oh."

"Oh yes, the cliché to end all clichés. My mother thought he hung the moon and instead all he hung was a baby on her."

"It's not a cliché, Avery. It's your life."

"Which is also why I have to tow the town line and tell you that your dad was a good man. Clearly misguided because he never found his way to bringing you here sooner, but a good man all the same."

Grier let out a heavy breath and watched the mist swirl in front of her face while she considered Avery's words. "It sounds different, coming from you. From Tasty, or from anyone else here in town, it sounds like a defense. From you, it just sounds honest."

"I am that." Avery started on another row of snow and Grier did the same, grateful to know about another side of her father.

"Since I am unflinchingly honest," Avery shouted over the heavy crunch of her shovel, "I can't help but notice that your sexy bush pilot didn't spend the night last night."

"He just came upstairs to check on me. Kate and I also left the room with quite a lot to discuss."

"The man wanted you."

And I wanted him, too, she wanted to add. "It's not the right time in my life for this."

"So when is the right time? When you're dead?"

"This sounds suspiciously like a lecture." Grier stopped at the edge of the lot and kicked her shovel to pack the snowbank in a pitiful attempt to hide from that unrelenting stare.

"I never lecture. It's bad form. What I am doing is trying to talk some sense into you. That man is so crazy about you, it blinks off him like the Christmas lights on Main Street."

"He should be blinking for someone else," Grier muttered. "I'm damaged goods. Oh wait, make that damaged goods that will be leaving in six weeks."

Whatever lighthearted note had tinged Avery's words up to that point turned serious as she walked over and wrapped an arm around Grier's waist. "You deserve love. You really, really do."

The tears she'd held back the night before welled up before Grier could stop them. "I know I do."

"Then why won't you reach out and take what's right in front of you?"

That arm never left her waist and Grier wondered how she'd come to trust this woman in so short a time. With a quick look around the empty parking lot, she took a deep breath.

Trust meant risk.

"You want to talk about clichés, Avery. I'm a walking cliché and you know it. My father's never been a part of my life and my mother sees relationships as a social tool. I'm not exactly a good bet."

"You can't—"

"Wait. If you want me to talk about this, you have to let me get it out."

Avery nodded, but her brown eyes, the color of rich sable, never wavered.

On a heavy breath, Grier swallowed around the constriction of tears in her throat. It was a new year and damn it, she was not going to cry every day. "I'm not exactly a good bet and I know that. But I also know, under the right circumstances, with the right person, I *could* be a good bet."

"I'm so glad to hear you say that. You mean it?"

"Yeah, I really do." Grier held up her mittened hand. "Scout's honor. You have to believe me on that. And you also have to believe me when I say the circumstances just aren't right here."

Avery's eyes narrowed. "If you're so sure about that, then why won't you just enjoy yourself with him for the next few weeks?"

"Because that's just selfish."

"Mick's a big boy. I think he's more than capable of handling a little selfish."

"It doesn't make it right." Before Avery could argue, Grier added, "I've been the one left behind, Avery. It damages you."

Avery's mouth opened, then closed again as a small

line marred her forehead. When she finally spoke, her lighthearted tone was absent. "I thought you didn't care about him."

"Jason? In hindsight, I really didn't. I mean, I cared for him—but I didn't love him. And it still hurt to be the one left. And if the way I do feel about Mick is any indication of how he feels about me, I just can't do that to him."

The two of them stood there for a long time in silence, breaths misting before them, both lost in thought.

And then Avery dropped her arm and stood before her. "You're sure about this?"

"About what?"

"Why you can't have it all. Why this isn't different from what happened with your ex."

"The time's not right."

Her new friend nodded but didn't press as she turned to walk back to finish off her nearly cleared area.

Avery and Sloan and even Mick seemed to think the time was *exactly* right. And so she didn't risk her heart and start believing them; she had to stay strong.

She simply couldn't give in and do something stupid.

Like fall in love with the man.

"My fingers are going to fall off." Grier leaned over to whisper it in Sloan's ear as they moved into their third hour of cutting out red construction paper hearts. Someone had unearthed a few sets of scissors from the elementary school and she'd used the small torture device for so long, her palm was actually cramping.

Sloan gritted her teeth and kept a proper Westchester smile on her face as she muttered back, "You do realize someone will have to hang these, too?"

"Oh good God."

"You gals having fun?" Julia cooed from the end of the table. She was unraveling a string of pink and red beads that Sophie had unearthed from a giant rubber tub.

"The best, Mrs. Forsyth," Sloan sang out.

"Do you know when we started this little event?"

"Um, no." Grier looked around the town hall at the various groupings of women. Another table was busy using a pattern to draw the hearts—in all three sizes they'd ultimately hang—and yet another where Avery sat unraveling the same type of beads Julia had.

"It was a celebration for Mick's parents when they got married. We'd so wanted a couple to get married on Valentine's Day in this town and they obliged us."

A delicate elbow hit her in the ribs as Sloan muttered, "Say something nice."

Grier shot her a dirty look back as she pried her fingers out of the small scissors and reached for a can of Coke someone had pressed on her. "That's really nice, Mrs. Forsyth."

"It wasn't just nice." Mary O'Shaughnessy floated over to their table as if she carried a radar device. "It was dreamy. Just as we'd hoped. Mick arrived the following November."

Grier almost choked on her soda. "That's great."

"His parents didn't waste any time making me a grandmother." Mary's beatific smile shone down on her and Grier had the sudden urge to scream, *Fire!* and flee the building.

When neither she nor Sloan said anything, Mary continued on as if there had never been a silence. "I've always thought Mick would make an excellent father."

"I agree." The words were out before she could stop them and Grier quickly realized she had no interest in holding back the compliment. "He's a wonderful man, Mrs. O'Shaughnessy. He'll make a great father."

Giant hearts practically floated from Julia's and Mary's eyes as they exchanged glances down the table. Grier wondered abstractly if she and Sloan came off nearly so scary when they got together.

If she was honest with herself, she sort of hoped they did.

And then slightly scary turned into completely diabolical as a deep male voice echoed—hale and hearty—through the hall. "Hello."

"Well, speak of the devil." Mary dropped her mouth into an *O* of surprise. "Mick is here and he's brought our supplies."

If the thought of a roomful of women staring on as she and Mick danced around each other was daunting, the image of more construction paper had Grier's stomach bunching up in knots.

"You mean there's more?"

"Why don't you go relieve the delivery boy?"

Grier shifted to avoid another one of Sloan's razor-sharp elbow pokes. "And why don't you mind your own business before I dig up some lefty scissors to really torture you with."

"Oh, come on, it's sweet. The grandmothers are playing cupid." Sloan pointed at their overflowing table. "It's oddly festive."

"I hate you."

Sloan offered up a mock sigh before reaching for another piece of construction paper. "It's a thin line between love and hate."

"Grier!" Mary waved her over. "You're on heart duty. Could you give me a hand?"

"You're being summoned, Ms. Thompson."

"Screw the thin line. I well and truly hate you." Grier stood to cross the room. The feeling wasn't unlike being naked as each and every eye in the Montgomery Meeting and Recreation Center focused on her.

So why was it the only eyes she could concentrate on were the vivid blue pair belonging to Mick O'Shaughnessy?

Chapter Six

"*A*nd would this be your idea of subtle, Grandma? Or simply crafty and opportunistic?"

Although his grandmother's eyes widened in mock innocence as her hands went up into a "who me?" pose, he wasn't buying the act for one moment.

Besides, she'd taught him that look when he was four.

"*Never admit guilt, Michael Patrick,*" she admonished him as she caught him with his hands full of melted chocolate chips from where he'd swiped a few fresh cookies off her stove. "*Make someone prove it.*"

Although his four-year-old's reasoning skills hadn't quite grasped the lesson, she'd exhibited the behavior enough times over the years for him to figure it out.

"Grier, dear. Mick's brought more supplies."

Grier never cracked a smile, but he didn't miss the lighthearted tone as she sized up the load of supply boxes he carried. "Oh good. Now we can make twenty thousand hearts instead of just ten."

"You can never have enough, dear. However"— Mary reached over and patted her arm—"you've been toiling away for hours. You must be famished."

"I'm positively light-headed."

"Mick, get this woman to the diner. She needs sustenance immediately."

Whatever joke was afoot was lost on him as he took in Grier's raised eyebrows, his grandmother's hopeful expression and the avid gazes of a roomful of women. "Of course. I could use a burger myself. I haven't eaten since breakfast."

"Perfect. It's all settled, then." Mary waved her arms. "Shoo now, before she passes out."

Mick's head was still spinning three minutes later as he ushered a bundled-up Grier out the door of the community center.

Mary watched the door to the meeting center slam closed with a satisfying thud. Although her money was on Mick, she couldn't quite shake the empathy that swamped her every time she looked at Jonas Winston's daughter.

So much wasted time.

"Nice job." Sophie sidled up next to her. "The scissors were a nice touch."

"Just a bit of extra incentive to get her running for the door when the opportunity arose to leave."

Mary hesitated for the briefest of moments, the indecision as foreign to her as the sudden swath of fear that lit up her spine.

"Am I doing the right thing?"

"Of course you are. They're crazy about each other."

"That girl has an awful lot of baggage. The hard kind that doesn't go away with the flick of a wrist. Am I only adding more?"

"But they care for each other. They just need to get out of their heads and in each other's way a bit more."

Sophie's cheery retort did nothing to assuage her concerns. "I know, but is it enough?"

The cheery smile fell into open-mouthed shock. "You don't believe that?"

"I do believe love can be enough, but what if she can't get past it? Her parents did a number on her and from what I can tell, whoever was in her life before she came here finished off the job. That girl's nursing a world of hurt."

"And the solution is our Mick."

Mary wanted to think it was that easy, but decades of living forced her to acknowledge that very few things ever were. And her grandson nursed his heart-aches, even if he had somehow figured out a way to control it and keep it hidden over the years.

What she didn't know was what Mick would do if he lost everything again.

"Mind telling me what that was all about?"

"Lesser of two evils," Grier whispered as she glanced back over her shoulder at the brightly lit community center.

"I'm sorry?"

"Your grandmother nearly crippled me tonight. I still can't feel my right wrist."

He reached for her hand automatically, the gesture as natural as breathing. "What happened?"

Satisfaction bloomed in his chest when her voice hitched, but she quickly righted herself. *And* left her

hand in his. "Elementary school scissors that were is-
sued when Eisenhower was president, for starters."

"So I'm less evil than school supplies?"

Her light gasp floated from her in a quick puff he
could see in the cold air. "I didn't mean you. I meant it
was far preferable to get out of there rather than being
stared at by a roomful of people while forced to use
small torture devices designed for five-year-old hands."

"I see."

"But the burgers are inspired."

"I know. I've seen you eat, remember?"

Grier giggled at that and he marveled that the
woman could be so *un*prickly about something most
women would have hit him for.

"Speaking of other things I know about you, I heard
you spent the afternoon with Tasty doing his accounting."

She turned toward him, her tilted face sweetly
framed by the ugliest gray beanie cap he'd ever laid
eyes on. "And for my troubles, I got my second copy of
this gorgeous piece of fashion."

"It's a winner."

"It's hideous."

Without thinking to censor himself, he leaned in and
pressed a quick kiss to her forehead. Or what passed
for her forehead under the thick wool of the cap. "But
you're not."

"Why do you do that?"

"Do what?"

"Say sweet things that make you very hard to resist."

He squeezed the small hand that still sat firmly in his. "Why are you trying so hard to resist me?"

"Why are you fighting me so hard on this?"

"Because I'm interested in you, Grier. And I want to spend time with you and get to know you better."

"We passed that step by sleeping with each other."

Her answer caught him up short and he stopped in the middle of the sidewalk, a few doors down from the diner. "What does that have to do with anything?"

"We crossed the line and made what's between us more serious. And it can't be that important."

He shook his head. "You've lost me."

"We jumped too fast. And now we're trying to make it more than it is. It was a fling, Mick. A fun, incredible, crazy ride. But it can't be more."

Images of that ride seared his memories. "Why can't it? Sloan and Walker started off hot and heavy, and look at them now."

"But I'm not staying here like Sloan is."

"You could."

"My life is somewhere else."

"A life that, by all accounts, you're not very interested in any longer."

Her eyes narrowed and Mick knew immediately he'd overstepped. "What's that supposed to mean?"

"You don't have a job. I've figured that much out based on the fact you've been here for well over six weeks. No one is allowed that much time away. What happened?"

"Nothing happened to me. I'm between jobs right now."

Mick had his suspicions it was something more but opted to let it go. "Fine. What about your family? You get into a pinch up here and you call a friend. What's that about?"

"Sloan's been my best friend for well over a decade. We're like family and we help each other out. That's what friends do."

"Which is my point. The very person who might tether you to New York isn't staying there any longer."

"I'm not just uprooting my life because you and I had a good time together."

The words had their intended effect as the painful truth of what she was telling him struck him like stinging needles. "I guess I thought we had something more between us. Clearly that was my mistake."

"And there we go again."

Again was right. Frustration rode Mick like a harsh tailwind, but unlike the laws of aerodynamics, he had no clue about what brewed and bubbled between them.

The woman was stubborn, a trait he knew he matched in spades.

But why did they keep coming back to this same impasse?

"Why don't I take a rain check on that burger?"

He swallowed the urge to protest. "I'll walk you back to the hotel."

Grier finished up the e-mail she'd promised Tasty the day before. A quick Internet search had turned up several links that would help him navigate some accounting basics. After one final read-through and an offer to come over and walk him through any questions he might have, she hit Send and sat back in her chair.

The walls of her hotel room had been closing in all morning and the e-mail to Indigo's most unique proprietor hadn't taken nearly as long as she'd have liked.

Of course, if she were fighting simple boredom, that would be one thing. But guilt layered underneath boredom was a recipe for oppressive thoughts that refused to quiet.

She'd been unfair to Mick and she owed him an apology.

The real question, to her mind, was how to make the apology without suggesting she was relenting on her point of view.

Or better, her conscious taunted, *how to get in and get out so he doesn't have time to change your point of view.*

The man was persuasive when he set his mind to it.

And no matter how many ways she tried to convince herself they didn't have a future together, an increasingly large part of her wanted to believe there was a way.

Mick allowed the heavy beat of Keith Richards's guitar to wash over him as he tightened up the engine of his DeHavilland. The ritual of getting underneath the hood of his planes dated back to his high school days and nothing had ever worked better for helping him think through a problem and clear his head.

And it had the added benefit of keeping his equipment in top working order.

He and Jack had a light day and Jack had opted to take their runs while using it as the perfect opportunity to take Jess into Fairbanks for a day of shopping.

Which was fine by him.

Mick reached for one of the wrenches he had stored in his back pocket and began to tighten the bolts he'd loosened earlier, finding satisfying the simple act of fixing what he'd taken apart.

Unlike the mystery of Grier.

He knew she was in pain and he wasn't trying to add to it.

Despite his continued pushing, if she asked him to walk away, he would. He wasn't one to stay where he wasn't wanted and he certainly wouldn't insist on spending time with a woman who wasn't interested. But he *knew* that wasn't it.

And no matter how he looked at it, he couldn't break through whatever it was that held her back.

"You're a man of many talents."

Mick looked down from the movable staircase he stood on to see the object of his thoughts staring up at him. Long, dark hair framed her delicate features and the bright, vivid gray of her eyes seemed to take up her whole face.

"Hey."

"You not only fly the planes, but you can fix them, too."

"No use flying something if you don't know how it works."

"That makes a surprising amount of sense." Grier nodded. "I come bearing lunch from the diner. I thought you might be hungry, and I owe you a rain check on those burgers."

"You thought right." Mick reached for the rag he'd thrown over the rim of the staircase and rubbed at the grease that stained his fingers. "How'd you get out here?"

"Avery let me borrow her car." She held up a bag and the scent of fresh-cooked burgers and hot fries wafted up toward him. "Where can I put this?"

He pointed to the kitchenette nestled into the far side of the hangar. "Go ahead and put everything on that small table. There are Cokes in the fridge. I'll be right down."

As she turned to cross the hangar, Mick took a moment to admire the view. Just like the night before, the thick coat did nothing to diminish his interest. And when she stopped behind the table to shrug out of her coat, he couldn't help but admire the small curvy frame clad in jeans and a pale green cashmere sweater.

How was it possible he went from competent and efficient to brain-dead just by looking at her? With a shake of his head, he turned back to the plane as he remembered he was mad at her.

More than that, he was hurt.

While the sight of her fired his blood, he wanted more than sex. And he thought of her as more than a good time.

He finished tightening the last bolt so there'd be no mistake of missing it later and then dropped the wrench into the toolbox that had been his grandfather's. The action was simple—and one he'd done more times in his life than he could count—but it held an odd sense of ceremony.

Grier waited for him.

He took the stairs and crossed to the sink to wash up. "So, what did I do to deserve lunch?"

"You mean aside from the fact that I owe you a giant apology for the way I acted last night?" She eyed him sideways as she opened the bag. The warm smell of grease and potatoes made his stomach growl, reminding him he'd skipped breakfast.

He reached for one of the Cokes and popped the tab, curious enough to say nothing and let her continue.

Once lunch was spread out between them, she took her seat and reached for the other Coke. "I realize I've been giving you a series of signals at best mixed and at worst terribly misleading."

She held his gaze when she spoke and her back was arrow straight. Although he had very little interest—or need—for an apology, he had to give her points for style.

Grier Thompson didn't back down from a fight. And she was mature enough to take on the hard stuff with grace and a matter-of-fact approach that was rather charming.

Curious, Mick took a sip of his soda, enjoying the cool slide of the sweet beverage as he fought the urge to smile. He knew she was being serious—and he knew he should take her comments that way—but damn if she didn't look about as appetizing as a tray of chocolate chip cookies.

He was even crazy about the small earnest line of worry that furrowed her brow.

"You're smiling."

"A little. But please, keep going."

"And not only do I owe you an apology, but I think it's only fair that we lay out a set of ground rules. I'm going to be in Indigo for the next month or so until my father's estate is wrapped up. Since I've come to think of you as a friend, there's no reason we can't hang out."

"Ground rules are good. And I'm glad to know you think of me as a friend."

"You've known Avery forever. And Sloan and Walker are here, too. There's no reason we all can't hang out together. Do the sort of friend things people our age do."

He took another sip of soda. "The things people our age do?"

"Sure. Dinners on Saturday evening. Nights out at the bar. Friend things."

"Hmmm. Those are nice."

"Exactly. There's no reason we shouldn't be able to go out and do those things. I don't exactly want to be a hermit for the time I'm here." As if satisfied she'd made her point, she reached for a fry.

"You're missing something fairly important."

"Bowling." Grier snapped her fingers. "I missed bowling. That's something else we can do."

Mick held back a bark of laughter as he reached for his burger. "That wasn't exactly what I was thinking of."

"You don't like bowling?"

"I do like bowling. But I was thinking more along the lines of sex."

"Oh."

"And I don't want to have sex with Avery or Sloan."

Mick couldn't resist poking holes in her friendship theory. "And I sure as hell don't want to have it with Walker, even if he does have a nice ass."

"You're really not letting this go, are you?"

"No, I'm not."

Grier reached for a fry and dipped it in a small pool of ketchup. "What if I told you I wanted you to? Let this go."

"Do you?"

"Yes."

"Then I walk away."

Her eyes shot up from where she focused on that lone fry. "You will?"

"Of course. I'd never force myself on a woman."

"You're not forcing yourself." She took a small bite. "Not in that way."

Whatever humor he'd felt faded. "Well, I won't in any way."

"I know that."

"So, what do you say? Do I need to walk away? Because"—he leaned over the table—"just between us friends, I really don't want to."

He watched the emotions flit across her face— frustration to desire to sadness—and wasn't immune to any of it. But how did he break through her resistance and encourage her to explore what was between them?

Of what could be between them.

"Can we work on the friendship part and think about the rest? I'm a good friend. And I know how to do that part of my life really, really well. Just ask Sloan and Avery."

Mick fought the disappointment that settled in his gut and focused on the positive. She was in a tough spot in her life and if he didn't give her space, he'd have nothing. "I'm not sure I'm up to the gossip requirements."

"So we'll talk about Walker's nice ass. That's a good place to start."

Grier took a deep breath as Mick's laughter echoed off the walls of the hangar. Whatever she'd expected coming here, the comfortable, easy acceptance he offered her wasn't it.

She did enjoy his company. The easy camaraderie was warm and welcome and rather unique in her life. She had several female friends but couldn't say she had all that many male friends. Of course, she didn't want to attack any of her female friends in a sexual frenzy, so perhaps the whole "let's be friends" theory needed work.

She reached for her burger and took a bite, willing some sort of answer from the delicious combination of beef and cheese. When all she got was a scrumptious mouthful of ecstasy that screamed, *Seize the moment of sin*, she figured the burger wasn't the best source of wisdom.

"What's up with the plane?"

"Routine maintenance."

"I noticed something on the flight up and again today. You really understand that flying the plane's only a part of being a pilot. You pay attention to your equipment and you seem to care about the plane as much as flying it."

"Let me let you in on a little secret."

Mick leaned forward and she found herself drawn inexorably toward him, his blue eyes pulling her in despite herself. "What's that?"

"I actually like to feel confident the plane's going to stay up in the air when I fly it."

The laughter filled the space between them again and Grier couldn't have held back the carefree feeling if she'd wanted to. "I can see how that would be of concern."

His smile faded as his gaze warmed. "It's good to see you smile."

A denial rose to her lips, but she held it back. Whatever feelings she fought for Mick, she couldn't fight the fact that he noticed things.

Because he actually *saw* her.

Saw her in a way no one else ever had.

"Why do you say that?"

"You've had a lot on your plate since coming here. A lot of missed years to sort through. And then there's Kate."

"Is it that obvious?"

"If you're looking."

Grier appreciated the honesty. It was raw and biting, but at least he wasn't hiding from the truth.

Mick continued. "I obviously couldn't hear what was said, but I could see your conversation with Kate didn't go all that well the other night."

"What gave you that idea? We didn't fight."

"It was the look on your face as you spoke to her."

Grier wadded her napkin into a tight ball. "What look?"

"Like she slowly chipped away at your heart with each and every word."

"Aren't you the poet?" When her joke didn't elicit a reply, she opted for the question she was suddenly desperate to know the answer to. "You saw that?"

"I did. What did she say?"

"It wasn't much, really. Just how much my father loved this time of year."

"He did love this time of year. Had the best light display on the entire block. Better than anyone in town, really."

Grier pictured the small A-frame on Spruce Street, lit from top to bottom. "See. That's a nice memory, told with a small smile and a glint of remembrance in your gaze. I can picture it in my mind and the thought of it makes me happy."

"That's good."

"It is. It makes me happy to think of him as a real person with real interests."

"But?"

"But from Kate, it was like she was trying to prove something to me. Like how well she knew him and all the private moments they shared together. Which, well, no shit. I *know* that already. The whole damn town knows it. I'm the bastard child he never knew."

"Grier—"

She waved a hand to stop him. "I don't mean that quite as sordidly as it sounds. But I do mean to say none of this is a secret, Mick. I'm the kid he never knew. Never took the time to know. Nothing can change that and frankly, I fucking resent that Kate can't see that."

"She's always been a bit brittle, if you know what I mean. Nice enough, but it's always been layered over a slight veneer of resentment."

"That's awfully astute of you."

"I hear way more than I want to hanging out all day with an airport full of the town's best gossips. And I listen to far more than they give me credit for." That bright twinkle was back in his eyes. "Shhh. Don't give away my secrets."

Grier made a quick cross over her chest with her finger. "I swear."

"Anyway, she can be as positive and happy about Jonas as she wants to now, but she also can't rewrite history. He was gone a lot of the time for work and it never set well with her. After her mother died, he tried to be home more, but by that time she was a teenager with her own thoughts and ideas."

Mick sat back and wadded up the waxed paper from his burger. "All I'm saying is that from an outsider's perspective, the two of them had their problems the same as other people. It might make her feel better to try to forget that now, but it doesn't change the facts."

If she was surprised at his frank words, she was even more puzzled by her reaction to them.

A small kernel of sympathy had opened for Kate and she wasn't quite sure what to do about it. "That's sort of sad."

"It is, actually. You can't do anything about your choices once someone's gone. That's why it's far better to fix things when you can."

"You believe that?"

"My attitude about life is pretty similar to my attitude about planes."

She glanced at the plane that sat on the opposite side of the hangar. "How so?"

"You do the maintenance to keep things running smoothly. It doesn't mean things don't break from time to time, but you make a point to fix them so they don't do any more damage."

Struck by the wisdom, Grier could only stare at the man. How he sat easily across from her, his large frame eating up the folding chair and his shoulders blocking the counter from view.

He was a special man. An honest one, too.

Despite her need to stay aloof and distant, with his simple words she knew with absolute certainty Mick O'Shaughnessy had chipped away at another piece of her heart.

Chapter Seven

Jason heard his flight announced in a soft, mild voice over the PA system. The gentle swell of conversation hummed around him in the airport executive lounge, but most of it was a dull blur as he thought through his strategy once more.

He didn't know what had taken him so long, but now that he had settled on a course of action, he wasn't going to be deterred.

He'd win Grier back. Groveling would be involved and while it wasn't an enticing prospect, he'd earned his punishment fair and square. He'd take his lumps like a man and at the end of it, he'd have his fiancée back and they could move on with their lives.

Or life together, as it were.

If that thought stuck in his gut in a tight knot, there was no help for it. A good man knew where he'd gone wrong and corrected his mistakes.

And he was a good man.

Add to it that he could combine this trip with a jaunt to the Seattle office to see one of their key Pacific Rim clients and he was hard-pressed to argue with the serendipity of it all. He'd spend a week in Seattle, then head for Alaska.

It was perfect.

He glanced at his BlackBerry once more and the note from Grier's mother.

JASON—SO LOVELY TO HEAR FROM YOU. I'D SUGGEST
A SURPRISE ATTACK AS GRIER'S BEEN A BIT PRICKLY
OF LATE. SHE'S STAYING AT THE INDIGO BLUE. . . .

It hadn't escaped him that the note held more orders than advice, but seeing as how they were all couched in Patrice Thompson's überpolite phrasing, Jason chalked it up to yet another round of punishment he needed to take with a smile.

With a last sip of the scotch he'd nursed since entering the airport lounge, he gathered up his things.

He was a good man.

Time to start acting like one.

The gentle hum of conversation at the Jitters did nothing to calm Grier's nerves. She reached for her spoon and stirred a couple of sugars into the frothy foam of her cappuccino, then lifted the mug to take a large sip.

It had been five days since she'd had her phone interview for the job and still had heard nothing.

Five long days in which she'd done nothing but read, catch up on the TV she'd missed for the last several months and balance her checkbook.

Twice.

She was going stir-crazy.

An old *Vanity Fair* sat on a nearby table and she reached for it, determined to enjoy her coffee and another endless hour of private time. She'd read the Proust questionnaire and enjoy it, damn it.

"I talked to Tasty."

Grier looked up into Chooch's bright gaze. She had had no idea the woman went anywhere without her husband, Hooch, by her side, but he was nowhere in sight. "Hello."

"Let me get my coffee and then we're going to have us a little chat."

"All—all right." Grier wondered at the sudden demand but wasn't going to argue. Company was company and she was sick to death of her own.

Within moments, the older woman was back at her side with a steaming mug of something resembling a candy bar.

"What is that?"

"Today's special. A caramel mocha."

"Is that a Twix bar for a stir stick?"

"Yep." Chooch smiled as she reached for the candy. "My own special invention."

Grier sent off a quick prayer the woman wasn't going to end up in a diabetic coma and put her best manners to use. "I'd say you're inspired."

"Hooch sure thinks so." She laughed and slapped her knee before leaning forward. "But you weren't asking about our sex lives."

"Um, no." Grier reached for her own coffee, her Upper East Side manners no match for an adequate response.

"I want you to do our taxes."

"I'm sorry?"

"Taxes. You know, we gotta pay 'em. I've been talking to Hooch and our eyesight's not what it once was. And he fucked 'em up so badly last year, we ended up owing. And you did help Tasty with that mess of stuff he's got in his computer. So I want you to do them."

"Well—"

"You are an accountant, aren't you?"

"Yes."

"We'll pay you."

"It's not about payment." Grier saw the woman's eyes narrow in glee and quickly added, "Not that I couldn't come up with a more-than-fair pricing structure. But what I meant was, are you sure you want me knowing your personal information?"

When Chooch just stared at her, Grier added, "Your annual income."

"Oh, that." Chooch waved a hand. "Don't matter if you do know. Hooch and I are right rich. He made a few million on the pipeline and we've invested well. Everyone knows that. No reason you can't know, too."

"Oh, okay. Well, then."

"I'll be by tomorrow with our receipts. We'll set up in the conference room at the hotel."

"Okay."

Chooch nodded and stood, clearly satisfied with the conversation. "I'm going to get this to go. Gotta get back out to the house before that man watches too many reruns of *America's Top Model* and gets ideas in his head. I've got things to accomplish today and I can't spend the whole damn afternoon in bed."

Grier wondered immediately what had possessed her to take a sip of her coffee before Chooch had finished speaking, but she managed just barely to keep from choking. Once she could speak again, she added a polite, "Of course not."

"I'll see you tomorrow. Ten o'clock?"

"Ten it is."

Grier watched Chooch swirl out of the coffee bar as fast as she came in, a to-go cup in her hand.

The thought flitted briefly through her mind to be careful what she wished for. But she couldn't deny her cappuccino and magazine were a whole lot more interesting now that she knew she had something to do tomorrow.

"Does this satisfy your need to do something social for the evening?" A small smile hovered on Avery's face as Ronnie, their bartender at Maguire's, lined up a row of tequila shots.

"This is exactly what I was talking about." Grier nodded as she licked her hand, then reached for the shaker of salt Ronnie placed next to the small glasses. "I've no interest in getting drunk, but a nice comfortable buzz with like-minded adults is just what the doctor ordered."

"I heard you've got a job tomorrow," Jess added as she took the saltshaker.

"Word travels fast," Grier couldn't resist adding with a dry tone.

Avery passed shot glasses from the bar, then held her own up. "To the small-town grapevine. May it forever bloom."

Grier clinked her glass with the two others, then drank down the rich tequila. She quickly reached for her lime to complete the ritualistic triumvirate practiced the world over and took a satisfied drag on the sour fruit. "Now that's a good start to girls' night out."

Her friends smiled as they all reached for the waiting beers that now lined the bar. "Thanks, Ronnie." Avery nodded as they each picked up their drinks and headed for an empty booth in the back.

"He likes you," Jess whispered as they slid into their seats a few moments later.

"Who?" Avery looked puzzled and it took all Grier had not to laugh outright.

"Um, Ronnie." Jess pointed back toward the bar where their bartender stood with a thoughtful look on his face. "He can't keep his eyes off you."

"Jess, he's about a decade younger than me."

"Which means his equipment is in prime condition," Grier added as she reached for a handful of pretzels.

"Ronnie?" Avery glanced back over her shoulder, only to turn a ripe shade of plum when he smiled broadly and winked. She turned back quickly. "You cannot be serious."

"Oh, we be serious," Jess said, warming up to the topic. "It's a long, cold winter and he'd be the perfect blanket. Trust me, I know about long, cold winters."

"Which you no longer have to suffer through," Avery added with a smile before laying her hand over Jess's. "A fact I am incredibly happy for you about, but um, Ronnie? No."

"Would you at least think about it?" Grier asked.

"I will if you seriously consider getting horizontal again with Mick."

"I can't do that."

"Yeah, well, I can't do that with Ronnie. I think I babysat him once."

"Eww." Grier lifted a hand. "Okay. Fair enough. We'll shut up."

"To small towns." Jess lifted her glass. "There's always baggage."

"Like dirty diapers," Grier added with a smile.

Avery threw a pretzel at her before clinking her beer merrily with the others. "To small towns."

Grier felt the bench seat buzzing before Jess reached for the phone in her back pocket. The bright smile that lit up her face was a huge clue as to who was on the other end. "Excuse me."

They watched her move across the bar to the quieter hallway that led to the restrooms, a spring in her step. "It's so good to see her like this," Avery said. "It was a long time coming."

"She had feelings for Jack for a while?"

"A few years. She never looked at him when he was married, but after Molly died, something happened between them. It took her a long time to open up about it. She was afraid the town would think she'd simply gone after a newly available bachelor."

"That's awful."

Avery's smile grew overly bright. "Yeah, well, people can think a lot of awful."

"I take it that's something you know a little about."

Grier knew the basics—that Avery and her high

school sweetheart, Roman, had parted ways years before when he left to join the National Hockey League. She also had a pretty good idea of how that had affected Avery.

What she didn't know was why it continued to affect her, all these years later.

"People believe what they want to." Avery's voice was thoughtful after a sip of her beer. "Sometimes it's easier to let them."

"Do you really believe that?"

"Absolutely."

"It still doesn't change the fact that Ronnie's been eyeing you like a thirsty man dying for water."

Avery glanced back over at the bar, a smile spreading across her face. "It certainly is nice to be noticed."

Grier lifted her beer. "I'll drink to that."

"Hear, hear."

"Where's Sloan?"

"She and Walker are over at Sophie's."

"And let me guess. Walker's grandmother has gone into full-on wedding planning mode?"

Grier smiled. "They've been engaged less than a month and the female urge to plan weddings is running rampant from New York to Alaska."

"It is one of the attributes that separates us from the animals," Avery added.

Jess rejoined them mid-discussion on hemlines and train lengths. "Jack and Mick are finished up out at the airfield. They'll be here shortly. I hope you don't hate me for expanding this beyond girls' night out."

As Grier looked into Jess's hopeful face, she knew

she couldn't be so unkind as to say no. And if the prospect of seeing Mick filled her with dangerous anticipation, well . . . maybe girls' night out was overrated.

Mick and Jack saw the three of them in a laughing heap in a back booth at Maguire's. Mick slapped his partner on the back. "You go on ahead and I'll snag us some longnecks at the bar."

"Will do."

He watched Jack walk away and couldn't quite stamp out the slash of envy that lanced through him at his friend's happy step. The man deserved it, Mick well knew. But damn, he wouldn't mind a piece of it for himself.

Which was the exact reason he needed to kick back with a few beers and shake off this maudlin attitude that had hit him on his midafternoon delivery in Talkeetna.

Petey Stone, the town dry goods owner, had meant well. Hell, Mick had known the man since he was a kid and the guy didn't have an unkind bone in his body.

It was just bad timing.

"How's your father doing, Mick? Haven't seen him for a while."

Mick had wanted to respond back with *That makes two of us*, but he'd held back and offered up a big smile. "He's been chasing wild things in Montana. I'll let him know you asked after him."

"You bet. Tell him I'm finally ready to part with that Winchester rifle he's had his eye on."

"Will do, Petey. How's Sandy doing?"

"Fine, real good."

"And I bet the grandkids are getting big. . . ."

The conversation faded off in his mind as he reached for the longnecks Ronnie held out to him. With a smile and a wave toward the back of the bar, he added, "I suspect we'll need another round before long as well."

He left his credit card, irritated when he couldn't quite shake off the afternoon.

A new rifle . . . Like hell he'd be sharing that bit of news with his father. Besides, he consoled himself as he shoved his wallet back in his pocket, by the time the old man managed to even get his ass back to town, it'd be summer. Petey would have sold the gun by then.

Which was fine by him.

Damn it. Mick shook his head as he crossed toward the back booth. He had to get past it.

Had to loosen up a bit.

And found it hard to be surprised when the sight of Grier, her cheeks bright with color and a broad smile on her lush mouth, managed to help him do just that.

The hard pit of grief that had been lodged inside him all afternoon eased, shrinking as he sat down next to her. The warmth of her body burned into his where they touched, shoulder to hip to leg, and Mick felt a different sort of tightness grip him.

She felt good.

And when she didn't scoot over or put room between them, that ball of lead in his stomach faded away entirely, replaced by the intoxicating thrill of being near her.

"I told Ronnie to send another round over when he gets a free minute."

The three women let out a loud burst of giggles and all he could do was stare at Jack in what had to be a matched expression of puzzlement.

"There's something funny about another round?"

"There is when it's Ronnie bringing it," Grier whispered. "He's got a crush on Avery."

"And has since he was about thirteen," Jack added. "He was just always afraid Roman would come back and beat the shit out of him."

"Like that would have happened. Besides, Roman wouldn't beat up a kid." Avery's quick leap to Roman's defense had Mick resisting the urge to smile. His old friend had fucked up royally when he'd walked out on Avery, but it was nice to see she could still defend him from time to time.

Mick had always thought it was a shame the two of them hadn't found a way to stay friends. And even as he thought it, he had to admit that friendship wouldn't be enough if Roman felt for Avery what Mick felt for Grier.

Maybe Avery and Roman had it right. Sever ties and move on.

The warmth of Grier's body continued to heat him and a low-grade burn settled under his skin.

He wanted her.

No matter how much he wanted to respect her wishes, he couldn't deny that. She had a powerful hold on him and he wanted to let loose with her.

"You sure you're ready for Chooch and Hooch to-morrow?"

Mick clued back in on the conversation as Grier's nervous laugh registered. "I'm not sure."

"What is this?"

Grier lifted an eyebrow as she turned toward him in the booth. "You mean there's actually someone in this town who doesn't know my business?"

"I've been out on runs all day."

"Well, I should be grateful it hasn't made it to the airstrip yet."

"You're doing Chooch and Hooch's taxes," Jack said dryly over his beer.

"Damn it! I do not believe it." Grier slapped a hand on the table. "News does travel fast."

"Maggie's got a bet going that their return this year will be over a cool million."

"No way," Jess breathed. "Have you seen that odd farm they live in? There's no way they've got that much money."

Jack held out a hand. "Wanna bet?"

"Well, whatever it is, I won't be sharing the number." Grier's voice was prim and that spine of steel was back. Mick couldn't help but admire the hell out of her convictions.

"Oh, we don't expect you to tell," Jack quickly reassured her. "Hooch'll be all around town with the number before you even get their return e-mailed to the IRS."

"You're really doing this?" Mick couldn't help asking.

"It's not like I had a choice. Chooch is sort of a whirling dervish. And I was an easy mark this morning over at the Jitters."

"How so?"

"I'm so bored, I'm about to start hand washing my clothes. With rocks," Grier added as an afterthought.

"You know. . . ." Jess leaned forward. "This isn't a bad idea. Lots of folks could use help with their taxes. You've got a bit of time on your hands. Why don't you set up shop and help them out?"

"This isn't exactly my thing," Grier said softly. "I'm a corporate accountant."

"But you know how to do income taxes," Jess said, pushing her point.

"Well, yeah. Of course. But it's not like . . ." She broke off. "I guess it's not a bad idea. And it would be nice to help out the people who have made me feel welcome here."

"I'm sure Walker would let you set up in the office. And we've got a secure area to lock up the files each day."

Mick felt the change in Grier almost immediately. A gentle hum vibrated off her as she turned the concept over in her mind. "You all really think this is a good idea?"

Mick turned toward her and laid a hand over hers. "I think it's a great idea."

Chapter Eight

"You don't have to walk me back. It's not that far." Grier turned toward Mick as they walked out of Maguire's. The hard bite of cold caught her by surprise—as it always did—and she rubbed her mittened hands together.

Damn, but she'd never known cold like this before. It infiltrated the bones and bit at the skin with sharp, gnawing teeth.

It was also strangely exhilarating.

"I could see Avery wasn't ready to turn in yet and it's clear you're ready to go."

"It doesn't make people feel all that comfortable when their accountant has a hangover."

"Funny thing, that. They feel pretty similar about their pilots." Mick pulled on a pair of heavy gloves. "So we both have a good reason to leave."

You could have an even better one than doing tax returns if you'd just let yourself see where things with him could go, her conscience taunted.

That damn voice had gotten louder with each boring day that left her with nothing but her own thoughts for company. Loud and insistent, it had no problem taunting her with the reminder that Mick would be ready, willing and able to help her pass the time.

And then it had gone and broken the sound barrier the moment Mick had sat down next to her in the booth, his long body edged alongside hers.

If only he weren't so hot. It was hard to ignore a man who radiated heat like a furnace.

Right. Because that was the *only* reason. She'd also heard there was some nice waterfront property just outside town that someone would sell her.

The street was quiet as they moved down the sidewalk, the sounds of the bar fading behind them into the night air.

"We're scheduled for another big storm. Look." Mick pointed upward. "No stars."

"Can you still fly?"

"Depends on the weather. If this is as bad as they expect it to be, we won't make any runs tomorrow."

Grier couldn't put her finger on what it was, but something tinged the edges of his words. It wasn't what he said, so much as something she sensed that hovered underneath. She'd felt it at the bar, too. He'd been quiet, smiling and nodding but not really saying much.

"You don't sound too upset about it."

"A day off'll be a welcome change."

"Is that all?" She wasn't sure why she pressed— couldn't have explained it if she'd tried.

"Sure, why?"

"I don't know. You seem, well, a little sad."

"Everything's fine." He reached for her elbow and pointed with his free hand. "Be careful there. Black ice."

Grier sidestepped the ice, leaning into him as he pulled her closer. "Thanks."

She didn't say anything else, curious to see what he'd do.

"Why do you think I'm sad?"

"Just a sense, really."

The hand at her elbow tightened reflexively and she wondered if Mick even noticed. "I ran into an old friend today on one of my runs. He said a few things and it just churned up a few memories. Nothing big."

"Want to talk about it?"

"Really. It's nothing." He pulled her to his side again, dropping her elbow to wrap a hand around her waist. "There's another patch. Watch it."

"Okay." She wanted to ask more—wanted to understand why something that wasn't a big deal had put him in a mood—but knew she had no right to push.

So instead, Grier reveled in the feel of his strong arm around her body and was glad when he didn't move away. The odd dance between them—a step forward, another back—had a funny sweetness to it she was loath to give up.

She didn't want to be a tease, but neither could she ignore the way he made her feel.

Safe and wanted. And special. Very, very special.

"You're awfully quiet." Mick's arm tightened on her waist.

"It's a quiet . . ."

Her words evaporated as her foot hit a patch of ice. On sheer instinct she turned toward him, her hands seeking purchase wherever she could get a good grip.

The movements were ineffective, doing nothing more than sending him off-balance so they both went sprawling.

"Night." Grier couldn't hold back the laughter as she inhaled a mouthful of leather from his jacket. Pushing on his arm, she tried to dislodge the heavy weight he made on her chest.

Mick scrambled, unable to get his footing on the slick surface. No sooner had he lifted himself off her than he fell right back down, his face landing on the heavy padding of the front of her coat. Another peal of laughter bubbled up before she could stop it and Grier's arms went around him in a gesture so natural, she barely realized she did it. "You're the graceful one."

"You have no idea."

He planted his hands on either side of her body and lifted himself above her. Although the weight lessened, she could still feel the solid length of him and the sensation shot heat straight to her core.

A wicked light glinted off his blue eyes and Grier knew she was in dangerous territory. She wanted this man.

Oh, how she wanted him.

Strands of desire bound them together as time seemed to slow. The feel of her in his arms—even covered in layers of down coat—was a heady aphrodisiac and Mick could feel her lithe form through the heavy material. Their breath puffed in quick exhalations between them as soft clouds of mist floated past their cheeks.

His body responded, hard and tight with need. One

long moment spun out after the next as they stared at each other under the light of the streetlamps, torturing each other with promises of all that could be between them.

It was that thought—of what could be—that finally pulled him back from the mindless oblivion. He'd been accused of a lot of things in his life, but horny bastard out for his own selfish ends had never been laid at his feet.

She'd said no and he'd respect that.

Even if it killed him.

Seeing as how he'd very nearly forgotten they were lying on a cold, ice-covered sidewalk in January, he knew he was dangerously close to that oblivion.

"Grier, I'm sorry. Let me help you up."

She squirmed underneath him as if coming back to her senses and he had to hold on to her shoulders to still her. "Hold on or we'll end up right back in the same spot."

Once she stopped moving, Mick looked for a patch on the sidewalk without ice. As soon as he found it, he planted one heavily booted foot and shifted to stand. Extending a hand, he bent down. "Come on now, nice and easy."

She trembled to her feet like a colt standing for the first time. As soon as she was steady, she dropped her hand from his.

"Come on. The hotel's not too far."

They continued on in the same direction, slower now in hopes of avoiding another slick patch. "You didn't hurt anything, did you?"

"No." Her breath whooshed out in a heavy puff as she added a sigh to punctuate the denial. "Nothing other than my pride."

"You'd be surprised by how many people end up on their ass in January in this town."

Another telltale puff of breath accompanied her soft-spoken words. "That's not what I'm talking about."

"Oh?"

They came to a halt at the edge of the Indigo Blue's parking lot. "I'm not a tease, Mick."

"I never said you were."

"It's not hard to read the subtext."

A surge of anger welled up. He hadn't thought of her as a tease and he'd be damned if he'd let her think he did. "There is no subtext other than good old-fashioned male frustration. I want you, Grier. I'm not going to go away and pretend that's not the case. I'm also not going to pretend I don't see the reciprocal interest."

"I know that. And, for the record, I'm blaming me, not you. You're like a drug and I'm the addict waiting for my next fix."

"I'm sorry?"

"My whole life has been built on the premise that good behavior begets good things. And you know what?" The words flew from her lips in a heated wave as fire burned in the depths of her gray eyes. "It's all bullshit!"

Mick reached for her, not quite sure what had prompted the sudden flash of rage. "Grier. Calm down. It's all right."

"No, Mick. It's not all right. It's anything but fucking all right."

She turned and began to pace and Mick was abstractly grateful Susan had seen to it the parking lot was clear of any snow and ice. Whatever bothered Grier had to come out. He suspected this was as good a time as any.

"You want to tell me what this is about?"

"I want you so bad I'm cross-eyed with it. I mean, for God's sake, we were just lying there on a frozen sidewalk and I wanted to strip your clothes off. Who does that?"

"Us, apparently?"

Her eyebrows narrowed and he didn't miss the telltale furrow that marred her forehead. "You're missing my point."

"Obviously."

"All my life I've done the right thing and it's gotten me here. To this place. Fucked up and out of answers. Totally and completely out of answers."

"You think I can't be one of those answers?"

"I don't know. I swear to God, Mick, I just don't know. But I do know I can't live with myself if I hurt you."

With that, she turned and walked into the Indigo Blue. It was at the very last moment—just before she walked through the door—that she turned back to look at him.

It wasn't much, but it was enough.

It had to be.

*   *   *

Grier reached for the carafe of coffee on the center of the conference room table and poured her third cup of the morning. She hadn't slept well and in the unique irony that only a sleepless night could provide, she'd now give her last nickel to crawl back into bed and sleep for a week.

"You're looking bright eyed this morning," Chooch declared as she marched into the conference room, a shoe box under her arm. "You sure you're up to this?"

"Of course."

"Word has it you spent the evening at Maguire's," Hooch added.

"I was back by ten," Grier answered, sitting up straighter in her chair. "I was simply out with a few friends."

"So that's what you're calling Mick, now?" Hooch smiled, but Chooch hushed him with a swift hit to the gut.

"Damn, woman. It's not a secret those two are crazy about each other."

Grier ignored the not-so-subtle attempt at garnering gossip and focused on the task at hand.

"Why don't you both take a seat and we'll get started. I usually wait until February to do taxes, but I presume you're not waiting on W-2s from an employer. Is that correct?"

"Yep."

"What about bank statements, investment statements, things like that?"

"Oh yeah, we're still waiting on those"—Hooch waved his hand—"but we figured it'd be best to get started sorting through everything. That's always what takes me the longest."

"Sorting through everything?" Grier eyed them over the rim of her mug as they each took a seat on the opposite side of the table.

"Yep." Chooch laid her shoe box on the table and Hooch set a matched one beside it. "All our receipts are in there."

"That's how you've kept track of your expenses?"

"Yep." Both nodded.

"That's the only way? For the entire year?"

Both nodded again.

Grier thought briefly about politely declining the work and sending them on their way and then remembered the sheer boredom of the last week. At least this would be boredom with a purpose. "All right, then. Let's get you set up and then you can leave this with me and I'll work through it."

"You sure about that?" Hooch looked skeptical. "I mean about us leaving things."

"Well." Grier hesitated, not sure if she should be annoyed at the lack of faith or fearful she'd have to sit with one or both of them opposite her for however long it took to sort through two shoe boxes of receipts. "I will leave everything as I found it, only sorted."

"Oh. Okay." Hooch nodded. "That should work."

"And you can come pick it all up at the end of each session if you'd like."

"Even better. I knew I liked you," Hooch added as an afterthought. "It's nice to look at you."

Grier looked up from her laptop and the tax program software she'd downloaded the day before. "I'm sorry?"

"It's like looking at your dad again. Well, a prettier version of him, but it's familiar, you know? Friendly. Boy, do I miss him," Hooch added with a last small sigh.

"You knew my father? I mean, I know you'd know him as a neighbor in town, but you sound like you really knew him. As a friend."

"We both worked the pipeline, at different times. I was one of the geologists who surveyed the area about a decade before he was up there. Chooch and I did some traveling after that, but we all ended up settling around here. Your father was a good man, Grier. A real good man."

She nodded, the words a lovely comfort as she watched the small smile dance across Hooch's mouth as he remembered her father. "Thank you for that."

"You're welcome. And, for the record"—Hooch leaned forward—"we're all pulling for you on the whole will thing. Kate's gotta get that damn stick outta her ass, if you ask me."

"No one's asking you, Hooch," Chooch said, shushing him once again.

"I'm entitled to my opinion."

It didn't take a crystal ball to see the battle brewing, so Grier pointed toward the computer. "Why don't we go ahead and get started." She tapped a few keys. "I need your full names and Social Security numbers first."

"Herbert Michael McGilvray," Hooch announced,

before wagging a finger at her. "But don't go telling anyone what my first name is."

"Oh, okay." Grier questioned the need for secrecy over his first name as opposed to the actual contents of his return, which he apparently broadcast with glee, but held her tongue. It was her job to take down the information, nothing more. She then tapped in the Social Security number he rattled off and tabbed over to the next field.

"I assume you're filing jointly?"

"We're married, aren't we?" Chooch demanded.

"Of course. I just needed to confirm."

Chooch nodded. "I suppose you need to follow the prompts. Which is probably why Hooch fucked it up last year," she added with a philosophical wink.

"Exactly."

"Okay, Chooch. I need the same information from you."

"Jennifer Mason McGilvray." Grier typed as the woman counted off her Social, but looked up at the heavy sigh that accompanied the last digit.

"Everything okay?"

"I need you to keep my name a secret, too."

Grier looked up, determined to nip whatever preconceived notions they'd walked in with firmly in the bud. "Everything we do here is a secret, just so you know. This is a confidential exchange of information that I wouldn't share for two reasons. First, because it's wrong. Second, because I could lose my license if I went around talking about my clients' returns. All that said, I'm not quite following all the secrecy around names."

"I sound like a cocktail waitress," Chooch said, then added, "And Hooch is named after the shitty president who got us into the Great Depression."

"You'd look awfully cute in a bunny outfit," Hooch guffawed, and leaned over to give his wife a big smacking kiss on the cheek.

Grier wasn't sure what the protocol here was as corporate tax clients rarely brought anyone along to the audit and, if they did, it certainly wasn't to make googly eyes at them. With stoic reserve, she did her best to ignore the comments across the table and just kept typing. "Okay. Next step is your address."

They made it through the next five minutes with relatively few comments and a minimum of fuss, although Grier figured she would have to live for a long time with the image of them discussing the joys of naked hot tubbing at their mountain cabin in Tahoe.

Grier looked up from the keyboard with a smile. "Okay. That wasn't too bad. Why don't you hand me those receipts and we'll get started."

Before the words were even out of her mouth, Chooch and Hooch had their shoe boxes open and upside down. As a mountain of receipts spilled onto the table, Grier held back the small scream that crawled up her throat.

"We left the other boxes in the car."

"Other?"

"Well, yeah." Hooch nodded, his gaze solemn and strangely knowing. "We didn't want to scare you off before we got started."

*   *   *

"How's it going?" Avery asked.

Grier held up a hand as she walked through the swinging doors of the Indigo Blue's kitchen. "You do not get to ask me that, especially since I know you've been spying on me with the conference room camera."

"It didn't look that bad, until Hooch dumped that fourth box on the table."

Grier snagged a Coke out of the Subzero. "Do not make me breach my professional ethics by groaning and/or agreeing with you."

"Seeing as how Hooch cackled his way through the lobby about all five shoe boxes and how he wouldn't have to be going through any of them this year, I think you're safe."

"They are eccentric—I'll give them that."

"And proof positive of something my grandmother always said. There is a lid for every pot."

The Coke opened with a satisfying pop as Grier snagged a few slices of bread off the counter and moved to stand next to Avery. "Thank God."

Avery hip bumped her before passing over a bowl of egg salad she'd just finished stirring up. "I've got some file folders in the office if that will help."

"I'm not confident an entire filing cabinet would help, but I'll take what I can get."

They moved to a small table with their sandwiches and sat in companionable silence for a few minutes.

"Did you get what Jack said last night?"

Grier glanced up. "About what?"

"About Ronnie being afraid of Roman. Do you think that's true?"

Grier hedged on saying anything that might hurt Avery, but she also couldn't bring herself to lie. "I can see Roman being an imposing figure for the other men around here. Sure."

"Do you think that's why I can't seem to get a date?"

"Do *you* think that's the reason?"

Avery reached down and toyed with the edge of her napkin, tearing off small pieces. "I didn't think it was, but I'm starting to wonder."

"Have you been interested in any of the men in town?"

"No one's quite blown my skirt up, but I wouldn't say no to a date now and again. But no one ever seems to ask. So it got me wondering after Jack said what he said."

"Well, you could certainly go out with Ronnie if you had a mind to."

"Grier, I wasn't joking last night. I did babysit him and change his diapers."

Grier couldn't hold back a grin. "It does have the whole Padmé-Anakin vibe to it. Maybe he'll turn into the Dark Lord of Indigo and you guys can have twins you shuttle off to the ends of the earth who then grow up to save the universe. Wouldn't that be fun?"

"You really are sick and twisted; you know that?"

"One of my finer points. But consider the positives. He is young and healthy and in his prime. It'd be a fun romp before the dark side of the force overtook him."

Avery's phone buzzed where she'd laid it on the counter and she picked it up, still laughing. "Mick. Hey."

Grier tried to stamp out the quick interest that flashed down her spine like heat lightning, but finally gave up. Even the man's name did things to her.

Why was she fighting it so hard?

As Avery agreed to something and hung up, Grier couldn't quite shake the image of lids and pots and how very well-suited she and Mick were.

Everything just *fit* when they were together. Like nothing else she'd ever known. It was comfortable spending time with him, even though she was wickedly *uncomfortable* the moment she got within a few feet of the man. Which made about as much sense as how Chooch and Hooch managed to fill five large shoe boxes with a year's worth of receipts, but it didn't make it any less true.

"Everything okay?"

"Yeah. Mick's got a visitor out at the airfield he's bringing over. The guy apparently tried calling a few times this morning and didn't get through and Mick offered to call and give me a heads-up."

"Oh. That's nice of him."

"I think it was an excuse."

"For what?"

"I think he's curious how your tax session went."

"Did you tell him the force has been sucking all life out of the vicinity and he should stay as far from its tractor beam as possible?"

Avery threw her half-torn napkin across the table. "You really need your head examined."

"I know." Grier picked up the napkin and laid it on

the table. "Listen. I don't want to shortchange what we were talking about. Are you really upset about what Jack said?"

"Not upset, exactly. I just don't want to let life pass me by—you know. And a lot of days I feel like it is."

"Yeah, I know."

And she did, Grier acknowledged to herself. That subtle feeling that something was missing, like a kaleidoscope without one of its colors. You couldn't quite tell it wasn't there until someone pointed it out, but once they did, it was all you noticed.

"I'm thinking about going to Ireland."

The rapid change in discussion had Grier leaning forward. "Ireland? What are you going to do there?"

"There's this exchange program I looked into. I could go to Ireland and work in a town's B and B and someone would come here and trade places with me for the same amount of time. It'd be short—only about three months. And then I could stay over there and travel a bit before I came home."

The enthusiasm that marked Avery's voice was unmistakable and Grier was caught up immediately in the excitement. "I think it's a great idea."

"It's a change of pace and sort of scary to think about doing it all by myself, but it's also scary to think about not doing it—you know?"

"It's inspired, Avery. In fact, I really have only one question."

"What's that?"

"What are you waiting for?"

*   *   *

Mick shot a sideways glance at the suit he'd flown up from Anchorage on his morning run. The guy had been a model passenger—quiet, composed and not airsick—but something had struck Mick as off.

For starters, he couldn't help but wonder what the guy was doing here. Italian loafers and expensive suits didn't exactly scream Indigo, Alaska. Add to it the man's reluctance to engage in any sort of conversation beyond whether the Seahawks had a decent shot in the play-offs and something rang Mick's bells.

The Indigo Blue loomed ahead of them and Mick pulled into the parking lot. They had gotten that snowfall the night before and he wasn't surprised to see Susan already had the parking lot cleared and ready for guests. "I called ahead. The Indigo Blue has your reservation and is ready for you."

"Great."

Mick found a spot and pulled in, cutting the engine.

"I can take it from here," the guy said, and Mick realized he'd forgotten his name. He wasn't sure why he even wondered about it as Maggie had likely broadcast it across town by now. It'd only be a matter of hours before the town's curious would be partaking in a happy-hour cocktail at the Indigo Blue to speculate on who the new visitor was.

"I've got a few things to take care of inside, so I'll give you a hand." Mick rounded the back of his SUV and dragged the designer luggage from the trunk.

Again, something tickled along the back of his neck, but Mick couldn't quite lay claim to what it was. He set the suitcase down next to the truck and the guy grabbed it with a muttered thank-you.

With a shrug, Mick followed him in. His passenger had been officially delivered and wasn't his problem any longer.

The light melody of women's voices floated toward him as Avery and Grier materialized from the hallway that extended off the lobby. Without conscious thought, his gaze zeroed in on Grier. Today she wore a bright blue cashmere sweater, which he knew would be baby-soft to his touch, over a pair of black slacks. The look was professional without sticking out as too fussy, unlike the suit he'd flown up here.

She fit in, he realized, as his gaze drank her in.

And more to the point, she fit with him.

Mick moved forward, curious to see if he could get her to share lunch with him. The itch that had ridden the back of his neck grew stronger and the moment expanded as if in slow motion.

The suit he'd driven up—*Jason*, that was his name—moved into his line of vision, walking right up to Grier and wrapping her in his arms.

Grier wrapped her arms around him in turn and her voice was crystal clear. "Jason."

Chapter Nine

"*Jason.*" Grier realized where her arms were and tried to pull away without looking too obvious. "What are you doing here?"

Jason gave one last squeeze before letting her go and smiled, if his strained expression could really be called that. "I've come to get you."

"I'm sorry?" Grier dropped her hands and tried to suck in air without being too obvious.

What the *hell* was Jason doing here? In the middle of Alaska? How had he found her?

As her gaze alighted on Mick's and Avery's twin looks of puzzlement, Grier put on her most patent society-girl smile.

The one that screamed she could conquer any social awkwardness.

The one that could level a social climber in one fell swoop.

The one that she prayed would convey to Mick that she was really, really sorry and would explain everything the moment they were alone.

"Get you?" Mick asked softly.

Before Jason could answer, Grier forced the introductions. "This is Jason Shriver. Jason," she said, extending a hand toward Mick and Avery, "you know Mick as he flew you up. And Avery Marks is the manager of the hotel."

She didn't miss the wealth of questions in Avery's gaze, but she also knew her friend was too much of a professional to do anything about it now. "Jason, I've got your reservation over here. Let's get you settled in."

Jason ignored the offer as he finally clued in to the male competition that filled the lobby with testosterone-laden awkwardness. "Yes, back. I've come to get Grier to bring her back home to New York."

Mick's voice was quiet. Commanding. "And why would she want to leave?"

"We've got some unfinished business to fix. If you'll excuse us."

Grier saw the light of battle hit Mick's eyes and she quickly cut in. "Actually, Jason, this is my home for the next several weeks. I'm sorry if you came all this way instead of just making a simple phone call to ask me what I wanted, but I'm staying put."

"Can we at least talk?"

"Why don't you get checked in and I'll come find you later. I've actually got a client commitment this afternoon."

"Client?"

Grier knew the stab of enjoyment she got at his puzzled expression was small and terrifically petty and she'd be damned if she'd spend one moment feeling bad about it. "Yes, I'm doing some tax returns while I'm here."

"Isn't it a bit early?"

"It's never too early to prepare properly. I'll see you down here later. Say four? At the bar?"

"That's fine. I need to catch up on some e-mails, anyway. The Glazer-Brown project has kicked into high gear."

She nodded and wanted to scream in frustration. Of course he had e-mails to catch up on. And of course he'd have to mention the high-profile project she'd been assigned to before.

"Then I'll see you later." Turning toward Mick, she added, "Do you have a few minutes?"

"I thought you'd never ask."

Mick focused all his concentration on the seemingly random piles of paper that covered the conference room table from one end to the other to avoid the driving desire to punch something.

Hard.

"Why don't you take a seat and I'll explain."

"I think I can figure it out for myself."

"No, you only think you can. Sit." As if catching herself, Grier added, "Please."

He took a seat at the head of the table and folded his hands over his stomach. "I'm all ears."

"First, I have absolutely no idea why he's here. Although I suspect my mother had something to do with it."

Mick didn't miss the way her hands fisted at her sides on the word "mother" and felt his stomach muscles relax ever so slightly.

She'd been blindsided and while he didn't appreciate *what* she'd been blindsided with, he couldn't mistake the stark look that covered her beautiful features and had her shoulders as stiff as the ice over a frozen lake in winter.

She was mad. And a little hurt, judging by the slight quaver that tinged the edges of her voice.

"Why don't you start at the beginning and tell me who Jason is."

"My ex-fiancé."

Whatever he'd expected, that wasn't it. "I didn't realize you'd ever had one of those."

Her strained laughter was tinny to his ears. "You mean that little tidbit hasn't managed to make its way around town?"

"No. Nor have you bothered to share it with me."

"I haven't shared it with a lot of people actually. The reasons why we are no longer engaged fall squarely into the camp of trite and embarrassing with a side of mortification."

"How so?"

Grier began to pace the edge of the table, running her hands lightly over the tops of the leather chairs. "I caught him getting a blow job. At the office. From our temp receptionist."

"You could have stopped at 'blow job.' "

She stopped behind one of the chairs and stared at him, her gaze the color of storm clouds. "You're right on that one."

"So? What came next?"

"I broke off our engagement. Which caused my esteemed firm, headed by my now no-longer future father-in-law, to sack me."

"You could probably argue that one if you'd wanted to. Legally."

Grier took the seat next to him at the corner of the table and pushed a pile of paper out of her way. "That's the funny part. I haven't really wanted to."

"Oh?"

"Exactly. The same week that happened, I got the news about my father. And suddenly whatever drama I was dealing with in New York seemed to pale in comparison."

"Or Jonas provided a convenient excuse to run away."

Those storm clouds flashed over and lightning sparked in her words. "Do you really think that?"

"It makes a funny sort of sense. You ran away from a problem at home to come up here. And all I've seen since you've been here is you running away from me."

"That is so unfair."

Mick unfolded his hands and stood. "But true. Add to it I've touched every single inch of your body and I didn't even know you had a fiancé and I'd say I'm spot on the mark, Grier."

"Ex-fiancé."

"Recent ex. And the timing doesn't make my point any less true."

"Mick—"

"Look. I've made my intentions more than clear. I want you. Despite today's surprise, I actually find I want you even more than before, and it's not to show up that little toady out in the lobby. Or not much," he added. "But it's your turn, Grier."

"My turn for what?"

"Your turn to decide what you want. To decide you're done with running and ready to take on something real. I think you've got the guts for it, but I don't get the feeling you agree."

She leaped out of the seat she'd just taken. "What the hell is that supposed to mean?"

"You tell me."

He didn't give her a chance to respond—refused to give her a moment's breathing room—but instead, he leaned in and took. With barely leashed ferocity, he captured her lips with his and channeled his own fury into the only thing that made sense between them.

Need—uncontrolled and dangerous—rose up between them as their lips met and clashed, gave and took with a desperate fervor. He refused to be gentle or slow things down as he fought to show her what she did to him.

What they did to each other.

Her tongue swept through his mouth, momentarily giving her the upper hand as her fingers kneaded his shoulders. Soft moans echoed from her throat, but he swallowed each and every one of them, absolutely greedy to take every bit she'd give him and more.

Harsh and demanding, he fought to regain control; knew he had it when her head fell back against his palm as she allowed him to take and plunder. Mindless, he drank from her lips, drawing a response that fired his blood and answered the only question he really cared to ask.

His hands itched to move lower—to cup the swell of her breasts or the wet heat at the apex of her thighs—and it was that knowledge that pulled him back.

Her small body quivered under his hands, her lips wet from his mouth. A passion-filled haze rode her eyes, turning them glassy. He had chased the storm clouds away, but that was no longer enough. He wanted more from her.

"It's time to decide, Grier."

He left before the confusion clouding their gray depths could pull him back or make him forget why he was so furious.

Grier sorted the receipts into piles by month, the simple exercise going a long way toward calming her shaking hands. Rationally, she knew why Mick was upset. And it had more to do with Jason actually being *in* Indigo rather than the idea of Jason.

She hoped.

But no matter how she spun it, she couldn't blame him for being upset. At the same time, no matter how many other ways she turned it in her mind, she wasn't sorry she hadn't mentioned Jason to Mick.

A woman was entitled to some dignity. And since Mick was the man who'd given it back to her, there was no way she wanted to discuss with him the one asshole who'd taken it away.

"Is it safe to come in?"

Grier glanced up at the heavy knock at the conference room door. "Chooch. Of course. Come on in."

"I left Hooch at home. I had a few things I wanted to say and couldn't say 'em this morning with him around."

Since the two seemed to be either joined at the hip or arguing, she figured Chooch's pronouncement didn't require a comment. "I've made a dent in the receipts but still don't have everything organized."

"Oh, honey, that'll take several days. Take your time."

Grier glanced at the endless piles that covered the table and thought Chooch was being awfully generous on her timetable. "If you're sure?"

"Of course. I only brought this stuff over so you'd have something to do."

A shot of heat suffused her neck and Grier knew an embarrassing blush was creeping up her cheeks. "What?"

"You're too smart a girl to sit around bored out of your gourd." Chooch pulled out one of the high-backed leather chairs that circled the table and sat down. "Come here and sit down with me for a minute."

"All right."

Grier braced herself for a lecture and couldn't have been more surprised by what came out next.

"I wasn't ever able to have children."

"Oh, Chooch—"

The normally gregarious woman waved a hand. "Let me get through this."

Grier nodded. She might not have fully known where

the conversation was going, but she did know when someone had something he or she needed to say. "All right."

"I spent a lot of years mad at the world because of it. Nearly drove my Hooch away because of it, too."

Afraid to say anything, Grier gave her another nod, encouraging her to continue.

"Point is, we all get some shitty deals in life. And it's okay to be pissed about 'em. But when you start fucking up the other things in your life that are good, you've got to start questioning if *you're* the shitty deal."

When Grier didn't say anything, Chooch added, "You gonna say anything?"

"Can I?"

The older woman cackled at that one, her smile broad. " 'Course."

"How do you know if it's you or the situation? Not to contradict anything you just said, but you had a great husband who loves you to distraction. I realize not being able to have kids was really hard, but you already had him. You two got off track for a while and then you got back on."

Chooch leaned forward and Grier felt weathered hands take her own in a surprisingly strong grip. "That's where you're wrong, sweetie. We had to get on a new track."

Before Grier could question her, Chooch added, "The track's never the same. If you want to move forward, you have to get on a new one. A new track, a new path, a new journey. The one you thought was right isn't any longer and you can't go backward."

"But I don't want to go backward. That's why I'm here."

Chooch's sharp brown gaze was unyielding. "Hiding in a conference room doing my taxes instead of spending time with Mick O'Shaughnessy?"

Mick's earlier words had a dangerous echo to Chooch's and Grier wondered for a moment if they'd planned this together.

"Why does everyone think this is about Mick?"

"It isn't about him. It's about you."

"Well, that doesn't seem fair to him."

"He can make up his own mind. In fact, I suspect he already has."

"What if I'm not made for this? Or him." As the words slipped from her lips, Grier wondered how she'd come to say the deepest fear in her heart to this odd little woman who hailed from one of the most remote—and harshest—locations on the planet.

"Then you're stupid."

Grier snapped back in her chair as her mouth dropped in surprise.

"Oh, don't look at me that way. I know you've got all those smarts. Natural God-given ones and college ones. So don't go being stupid over a man. Especially not one as delicious as Mick O'Shaughnessy."

"You noticed that?"

Whatever compassion or thoughtfulness the woman had shown evaporated like smoke. "I'm not dead. And have you seen those feet?"

"Well, yeah."

"They're huge and you know what they say about

feet. I, for one, have no doubt that man's got quite a package and the moves to go with it."

Grier sputtered, desperate for some response as Chooch's words floated over her.

And came up with exactly nothing because damn it all if the woman hadn't hit the target square on the bull's eye.

"Um, well—"

"Um . . . well . . . nothing. Mary'd die if she knew I was talking about her grandson that way. Add to it I saw that man the week he came home from the hospital thirty-five years ago and I have no business acting like a horny old woman over his assets. But what I will tell you . . ." Her gaze was so sharp, Grier could have sworn she felt herself pinned to her chair.

"What's that?"

"There aren't many finer than Mick O'Shaughnessy. And I'm not just talking about his body."

"I know Mick's a good man."

"The best."

Grier hesitated for the briefest moment, then said what she thought before she could chicken out. "Why is all of this easier to hear from you?"

"Sometimes the people who don't know us very well make better mirrors. Too often, our friends feel they have to stand off to the side so they can protect us from the hurt of seeing our true selves."

"Or what an ass we're being," Grier muttered.

The sly grin was back, along with a heavy cackle. "Now there you have it. That's my job with Hooch and

I do it with gusto. Speaking of that man, if I don't get home, he'll think I've gotten up to something."

"Don't you want your boxes?"

Chooch shot her a wink. "You keep 'em. I trust you."

"I'll do that."

Grier smiled as the woman crossed toward the door and had almost turned back to her computer when Chooch's voice stopped her. "You want to know something else?"

"What?"

"In all those thirty-five years I've known Mick O'Shaughnessy, I've never seen that man set his cap for anyone the way he's set his for you."

And with that pronouncement, she turned on her heel and walked out of the room, her gleeful laughter following in her wake.

Chapter Ten

*J*ason hadn't felt this nervous and uncomfortable since his first presentation to the partnership. He took a tense sip of his scotch, well aware the people who'd assembled in the lobby bar of the Indigo Blue hotel were checking him out.

It was creepy, in an Alfred Hitchcock *The Birds* sort of way. And like the birds that had gathered on the swing set in Hitchcock's masterpiece, the residents of this backwoods town Grier had ensconced herself in had started to multiply.

Two in the lobby. Then four. Then eight.

On a slight shiver he couldn't quite chalk up to cold, he took another sip of his drink.

Where was Grier, anyway?

The urge to turn around and look for her was strong, but he tamped down on it, reaching for his BlackBerry instead. At least the CrackBerry would let him look busy, even if he'd just checked it before coming downstairs.

The birds—no, the *residents*—didn't know that.

A movement at the corner of his eye caught his attention and he looked up from the device, thinking it was Grier come to rescue him.

And instead he stared at a profile as startling as it was familiar.

"Grier?"

The small woman who stood next to him at the bar waiting for a drink glanced sideways, her irritation at being called another woman's name more than evident. "No, I'm Kate."

"But—" Jason broke off, at a loss for words. While he could clearly see the woman standing next to him wasn't Grier, the resemblance was shocking.

On a small sigh, the woman extended her hand as the irritation that rode her striking features dimmed. "I'm Grier's half sister."

"What?"

"Which word didn't you understand?"

If the lobby's patrons had him thinking of *The Birds*, the sheer disorientation he felt staring at this woman was straight out of *Vertigo*. "You're her sister?"

The woman smiled, her gray eyes crinkling at the corners. "Half sister. And you mean you haven't heard of me? And here I thought you were a good friend of Grier's. A very good friend, if you trust the town gossip."

"She and I have a bit of catching up to do."

"Is that what they call groveling these days?"

An irresistible tug of interest pulled at him as he stared into Kate's face. The resemblance to Grier was oddly unsettling, but underneath the discomfort beat the insistent drum of instant attraction.

Ignoring the spark, he focused on her words. "I haven't told anyone why I'm here. And Grier's so private, I can't imagine she has, either."

"Neither of you had to say anything. I know how to use the Internet." A light, flirty smile played at the corners of her mouth and his interest ratcheted up another notch.

"I didn't put my trip on the Internet." The words were inane, but for the life of him he had no idea what the Internet had to do with his visit to Indigo to win back his fiancée; nor did he have any idea why puzzling through this woman's mysterious words felt like so much fun.

Kate leaned in and the light scent of her swamped his senses, a barely there peach that was just indistinct enough to intrigue. "No, but those fancy New York papers did put your engagement on the Internet. And seeing as how Grier's been here for almost two months and you've been nowhere in sight, my powerful skills of logic and deduction have figured out the real story."

"Oh." He reached for his drink, not sure what else there was to say but enjoying the conspiratorial way she leaned toward him. "Well, what do your amazing powers of deduction tell you I'm up here groveling about?"

"Two months apart is a long time in the land of the happily engaged. You must have done something to piss my big sister off."

The sweet moment was broken by the reality of why he was here, flirting with someone other than the woman he wanted to win back. And as Jason looked into the charming, sexy face next to him, for the first time he felt more than embarrassment for his actions with the office temp.

He felt shame.

* * *

The apocalypse was upon them, Grier thought in panic as she took in the sight of her half sister sitting next to her ex-fiancé while sharing happy-hour cocktails.

Somewhere in the depths of her heart she tried to muster up a tiny smattering of jealousy, or annoyance or, hell, she'd even take a slight case of indigestion.

But nope . . . nothing.

In fact, the only thing that actually did register was what a cute couple Jason and Kate made.

Which was just insane.

And most likely another mark in the petty column for her, since pushing her cheating ex-fiancé off on her prickly half sister was an insult to the sisterhood of all women.

Once a cheater, always a cheater floated through her mind. She'd heard the adage through the years, but each time she'd tried to use that as an argument to herself for what a jerk Jason was, something held her back.

While she didn't want him any longer, she also couldn't quite shake the fact that Jason wasn't really an asshole. And she never could really reconcile her discovery of him in flagrante with the man she knew him to be.

"Jason. Kate. I'm glad to see you two have met."

The bar behind her was so quiet, Grier thought she might have heard the snow falling outside the window.

"Grier!" Jason's voice was overly bright in the tense silence as he stood to press a light kiss on her cheek. "You never told me you had a sister."

With an overly bright smile to match his tone, she

kept her voice low, hoping beyond hope he'd get the message. She'd always hated his "let's address the partnership" tone, a trait that hadn't changed in three months.

"That's because I didn't know I had one."

Jason's impeccable manners and good breeding finally kicked in and he scooted down and offered her his seat. "I'm sure it's been a difficult few months for both of you."

Kate shot her the gimlet eye and Grier had the insane urge to laugh as she pulled Jason's barstool out to create a half circle. Her sister clearly wasn't going anywhere.

And difficult?

That was a polite understatement. Being kept from Jonas's things while she and Kate hammered her father's will out in the legal system had been more challenging than she could have ever expected.

Of course, Jason didn't know that and she wasn't interested in having him know any more about her new life. He was part of her past and she couldn't shake the subtle feeling that he was trespassing on her new one.

So she opted for politely bland. "Grief is a difficult thing."

The three of them sat there in stilted silence and Grier had the perverse thought to keep her mouth shut, just to see how long they could possibly sit there, quiet as church mice.

And then there wasn't any silence, because an incredibly familiar voice piped up from behind her.

"Well, look what the cat dragged in."

*   *   *

Grier swirled her wine around in her glass to avoid looking at Jason. Avery had unlocked the conference room for her again and they currently sat at opposite sides of the table, as far away as possible from the snow-fall of receipts that littered the other end.

"You said you wanted to talk."

"Grier—" Jason broke off.

She sat and watched him compose himself. It was odd, actually, to watch him struggle for something to say. He usually knew exactly the perfect thing to say, or do, or think.

"Clearly Sloan doesn't think all that much of me." He laughed, emitting a harsh bark that broke the silence of the room. "She never did think much of me, anyway, so I suppose that's no surprise."

Grier inwardly cringed at Sloan's unwelcome greeting in the bar before they'd managed to escape to the conference room. "What makes you say that?"

"She never liked me. She put on a good face for you, but it wasn't hard to see."

"See what?"

"That she wanted to scrape me off her shoe like a piece of gum."

Not for the first time Grier wondered how she could have been so incredibly blind. How had she missed all the signs? She'd ignored her own doubts, which was bad enough.

But how had she ignored the apparently not-so-subtle cues from someone she loved and respected as much as she did Sloan?

All for what?

"I owe you an apology." Jason's words broke into her thoughts.

"You said you were sorry about six hundred times before I left New York. Did you really need to travel four thousand miles to say it again? Besides, they do have phones up here, if you were that concerned about repeating it one more time."

"This is about more than saying I'm sorry."

She glanced up at that. "What more is there to say?"

"I want you back."

A resounding *Hell no!* rose up in her throat, but she held back, curiosity rapidly replacing the horror that he might be serious.

"That feeling is far from mutual."

"I know you've had a lot going on, but surely we can figure this out."

"We have figured it out. And the equation was a division of our relationship."

He sat up straighter at that and the competitive edge she'd always seen in him came roaring to life. "How can you throw away what we had? We were almost married, for fuck's sake."

"You threw it away, Jason. The moment you made the decision to have sex with someone who wasn't me."

"I didn't have sex with her."

Grier stood, the anger she'd managed to keep on a low simmer flaring bonfire-high. "If you're going to sit there and tell me some woman who is not me, wrapping her tongue around your dick isn't sex, this conversation is over."

"Wait, wait, wait." He stood as well and pointed to her seat. "That was cheap of me and not true. I'm not a politician and I didn't come up here to make excuses to you."

"Then why did you come up here?"

"To fix things."

"Did you ever think maybe they were broken for a reason?"

His dark brown gaze shot to hers. "Do you really think that?"

She sat again on a sigh. She'd promised to have a conversation with him and there was no reason not to have it. "I do now. And if I'm honest with myself, I did see it before, but I kept ignoring the signs."

In hindsight, that should have been a bright, blinking clue that the two of them weren't the best match— the restless questions and the sleepless nights—but she'd overlooked it. Had told herself it was silly and immature to want the spark.

So she'd focused again and again on how compatible they were. And how stable their life was, since they never argued or fought or even disagreed. And she spent all of her time reassuring the increasingly loud voice of her subconscious as it whispered late at night in her ear that it was all so very *mature* of her to make a decision about her future with her head.

"Why didn't you say anything? Why didn't you try to talk to me about it?"

"Because there was an engagement announcement and wedding plans and it was all completely out of control. And every time I listened to that small voice in my head trying to tell me something was wrong, you and I were off doing something else like picking china or scoping out honeymoon spots, and I told myself it was just cold feet."

"So how can I make it up to you?"

"You can't, Jason." Chooch's words came flooding back from earlier and she found herself selecting bits and pieces to make her point. "We were on the same path for a while, but we got off. And we can't go back to it."

"You have to believe me; that wasn't me." He held up a hand before she could say anything. "Hear me out, please. What I did was me and I take responsibility for that choice. But you have to understand something. I don't act that way. In fact, I've never acted that way. It's disrespectful and it's not part of how I treat the women I'm involved with."

"So why did you do it?"

"I don't know." He ran a hand through his hair, tugging on the ends. "I fucking do not know."

"Maybe it's the only way you knew how to get out."

He looked up at that. "I don't want out. That's why I'm up here. I want you back in my life."

"Do you really, Jason?"

Grier stood and reached for her wine. "All I can tell you is this. I forgive you. In fact, as I've thought about it, I pretty much forgave you the moment I pulled that engagement ring off my finger and the weight of the world lifted off my chest."

"You really felt that way? Like everything was bearing down on you?"

"I really did." She crossed around the table and leaned down to press a kiss on his cheek. "And I bet if you dig way down in your heart, you'll agree with me."

Mick tried to concentrate on whatever it was Walker and Doc Cloud were saying about the upcoming playoff games this weekend, but the sounds of their voices were a heavy blur. He was on the verge of walking down the hotel's hallway toward the conference room and doing physical harm to that fucking interloper from New York.

The only thing that kept him in his seat was the fact that no matter how many ways he tried to twist it, he had no claim on Grier. And he had no right to interfere with whatever history had to be cleared up with that asshole.

He took another long drag on his beer and tried desperately to come up with some recollection of why the Patriots' defense would whip the Raiders' offense.

Or why he should care.

And then he saw her walk back into the lobby —sans the asshole— and the murderous haze coloring his vision receded slightly. Grier's smoky gaze settled on his before she crossed to their small conversation circle and took an empty seat between him and Sloan.

He lifted the bottle that sat on the table. "Need a refill?"

"God yes." Grier smiled, but he didn't miss the tension lines that still bracketed her mouth. And he really didn't miss the overly cheerful tone that came out seconds later.

"So, what did I miss?"

"The over-under on the Pats/Raiders game and Walker's rhapsodic chants about the appetizers on the menu for our reception."

The heavy-handed cadence eased a bit and he saw the first genuine smile cross Grier's face since she'd walked back in. "So what is on the menu?"

"I am a man of simple tastes and I think my request was simple, too." Walker took a swig of his beer. "Although I think I nearly gave Sloan's mother a heart attack when I told her I had only two requests for the wedding."

"What were they?" Grier probed.

"Mass quantities of pigs in a blanket and her daughter at the end of the aisle. Not in that order of importance."

Mick practically saw the sighs rise up in little hearts around each woman and he couldn't resist giving his friend a hard time. "You're going to make the rest of us look bad, buddy."

"Some people can do that all on their own," Sloan added with a pointed look toward the bar and the now-absent Jason.

Grier shot her a dark look. "That's not nice."

"It wasn't meant to be. Did you have any idea he was going to show up here?" Sloan shot the bar area—and her imagined target—one final parting glare before turning back to pick up her wine.

Grier reached for her glass. "Of course not! I was shocked nearly speechless when I walked into the lobby earlier today and saw him standing there with Mick."

"When did he get here?" Sloan seemed unwilling to drop the subject and Mick felt a small stab of annoyance that they were wasting time even discussing this.

"This morning." Mick set his empty bottle on the small table next to their open wine bottle and reached for the freshie Avery had deposited a few minutes earlier. "I brought him up from Anchorage."

"You should have left his ass there," Sloan grumbled, clearly dissatisfied with Indigo's newest visitor.

"Believe me, had I known who he was, I'd have given it serious consideration."

"I don't know which one of you is worse than the other." Grier's voice was soft as she stared into her wine.

"He's the asshole, Grier," Sloan argued. "Don't tell me you're thinking of forgiving him?"

Mick didn't miss the tension between the women and wondered at the sudden change. From the moment he'd first seen them together, they were completely in tune with each other, so it was a surprise to see such dark emotions swirling around the two of them.

"You know, it's all well and good of you to tell me that now," Grier muttered. "I don't want anything to do with him anymore. Where was the help a year ago?"

"You were engaged a year ago."

Mick and Walker exchanged glances as the conversation veered and made landfall.

"Right. When knowing your true feelings would have done me a hell of a lot more good." Grier set her glass down on their small table with a heavy thunk.

Before any of them realized what was happening, Grier stood and was halfway across the lobby.

Sloan got up to follow after her, but Walker had his hand on her arm, holding her in place.

"Walker. I need to go apologize."

"You can do that later." Walker kept his voice low and allowed his gaze to briefly roam the room. "Look around. She's got a lot of witnesses and she's a little raw right now."

"But—"

"She's embarrassed, Sloan," Mick said, unable to help interjecting.

Without waiting for a response, he set his beer on the table and followed the same snaking path Grier had taken through the lobby.

Chapter Eleven

*A*nger carried her through the lobby and past the front desk, but sheer practicality had Grier stopping at the door. It was January in Alaska.

Shit, she needed a coat.

A quick glance behind the concierge desk turned up the heavy down coat Chris the handyman used when he had to go outside. Remembering he was off duty and enjoying a few beers in the bar with Bear and Tommy, she grabbed the coat, vowing to take it for only a few minutes.

She needed air.

And she needed to catch her breath.

Although it was early evening, the sun had long since vanished and the dark, overcast sky did nothing for her mood. Heavy flakes of snow drifted down and she burrowed farther into the oversized coat that she could have wrapped around herself twice.

With each step that took her farther from the hotel, Grier allowed her self-righteous indignation free rein.

Damn it, where did Sloan come off? She wasn't the one who had to sit there and look her cheating ex-fiancé in the eye—in front of a roomful of people, no less.

"Watch out for the ice."

Grier whirled at the sound of another voice, slamming her hand against her heart. She'd been so wrapped up in her personal misery, she hadn't even heard footsteps behind her.

She knew she shouldn't be surprised to see Mick. She wasn't even surprised at the sly curl of desire that fluttered through her body and she attempted to push away the anger that filled her.

She was, however, surprised he'd come instead of Sloan.

"Why are you here?"

"You looked upset."

"I *am* upset."

"At Sloan?" Mick waited a beat. "Or is it something else?"

Grier couldn't hold back the laugh that came out in a half-strangled choking sound. "*Something* else? How about everything else?"

"So what are you doing about it?"

"Oh, I don't know. For the record, all I was trying to do was sit there and have a few drinks with my friends when Sloan went and shoved it in my face that Jason, my poor excuse for a fiancé, was here."

"Ex-fiancé."

Another one of those sly fingers of need floated through her, rolling through her stomach in fluttery waves.

"Exactly."

"For what it's worth, I thought the point you made back there was a valid one."

Grier glanced up from where she kicked at a snow-drift with her foot. "What?"

"About how Sloan felt about him. If she disliked him that bad, she should have told you."

"The girlfriend code often prevents that sort of honesty."

"Why?"

"A friend can say only so much. Or family, too. People are entitled to make their own decisions about what they're going to do with their lives. That's extra true of whom they plan to marry."

"That sounds like a bullshit cop-out to me."

Grier's mouth dropped open. "Excuse me?"

"It's bullshit. If people put more energy into their relationships instead of avoiding difficult conversations, they'd be a lot better off."

While his words had a distinct ring of truth to them, she couldn't help but defend her friend. "And what should Sloan have done? Tell me what she really thought of Jason and risk having us not be friends any longer?"

"Would you have dropped her?"

"No." Grier paused, unwilling to be anything less than honest. "But it would have made things awkward. So I'd likely have avoided inviting her to things that included couples."

"You'd have done that anyway if Wall Street had any say in it."

Again, she felt her mouth dropping and wondered when she'd turned into a gaping fish. "What makes you think that?"

"He's looking for a fancy dinner partner, not a wife. And your very eligible friend, which she was at the time, wouldn't have been a suitable person for his married dinner partner to hang out with on a regular basis."

"You don't even know him. He wouldn't have asked that of me."

"It'd have been slow and subtle," Mick pushed on. "But it would have happened. And one day you'd have looked up and you and Sloan would have just drifted apart."

Grier thought about all the long nights over the last few months. Those endless hours with nothing but her thoughts, when she tried to piece together what had gone wrong.

And more than once, she'd been unable to shake the idea that she and Jason had been in a relationship based on something other than love. Had anyone asked her at the time, she'd have said she was in love.

But he'd been surprisingly easy to get over.

Unlike Mick.

On a soft sigh, she pushed the thought away, loath to compare Jason and Mick. Jason was her past and Mick—well, he was his own man.

"That doesn't paint a very nice picture of me. Or of how I value my friends."

"But it likely would have been your life, Grier. Which is why you're more embarrassed than hurt about what she said."

"Aren't you full of opinions."

"I'm just calling them like I see them."

"Well, you've got one thing right. I am embarrassed

and I feel like a fool. As though everyone knew what was going on but me."

"You're not a fool."

"Yes, but I *feel* like one. Which is really all that matters."

Mick threw up his hands and she nearly laughed at the disgusted look that rode his features as he kicked at a pile of snow in a move strangely reminiscent of hers. "And people wonder why I like my orderly, logical planes."

"I'm sorry."

"Seriously. Life's not about making one perfect decision after another, Grier. There's no scorecard. We're not fools when we make a bad decision and geniuses when we make a good one."

"But making good decisions doesn't make us feel bad."

He whirled on her from where he focused on the snow and Grier took a step back at the feral gleam in his eye. "Oh no? Because I think you and I made a pretty damn good decision last month and you've been running from it ever since."

"This conversation has nothing to do with that night."

Even as she said the words, Grier wondered how her nose wasn't growing.

That night. That single, glorious night when she'd put her brain on hold and let her heart make the decisions.

She'd changed in those long hours in his arms. She'd given in and taken what she'd wanted, instead of behaving like the person she was expected to be.

And it had been perfect.

Until she'd run. Because actions had consequences and how the hell could she, a New Yorker to the core, carry on an affair with a bush pilot from Alaska?

Or worse, how could she fall in love with him?

"This conversation has everything to do with that night."

Mick had sworn to himself he wasn't going there. He wasn't going to goad her and force her to explain what had happened after that amazing night they'd spent together.

And what had he gone and done after three minutes in her company?

He'd fucking gone there.

"That just . . . happened. And it was wonderful and amazing."

The anger that pulsed in his blood flashed over to out-and-out rage. "Do. Not. Pacify. Me."

Whatever he was feeling reflected right back at him in the sheer ire that tightened her lips and had her spine going rigid.

"What do you want me to say? That it was the most amazing night of my life? That you gave me back a piece of myself, Mick? Because last time I checked, men didn't want to hear that sort of flowery shit from the women they have a one-night stand with in the middle of a damn sauna."

She stormed off before his addled brain could register she'd left.

Was that really how she'd seen that evening? As a one-night stand?

And how had such an amazing, vibrant woman thought there was something missing in her? His earlier dark thoughts about Jason took a dip further toward murderous rage as he began to understand the true depths of what the asshole had done to Grier emotionally.

His jumbled thoughts parted as he registered her walking away from him and he moved after her, nearly slipping on the slick parking lot. He regained his balance, thankful his long legs gave him one stride for every two of hers, and caught up with her. "If you think you're dropping a bomb like that and walking away, guess again."

"There is no bomb, Mick. Just like there is no us. There was hot sex and an amazing night together. Thank you for it and the smorgasbord of orgasms you managed to serve up."

Mick reached for her hand, holding tight until she turned to look at him.

He didn't say anything—he couldn't even find words as he stared into her dark gray eyes. So much pain there. And anger. And a hurt that lanced through him and made him wish he could change things for her.

But he knew better than anyone there were some roads you had to walk on your own.

So he fell back on the two things he'd always had in spades.

Honesty and humor.

"Smorgasbord?"

Her pink cheeks turned a delightful shade of red. "It seemed an apt term."

"It's unique, I'll give you that. Just like you."

A soft sigh escaped her lips. "Why do you keep pushing? I'm not really worth the trouble."

Mick moved in and wrapped his arms around her. As his mouth met hers, he murmured against her lips. "You are so worth it."

He felt the briefest hesitation before she melted in his arms. The hard set of her shoulders relaxed as she wrapped her arms around his waist and her lips opened beneath his.

He reacted in kind, pulling her more tightly against his body. Moments as fragile as the snowflakes that fell around them knit themselves together as he made love to her with his mouth.

The heavy gloves that covered his hands restricted his movements as the urge to touch her consumed him. And the seducer became the seduced as her tongue slid past his lips to tangle with his. Fire shot through his body straight to his groin as the sweet taste of her lit up his senses.

Good God, how he wanted her.

Which was the exact reason he needed to pull back.

Mick lifted his head but kept his hands on her. "And baby, for the record, what we shared wasn't a one-night stand."

She blinked a few times as the sensual haze receded from her gray eyes. "It wasn't?"

With as much finesse as he could muster while his body screamed at him in frustration, he leaned in and planted a kiss against her jaw, then worked his way slowly up toward her ear. "No, it wasn't," he whispered hotly in her ear, satisfied when she shivered in his arms.

"How can you say that?" she mumbled back as her hands reached under his jacket and fisted in the heavy flannel of his shirt where it hung past his waist.

Her fingers brushed against his skin and almost had him throwing restraint to the wind, but he forced himself to focus. "Because I'm most definitely getting my hands on you again."

Kate took her favorite chair in the back of the Jitters and opened her book. As outings went, it was a far cry from the nights she'd always imagined she'd have growing up, but at least it wasn't the inside of her house.

She was sick of her house.

And she was sick to death of her own company.

Lifting the decadent mocha she permitted herself once a week, Kate allowed her gaze to roam the room briefly. The coffeehouse was quiet tonight, the few people in evidence huddled into small conversation groups. She'd smiled and said her hellos on her way in. She was thankful no one had tried to follow her to her seat or make small talk.

If it was possible, she was more sick of small talk than she was of the inside of the house.

After another quick sip of her mocha, she reached for the book in her lap, determined to settle in to someone else's problems. One of her students had sighed dramatically through a book report over teen vampires and she'd picked up *Vampire Academy* on a whim. Four books later, she was hooked and desperate to know whether Dimitri would stay a soulless vampire or whether he could somehow be saved.

Smack in the middle of one of his odes to the heroine, a deep voice interrupted her. "Are you all right?"

The light hand on her shoulder had a shriek bubbling to her lips as Kate dropped her book.

"What?"

"I'm sorry."

The man from the Indigo's lobby bar—Jason—was already bending down for her book that had fallen from her lap. Without thinking, she followed him down and their heads collided.

For the briefest instant her hand covered the back of his head, the soft strands of his hair against the pads of her fingers, before they both pulled away as if having been singed.

"I'm really sorry."

"It's fine." Kate dropped her hand and grabbed the book, embarrassed to be caught touching him *and* reading teen fiction. "You just startled me."

"Can I sit down?"

"Sure."

"Why'd you ask me if I was all right?"

"You looked as if you were about to jump out of your skin." He pointed to the book. "That must be one incredible story. I should give it a try."

"It's a YA." At his confused look, she added, "Young adult. About vampires. One of my students recommended it. I doubt it's your cup of tea. Or coffee."

"Since my body's still on New York time and I've not slept for two days, I'd be willing to give it a try anyway."

His smile was as warm and friendly as she'd remembered from the bar and Kate fought the interest that prickled the back of her neck.

"It's part of a series." Kate fought the urge to smack her forehead at the inane chatter.

"Even better. Hours' and hours' worth of reading material."

"What are you doing here?" On a rush, she added, "I mean, besides dealing with jet lag?"

"I didn't feel all that welcome in the hotel lobby and there's not much else open."

"Small towns have a unique way of welcoming outsiders. Out-and-out acceptance that borders on parade-worthy or flat-out rejection. Unfortunately, you've gotten the latter." The real question, to her mind, was *why*.

And if her curiosity at Dimitri's eventual fate was high, it was off the charts for the man sitting opposite her. What had brought him all the way here? And why was Grier's reception so chilly?

"You're from New York?"

"I am."

"We seem to be getting a lot of New Yorkers these days. They're going to need to add a direct flight."

Stop babbling, Winston. Your country bumpkin roots are showing. In vivid detail.

"You're Grier's sister?"

"Half sister."

He leaned forward and she had the insane urge to run her fingers through his dark hair again. This time on purpose.

"You said that before. In the exact same way."

"Sorry."

Jason didn't move back and she couldn't help but notice how the day's growth of beard roughened his cheeks slightly. Or how thin lines radiated from the corners of his eyes. "Nothing to apologize for. It just sounds complicated."

"You have no idea." When he just waited for her to continue, she reached for her drink and took another fortifying sip, measuring her words. "Neither of us knew the other existed until a few months ago."

His eyebrows rose. "That explains a lot."

"I thought you were her friend. Didn't she tell you?"

"Would you consider me unoriginal if I said it's complicated?"

"Not much about Grier isn't complicated. But I don't need a blinking neon sign to understand that's code for a previous relationship."

Whatever interest sparked in her veins fizzled at the evidence he was likely in Indigo to win Grier back. What was harder to understand was why the thought was so disappointing.

"We did have a relationship. But it's been over for a while."

Kate fought the urge to squirm in her chair as the moment grew awkward with the knowledge he'd had a relationship with her sister and she knew he felt it, too, when he stood up.

"I should probably let you get back to your book. I can get this to go, right?"

"Oh sure. They've got cups over there." She pointed across the café.

"I'll see you around."

"Sure." He had taken a few steps before a question rose to her lips. "Why are you here?"

When Jason turned, she could have sworn she saw an ocean of regret in the dark depths of his eyes. But it was the lonely timbre of his voice that confirmed it. "I'm not quite so sure anymore."

The first thing Grier saw as she walked through the door of her hotel room was Sloan and Avery sitting on her bed, a plate of cookies between them. Before she could even say anything, Sloan was up and across the room. "I'm so sorry for what I said."

"I know." Grier reached out and pulled her into a tight embrace. "I know," she whispered again against the soft blond hair at Sloan's temple.

As Sloan pulled back, Grier couldn't help adding, "But how'd you know I'd be coming back to this room alone?"

A sheepish grin stole across Sloan's face. "Avery and I were up in her apartment. Walker texted me from the lobby and let me know you were by yourself."

Grier shook her head in mock disgust. "Sold up the river by my lawyer."

"We actually made a bet on it," Avery said. She extended what looked like a twenty toward Sloan. "Doubtful bitch here won."

Sloan waved the twenty like a flag. "And before you take that as an insult on your charm, grace and all-around wonderfulness, I have absolutely no doubt the two of you *will* have sex again. I just didn't think it would be tonight. So I'm going to double this twenty and say it'll be by the end of the week."

"Sloan!" Grier crossed to the bed and picked up a cookie. "What do you take me for?"

"A woman who's got a date for hot sex with Mick O-yeah O'Shaughnessy."

"You know, I never got that before," Avery said thoughtfully as she reached for a cookie. "Isn't it funny, orgasm and O'Shaughnessy both start with the same letter?"

Grier dropped onto the bed and reached for a pillow, tossing it at Avery's head. "You've got a one-track mind."

"It's a rare and awesome gift. And like all gifts, it must be protected, nurtured and treated with the utmost respect."

"He *is* more than a hot package," Grier argued.

"Of course he is." Avery reached for a cookie. "That's just the fun part to focus on. Mick's a great guy and always has been. In high school, he used to tutor everyone in physics."

"Physics?" Fascinated at this glimpse into his past, Grier reached for her own cookie. "Really?"

"Oh yeah. By the middle of the year it was evident Mick understood it better than the teacher. Small town and all that. I think it has something to do with the flying."

"Well, that makes sense." Grier smacked her head lightly. "I'd hope someone who flew planes for a living understood the properties of physics."

"Anyway, my point is, even back then, Mick was

quick to share his knowledge. Quick to include every-one."

Sloan let out a small sigh. "That's so sexy. Why don't more people understand that? Inclusion beats exclusion every time."

"He also ran errands for some of Mary's older neighbors. Still does. He's just the guy who jumps in and does what needs to be done."

Another piece of her heart crumpled to a hopeless pile of dust at further evidence of just how wonderful Mick was. "He's a good man."

Avery smiled and reached for another cookie. Although she said nothing, it would have been impossible to miss the *I told you so* from a mile away.

"So, catch me up on what I've missed." Sloan resettled herself on the bed. "Like for starters, what was Kate doing in the bar with you and Jason?"

"You've got me there." Grier couldn't resist another cookie. "I told him I'd meet him at four and when I showed up, the two of them were sitting there."

"An oddly poetic match," Avery added.

Grier leaned forward. "Want to know something? I actually had the exact same thought. Well, not the snarky poetic part, but the match part. They're quite attractive together."

Sloan's tone was careful, clearly a nod to her earlier haste. "That doesn't bother you?"

"Well, if he pulled the same sort of shit on her that he did on me, that would make me go all big sister on his ass. But assuming that was a one-time fuckup"— Grier paused—"which I still think it was . . ."

It was Avery's turn to wave a hand. "Did I actually just hear you defend Kate?"

"I guess so."

"Why?"

"Well, because—" Grier broke off. How could she explain it to them when she couldn't even explain it to herself? "Just because. She's my sister and blood's thicker and all that mushy shit."

"Fair enough." Avery nodded.

Grier kicked her foot out as she got comfortable and connected with the end table next to the bed. A heavy thud had her up and moving, only to see that a large padded envelope lay on the floor. "What's that?"

"I forgot. We brought it up before." Sloan leaned down to pick up the package. "Avery got it earlier today."

Grier reached for it, an odd charge shooting through her fingertips as she touched the package. "Who's it from?"

"I'm not sure," Avery said as she sat up. "Chris took it. Want me to call downstairs?"

"Please."

Grier turned the padded envelope over in her hands as Avery made the call. Those odd sparks continued to fire up beneath her skin, growing in intensity.

She abstractedly heard Avery say, "Really?" before she replaced the phone in the cradle after a quick thanks.

"Who's it from?" Even as she asked the question, Grier knew she held something big in her hands.

"Your aunt."

* * *

Kate finished scrubbing off her makeup and dried her face. She'd always taken comfort in ritual and that feeling had only grown since losing her father.

Order amidst chaos.

Every night, she kept to the same routine. She changed her clothes, then carefully brushed her teeth and finished by washing her face.

So why couldn't she find any peace in the ceremony of it tonight?

On a heavy sigh, she burrowed under the covers.

She knew exactly why. And the reason sported Italian loafers, a killer smile and a heart that beat for her sister.

How could it be even remotely possible that the one man she'd had more than a passing interest in could be Grier's fiancé?

Well, ex-fiancé if she'd put the pieces together correctly.

But even if she had, Jason Shriver clearly wasn't in the middle of Alaska to see an ex. He was here to win Grier back.

A cold sensation unfurled in her stomach as she thought about Grier. The feeling was less about her sister and more about the way she'd treated her since the woman had arrived in Indigo.

And while she'd like to chalk it up to anger, pure and simple, Kate knew it was something more. She might smile and offer polite platitudes to most everyone else, but she made it a rule never to lie to herself.

Grier was a threat.

A threat to her relationship with her father and the bond they'd shared.

Or so she'd thought.

As Kate had observed Grier over the past few months, her thoughts had begun to change. It had been subtle at first—the woman's clumsy attempts at striking up a tentative friendship had been earnest and more than a little sweet.

But when Sloan, Grier's friend, came to town and the two had struck up a threesome with Avery Marks, Kate had actually grown a little jealous.

Every time she saw them together, the three of them looked like they were having fun.

Snowball fights on the town square or laughter over a bottle of wine at the Indigo Blue or coffee at the Jitters.

Grier *had* sisters. Of the heart. And Kate had increasingly found herself wishing she could take part.

The phone rang and she jumped as the sound punctuated the silence. Her anxiety ratcheted another notch higher as she saw her aunt's name on the caller ID.

"Aunt Maeve. What's wrong?"

Her father's sister lived past the edge of town. Maeve had spent most of her life out there after her husband died, puttering around and keeping to herself. Even with the short distance between them, Kate had to make the weekly effort to go out to see her as the woman rarely made it into town.

"Nothing's wrong."

"Well, good. How are you? Is everything all right with the house? This latest storm hit us pretty hard today."

"I'm good. I've got what I need."

Kate smiled to herself. Didn't she know it. Her aunt had a stocked pantry full of enough food to see her into the next millennium. Her husband had set her up well financially and Jonas had seen to some home improvements a few summers back.

Barring an unexpected illness, Maeve was set up comfortably enough.

Kate struggled for something to say. While they found enough to talk about on their weekly visits, her aunt usually called once a year and that was to decline their Thanksgiving dinner invitation. "I'll be out to visit on Thursday. Can I bring you anything?"

"No, I'm fine. I'll e-mail you if I think of anything."

"All right." Kate paused a moment. While the urge was strong, she knew hanging up would be a mistake. "Are you sure everything's okay?"

"It is, Katie. But I need to tell you something. And I hope you'll forgive me."

Kate sat straight up in bed. "What is it?"

Chapter Twelve

"A notebook and sixteen letters." Grier laid the last faded letter on top of the stack.

"Don't forget the letter that came with the package," Avery added.

That one looked fresh and had her name on it, but Grier hadn't opened it yet. She couldn't explain why, but she wanted some time alone with the contents of the package.

As if reading her mind, Sloan patted her shoulder. "We'll let you get to it. We're here if you need to talk."

Avery added a hand to her other shoulder. "Whenever you need us."

Her throat tightened at the show of support and Grier stood to grab both of them in a three-way hug. "You guys are the best. I'm probably just being a loon. I'm sure there's not much here."

"It doesn't matter what's here." Sloan patted her back. "It's yours to discover. We'll talk to you later."

"And we'll leave the cookies," Avery added with a wink.

The two of them slipped from the room and Grier was left with the past.

Unable to wait another moment, she slit open the letter and pulled out a fresh sheet of paper, covered in neat, even rows of cursive writing.

She saw Maeve's name first, larger than the other lines in a heavy scrawl at the bottom of the page, and thought about her aunt.

Walker had told her early on she had an aunt—her father's sister. She'd tried making an outreach several times but hadn't gotten anywhere, despite leaving phone messages and sending e-mails. Although the urge to go out to the woman's house had been strong, she knew where she wasn't wanted and she hadn't been all that willing to face yet another cold, unfriendly face.

Especially when that face belonged to a blood relative.

She'd also asked around about Maeve and had gotten more than a few raised eyebrows. The term "recluse" was the kindest she'd heard, with "a little off" bringing up the rear. No one had used the word "crazy" outright, but it hadn't been too big a leap to make to pull that from the subtext.

On a sigh, she settled back in her chair.

Might as well see if she really was as crazy as the common wisdom suggested.

Dear Grier:

Forgive the delayed note, but I've struggled with the best way to reach out to you. I've appreciated your calls and your e-mails, but as with most things in life, if you're not ready to do something, it's best to wait until you are ready to do it.

I have some things that belonged to your father that now belong to you. I've hesitated to give them to you because doing so unequivocally revokes Kate's claims in court. While I'd have come forward eventually to ensure you have a right to what's yours, I've had a hard time coming to grips with what my actions will mean to that child.

Jonas often worried about her to me. He worried that her prickly personality hid a deeper fear of life and how to live it. Oh, she's always done the right things and said the right things and put on a good face, but Jonas worried, especially after Kate's mama died.

I'd hoped she'd come around and drop this ridiculous fight to keep you from his things, but since that's not happened, it's time to end it.

For her good and for yours.

Your father loved you and he loved your mother. That also might not be very evident by his actions, but don't you spend one more day thinking otherwise.

That man loved you.

He just never knew how to tell you.

The enclosed notes are all the proof you need that you are his daughter.

If I might make one other suggestion, there's a man in Barrow named Brett Crane. He was a good friend of your father's and they worked together around the time you were conceived. I've enclosed his contact information in the envelope. Give him a call. He can testify on your behalf and get this ridiculous court nonsense finished.

One final suggestion. Go visit your father's grave.

I know you haven't been out there and while I don't think he deserves much from you, he does deserve that.

Give me a call when you get back. I'd like to have a visit with my niece.

Maeve Price

Grier folded the letter and set it aside, afraid of getting it wet with her tears.

She glanced at the faded letters and the leather-bound journal. As her gaze danced over the address on the letters, she realized it was her mother's handwriting. Curiosity rose up, swamping her as she reached for the one that lay on top.

A New York City postmark ran along the top edge and the date was about two months after her birth.

With shaking hands, she slid the note out and saw the baby photo of herself, worn and slightly crinkled, as if it had been touched too often. Setting the photo aside, she unfolded the letter and saw her mother's small, efficient script.

The letter was short and to the point.

Jonas:

I can't see you again and I hope you will allow me to raise Grier as I see fit. I can't make a life with you and I won't go through my reasons again.

I will see that you receive photographs of our daughter, but I need to ask that you respect my wishes and stay away.

Patrice

Whatever Grier had expected, this cold, horrible note from her mother wasn't it.

Since this whole mess had started, Patrice had artfully managed to stay above it. She'd refused to engage in conversation about "her past" and she'd been unwilling to offer any assistance, including a signed affidavit or any form of testimony confirming she and Jonas Winston had conceived a child.

Although hurt, Grier had thought it unkind of her to ask her mother to open up her past grief and she had agreed to do this on her own. She'd been willing to fight this battle alone because she'd believed Patrice hid the scars of a deep and painful past.

But this?

Her gaze alighted on the letter once more.

I need to ask that you respect my wishes and stay away.

Grier had always thought her mother cold and distant, but she'd at least believed something hopeful lived within her. Something that gave her a life of purpose.

How wrong she had been.

Avery wiped down a table, delighted the small crowd who'd been in the bar earlier had all left. Susan had covered things while she was upstairs with Grier and Sloan, and it was easy enough to collect the last of the glasses and get everything locked up for the night.

She moved to another table and heard Susan's voice from where it echoed out of the office. Something struck her as slightly off. While she wasn't an unhappy person, Susan was pretty even-keeled and not much got her chattering away in a high, excited voice.

Except Roman.

Or showing off pictures of her grandchildren, courtesy of Roman's younger sister, Riley.

It had to be a story about the kids. Maybe Madison was getting the hang of potty training or Connor had had a good game of peewee hockey.

Because it couldn't be about Roman.

He'd just been here, for God's sake. There was no way the league would give him enough time off twice during the season. And even when they got the occasional stretch of days off, he never had enough time to get all the way up to Alaska for a visit.

Susan's voice broke into her thoughts as she danced into the lobby. "You'll never believe what happened!"

"You sound excited. Did Connor have a good game?"

"It's even better news."

She knew the answer before the words even left Susan's lips.

"Roman's coming. Twice in one season, do you believe it?"

Susan's chatter ensured she wasn't really required to give an answer, so Avery moved on to the next table.

"He's coming up because one of the big sports channels is doing a special on him and the amazing season he's having. They want to get a few live shots of him at home, so they're flying him up here on a private jet."

Avery didn't have the heart to stomp on Susan's happiness, and it certainly wasn't her place to tell her employer she wished her son would just stay away.

But seriously?

She and Roman got along just fine with an entire

continent between them. And on the occasions when he was home, she managed to find ways to avoid him for the duration. Her alcoholic mother had actually been a blessing in that sense—one of the rare occasions when she was—but that excuse was now gone and she hadn't yet cooked up a new one.

"Avery, did you hear me? They're going to film right here. And they want to interview us."

"You. I'm sure they want to interview you. I'm just the hired help."

"You're so much more than that and you know it."

Avery swallowed at the lump that always rose up in her throat every time Susan pulled the mother routine on her, and she tried for a smile instead. The truth was, Susan Forsyth was the closest thing she'd ever had to warm and nurturing, and she hated to disappoint her.

Even if a small part of her twisted up in grief and pain at the fact that she'd had to turn to someone else to find the warmth her own mother was incapable of giving.

The fact that the source of that warmth was her ex's mother, well . . . life was a freaking circus, even on good days.

And since the woman had a blind spot the size of the North Slope when it came her son and her hotel manager, Avery walked a tightrope when it came to the subject of Roman.

The two of them weren't teenagers any longer—and hadn't been for a very long time. Whatever bright, shiny happily-ever-after Susan still envisioned for the two of them wasn't possible any longer.

But no matter how many ways she tried to explain that, Susan would not be convinced.

"What's going on?" Sloan stood on the other side of the door, her flannel PJs peeking out of the bottom of her padded coat. "I came as fast as I could."

"Is Walker downstairs?"

"Yeah. I know it's just a walk across the square, but he insisted."

"You can tell him to come up."

"He's fine"—Sloan waved a hand—"and before you push it, he understands. Just tell me what's going on."

"Here." Grier thrust the first letter she'd read from her mother into Sloan's hands. "Read it."

She watched the expressions flit across Sloan's face—curiosity, frustration and finally, anger—and realized the order matched her own processing of the document's contents.

"Grier, I'm sorry. I know I overstep all too often when it comes to your mom, but that is beyond cold. Heartless."

"I know."

Sloan shrugged out of her coat and threw it onto one of the room's chairs before hopping on the bed. "Did you read the rest?"

"Yeah. The next one, written about a month later, is clearly in reaction to his writing back to her. In it she tells him she's marrying my stepfather."

"What about the others?"

"They're all before she left Alaska."

"Oh."

At Sloan's probing gaze, Grier nodded. "They're love letters."

"Really sexy love letters?"

"Passionate and flowery, yet nothing too specific on the creepy, eww, this-is-my-parents front. But—"

"But what?"

"But it feels like a violation somehow. To think that my aunt read them and now I'm reading them. It feels intrusive."

"Maybe your aunt didn't read them."

Grier shrugged. "True. But it still feels weird that I have. I mean, it sounded like she really loved him. And there was this passion in them. If I didn't know my mother's handwriting so well, I'd say they were written by someone else."

"Maybe she was someone else then. Someone who was in love."

"So what happened?" Grier picked up the letter where Sloan had laid it on the desk. "What happened between love and passion and a baby and this?"

"You'll have to ask her."

"She refuses to talk about it."

Sloan pointed to the pile on the bed. "It looks like you finally have the proof you need to make her talk. Up to now, you've given her the benefit of the doubt of her privacy. But this? You're entitled to know why your mother refused to let Jonas see you."

Of all the things Mick had expected after a restless, sleepless night, none of them involved Grier Thompson standing over his table at six o'clock the following morning in the middle of the Indigo Café.

"I need to go to Barrow."

"Well, good morning to you, too."

She impatiently dragged off her padded coat and threw it across the bench seat that made up her side of the booth. Before dropping into her seat, she leaned forward and pressed a hard kiss to his mouth. "Please."

"You don't play fair." He reached for his coffee, his hungry gaze devouring her small form as she slid into the booth, his lips buzzing from that kiss.

"I'm not trying to play fair. I need to go to Barrow."

"Why do you want to go to the North Slope?"

"Would you accept sightseeing as an answer?"

He shot her a dark gaze as he sipped his coffee. After swallowing it down, he added, "No."

"I need to go see a man who knew my father."

Mick sat up straighter in his seat, the caffeine and the reality of what she wanted to do waking him up. "Grier. Where did this come from?"

"My aunt. My father's sister."

"What does Maeve Price have to do with a trip up to the North Slope?"

As Grier began to tell him about a package and old letters and Maeve's move behind Kate's back, Mick could only hold up his cup to gesture to their waitress for more coffee.

And fifteen minutes later as their waitress set down matched stacks of pancakes before each of them, Mick still couldn't quite process it all.

"But you have all you need. The letters definitely prove you're Jonas's daughter and that he wanted you as part of his life. Kate has no claim otherwise and there's nothing further she can use to waylay the processing of the will. Give them to Walker. He can have them before the court today and you'll be on your way. The injunction will be lifted. You and Kate can split the contents of the will and you're off to the races."

And off to New York. The morose thought hit him as he spread the butter across the top of his breakfast, pulling him up short.

She'd gotten what she'd come here for and she'd be leaving.

"But I want to meet this Brett. Talk to him about my father. He knew him, Mick. Really knew him."

"We all knew him, Grier. Just ask any of us."

"None of you knew him when he knew my mother. Brett Crane does."

He saw the need in her eyes—would have been blind to have missed it. "Do you have any idea what it's like up there in January?"

"No sunlight."

"Pretty much."

"And it's inside the Arctic Circle, so it'll be even colder than Indigo, if that's even possible. Can you fly there?"

Mick tamped down on the indignity that reared up at her question. "Yes, I can fly there."

"Have you flown there?"

He grinned at that. "Darlin'. There's nowhere in Alaska I haven't flown."

"Don't get cocky," she muttered as she dug into her pancakes like a lumberjack.

Damn, but she made him smile. And got his insides so fucking twisted, he didn't know if he was coming or going.

Of course he'd take her up to Barrow. He'd be damned if he'd let anyone else do it and the determination in her eye wasn't to be taken lightly.

"How do you eat like that?"

She looked up from the forkful of fluffy pancake, drenched in syrup. "Why does everyone ask me that?"

"Maybe because you've got an ass that makes the angels weep and the rest of you is even finer than that."

"Um, thank you?"

Despite the sass, he didn't miss the lopsided grin she fought to hide as she took her bite.

Mick reached across the table and snatched a piece of her bacon.

On a huff, she added, "I do work out."

"How often?"

"Every day. I just don't make a big deal out of it. I hate those people who run around talking about how healthy they are."

"The wheat germ people."

She snapped her fingers. "That's a good name for them. What's the point of working out if you can't eat stuff like this?"

"I couldn't agree more." He snatched one more piece of bacon and settled back. "So, when do you want to leave?"

Chapter Thirteen

*G*rier flipped through the fourth-quarter folder she'd created for Chooch and Hooch and sighed. How much dog food did these people buy? As she thought about their brood of huskies, she had to acknowledge they required quite a lot. Add in vet bills and you had one very expensive hobby.

"You look like you've gotten through most of that," Chooch interrupted from the doorway of the conference room.

Grier glanced up and nodded, but she didn't say anything as she finished tallying up her last stack. She'd dragged an adding machine in earlier from the hotel's office and the monumental task of sorting Chooch and Hooch's receipts had gone a lot faster.

The satisfying hum of the adding machine clicked as she finished tallying up the receipts, the gentle whirl of printed paper falling out the back. She missed this, Grier acknowledged to herself as the last of the paper spooled off the machine. More than she had realized.

"You look like you've gotten through nearly all of them."

"These pet receipts were the last of it. I'll get them

input later and once you've got your bank statements, we'll be ready to get you and Hooch filed."

"Damn, but you were quick."

"I enjoy it and I'm going out of town for a few days."

Chooch grabbed a seat, the lure of being in the know clearly catching her fancy. "Where are you going? Or more to the point, who are you going with?"

"Mick's taking me up to Fairbanks for a few days."

Although she hated to lie, she and Mick had agreed that the fewer people who knew what they were doing, the better. She'd done her level best to keep her situation with her inheritance from her father private and she'd be damned if she'd start blabbing all over town any new details.

Besides, they technically *were* going to Fairbanks. Mick had several runs he could make as part of the trip, so they'd spend tomorrow night there, refueling the plane and staying overnight before heading to Barrow the next day.

"Sounds like a romantic getaway to me."

"I'm doing some sightseeing."

"And what glorious sights they are," Chooch said on a reverent whisper.

"Chooch!" Grier threw a wadded-up receipt at the woman. "What is it with this entire town? Everyone wants Mick and me to have sex."

"Lots of it, too. The women of this town are living vicariously through you, my dear. Please don't take away our enjoyment."

Grier snorted at that. "Oh come on. Surely the man's had girlfriends before. I can't be the first woman he's

ever dated." As she said the words—and put a defini-
tion on them—a heavy flutter hit her stomach.

Dating? Girlfriends? Was she really willing to go
there?

She wasn't so resistant to think they didn't have a
personal relationship, but definitions like those were
serious.

"That man's more private than you are. Other than
how gaga he is over you, none of us has ever seen him
all that fussed up about a woman."

"Surely he's dated."

"Of course. There have been rumors aplenty—even
a sighting or two over the years—but Mick O'Shaughnessy has steered clear of the women of this town since
the ninth grade when he dated Jenny Stewart." Chooch
sniffed. "It'd be insulting if he weren't so damn lovable."

Grier struggled with the description of Mick's love
life versus the virile, vibrant man she'd come to know.
Clearly he was discreetly enjoying his time outside the
prying eyes of Indigo.

"Now"—with a fingernail Grier tapped one of the
many folders she'd sorted the receipts into—"these are all
in order and ready to file away. I want you to take these
home and keep them in a safe place in case I need to see
them again before we file your return. And you really
should keep them anyway in the event of an audit."

"Do you want a puppy?"

Grier stopped in her tracks where she'd organized
the file folders together into a neat pile. "I'm sorry?"

"Well, you talked about the dog receipts. And we're

about to have a new litter. And Mick's got his sights set on you. A puppy's the next step."

A puppy was *so* not the next step, but Grier wasn't sure she could get those words out past the stranglehold of panic that had seized her.

"Um, I'm sorry, but I'm going to need to pass on the puppy." As Chooch's face fell, she quickly rushed on. "I'm sure it'll be a beautiful litter, but a puppy's not going to do very well in a Manhattan apartment."

Chooch's eyes narrowed and Grier wished she could bite back the words. "You're going back?"

"Well, yes. I haven't moved to Indigo permanently."

"But what about Mick?"

"That's for him and me to decide."

The older woman stood and Grier didn't have to wonder where the sudden frost came from. Chooch gathered up her folders and marched for the door. As she crossed over the threshold, she hollered back over her shoulder, "Enjoy the trip."

Mick sat in the terminal and pored over his flight plans as he drank a cup of coffee. He'd finished up a little earlier than he'd expected and the extra time had turned out to be a boon. He hadn't lied to Grier—he had been all over Alaska and back—but he hadn't been to Barrow in a few years. A bit of extra time to check his maps and work out a few routes was welcome.

"Do you know Grier is headed back to New York?"

Maggie stood next to the table, her hands on her hips and an expectant expression riding her gaze. A gaze, he added to himself, that was made positively frightening by the mint green eye shadow that covered her eyelids.

"Now?"

"No. When she's ready to go home."

He reached for his mug and leaned back in his chair, well aware his comments in the next few minutes would dictate the messages that ran up and down the town's grapevine for the next forty-eight hours. "She's said as much."

"Well, you can't let her do that."

"I don't think I have all that much say in it."

"Of course you do. You're a catch and you're crazy about each other and you need to convince her to stay. She'd be a fool to walk away from you."

He did believe Grier's stubborn resistance to what was between them was a mistake and he was going to do his level best to prove that to her over the coming days.

But Maggie's approach?

No way.

"Maggie, I presume you do realize it's 2013? A woman can make up her own mind about who she wants to date."

"Well then, put your game face on. You've got more charm in that little finger than most men do in their whole damn body." She wagged a brightly painted fingernail at him. "I suggest you put it to good use."

With that she marched off, her heavy footfalls echoing through the empty terminal.

"You give me far too much credit," he muttered to himself as he stood and rolled up his plans.

While the idea of Grier's leaving left a painful, gaping hole in his stomach every time he thought about it, Mick would be damned if he let the town dictate his course of action.

Hell, he wanted Grier to stay and he knew everyone else had grown rather fond of her as well. But he'd be damned if he'd be goaded into keeping her like some bad sixties sex comedy.

He was still fuming fifteen minutes later as he slammed into Walker's office. "I don't have any more runs today, so please tell me you have scotch, whiskey or bourbon in that filing cabinet over there."

"I've got all three. What do you want?"

"Bourbon," Mick ground out as he dropped into one of the chairs opposite Walker's desk.

"Let me guess." Walker handed him the bourbon, then sat down in the chair next to him and raised his own glass. "Grier's headed back to New York."

"Fuck, shit and damn," Mick muttered as he knocked back a large sip of the bourbon. "Word travels even faster than I realized."

They both glanced at the door of Walker's office, then said in unison, "Myrtle."

Myrtle Driver was Walker's secretary. She'd been working for him since the day he'd opened his practice, fresh out of law school. She'd stood at the front door, telling him how things were going to work between them.

Best Mick could tell, the woman did little work, was obsessed with spider solitaire and was one of the key nodes on the town grapevine. The only reason Walker hadn't ever fired her was because the woman had an unshakeable faith in the legal system and wouldn't breathe a word to anyone about what went on in the office.

Anything outside the files of Walker's law firm, however, was more than fair game.

"I hear ya talking about me," came a loud voice from the outer office. "And if you don't do something about that girl, Michael Patrick O'Shaughnessy, you're not the man I thought you were."

Mick rubbed his eyes and groaned inwardly. "What is wrong with this town?"

Walker stood and crossed the room, closing his office door with a definitive snap. "Do you want me to start making a list?"

"No, seriously." Mick lifted his head. "What is wrong with them? I thought it was only the grand-mothers, but it's all of them. The women of this town are bat-shit crazy about love."

"It's definitely in the air."

"No thanks to you." Mick shot his best friend a dark look. "Hell, Grier and I aren't married. We're barely dating. What would make anyone think the woman was staying here?"

"I think the better question is, do you want her to stay here?"

Mick saw how neatly Walker had boxed him in and refrained from indulging the urge to break something.

"That's a shitty question, Counselor. Isn't that lead-ing the witness or something?"

Walker shrugged, clearly enjoying himself. "Does the witness want to be led?"

"Bite me."

Grier thought back over every scary thing she'd done in her life. Skydiving had been terrifying but exhilarating. Traveling out of Romania during a coup while on a business trip had been particularly daunting. And presenting at an annual meeting of the partnership had turned her insides to mush for days.

But she knew none of these had come close to answering the summons to dinner that had appeared for her at the hotel at three o'clock that afternoon.

Oh, the invitation looked innocent enough, Grier knew. But the pleasant order layered underneath it was clear.

Mary O'Shaughnessy was inviting her, Avery and Sloan, as well as Walker and Mick, to dinner.

And there was no number to extend her regrets.

Grier walked in front of the mirror once more, smoothing her skirt with shaking hands. She'd almost left this skirt at home and thanked whichever god looked out for women headed into scary family situations that she'd thought to pack it.

A brief knock on the door had her turning away from the mirror and she knew the time for stalling was done.

She opened the door and nearly lost her breath as she took in Mick on the other side. He wore a gray dress shirt, tucked neatly into pressed black slacks. His blue tie set off his eyes to absolute perfection and she had a brief, pressing urge to wrap both hands around that tie and pull him inside the room.

Of course, an action like that would only reinforce why she was being summoned to dinner, but now that the image had taken hold, Grier couldn't quite shake it.

"You look beautiful."

"Thank you. You look very handsome." *And sinful,* her overactive imagination added.

Mick helped her into her coat and she didn't miss the veneer of nerves that coated his words. "I didn't know she was going to do this."

"I know."

"I got the call this afternoon. Her words were stern as she warned me that there was no such thing as free milk and the least I could do was bring a woman I was dating over to see her."

Grier wanted to wince at the free-milk comment, but it was hard to be embarrassed when the entire town kept encouraging them. "She found out about the trip."

Mick raised his eyebrows. "Since you and I have been the subject of nearly every other conversation that's happened in this town for the last three days, I'd say that's a safe bet."

"Why'd she invite Sloan and Avery along?"

"My grandmother may be scary, but she's fair." He opened the door and gestured her through.

"What's fair got to do with it?"

"She clearly wanted you to have reinforcements as you walked into battle."

Grier felt her stomach drop as her hotel door slammed shut behind them.

The party was already in high gear when they arrived at Mary O'Shaughnessy's house ten minutes later. Mick helped her out of his SUV and as her booted feet slid into a slushy pile of snow, she inwardly offered up thanks that she'd remembered to pack her heels in a separate bag.

"You okay?"

"I'm good. And very glad I'm in boots."

He escorted her up the walkway of his grandmother's house and Grier took in the beautiful lines of the large home. Heavy logs framed the structure and bright, warm light shone from each window.

"It's a log cabin. Well, cabin's a stretch, but it's the same idea."

"My grandfather built it."

"It's gorgeous. And welcoming," she added as they got to the front door.

"That's about the biggest compliment you can give my grandmother."

The door swung open on his words and Mary O'Shaughnessy's bright, smiling face greeted them. "What compliment is that?"

"Your home, Mrs. O'Shaughnessy," Grier said as she stepped into the large foyer. "It's warm and welcoming."

Mary leaned forward and kissed her cheek. "Thank you, dear. That's the nicest thing you can say about a home."

Mick pulled Mary into a tight hug and Grier reveled in the brief moment as observer. It was a welcome change from the ever-present gazes that focused on her, and his ready and simple affection for his grandmother was refreshing.

While she had no doubt the woman drove him crazy half the time, the love, respect and genuine affection the two of them clearly held for each other were lovely to see in action.

"Well, come on in, then." Mary gestured. "It's too cold to stand out here."

They were quickly escorted down a long hallway that led to the kitchen. Heavy wood framed the ceiling that arched above them and the various guests were assembled around a large round table or the large island that dominated the center of the kitchen.

Grier did a quick count and noted that in addition to the guests she'd expected, Julia and Sophie were there, along with Doc Cloud and Jess and Jack.

Mary had her hand in a firm grip and led her straight to the island. "Let's get Grier fixed up with a drink and then I want to finish hearing all about the wedding plans."

Avery thrust a glass of wine in her hands and Sloan patted her arm, and Grier quickly found herself enveloped in a friendly, engaged circle of women as they discussed wedding dress material, bridesmaid colors and cake-filling flavors.

It was several long minutes later before she even thought to look for Mick. He stood with the other men near the entrance to a large family room, a big screen behind him showing a hockey game. Intermittent shouts or groans would go up from their group from time to time, but the low, steady hum of their voices was a pleasant counterpoint to the wedding chatter.

Several barstools had been strategically arranged around the island for the older women and Mary settled herself on the one closest. Grier smiled as Sloan described a wedding dress she'd found in a magazine, happy to see someone she loved so excited.

As she watched Sloan's animated face, she felt Mary take her hand and give it a small squeeze.

Grier squeezed back, the nerves she'd walked in with a distant memory.

Jason sat in the overstuffed chair in the corner of the Jitters, his iPad open on his lap. He'd thought to distract himself with the *Wall Street Journal*, but the only thing he'd managed to do was play a few rousing rounds of Angry Birds.

He was stalling and he knew it.

He'd come here to win Grier back, but so far he'd spent every free moment watching TV, answering e-mail or playing on the damn tablet.

Or thinking fleeting thoughts about gray eyes—so familiar, yet not—that probed and penetrated and saw slightly too much.

On a harsh sigh, he refocused his wayward thoughts toward Grier. She'd made it abundantly clear she had no interest in getting back together when they'd spoken the other night. Add in her forgiveness—which actually seemed quite genuine—and he should be relieved.

Like a tantalizing breath of fresh air after being shut up inside for days on end, he wanted to take her at her word and move on. But there was no way in hell he could come back from Indigo without his fiancée in tow.

He glanced back down at the device in his lap. Although he had maintained a steady check on e-mail, the office had been abnormally quiet, his team all actively working on their outstanding projects. Maybe there really was some merit to working your ass off to make partner, he thought with no small measure of satisfaction.

Or maybe the old man told everyone to leave you the hell alone while you were groveling.

Ignoring the sinking feeling that the answer was housed in his father's almighty influence, Jason closed the game app and opened up the *Journal*.

His eyes had nearly glazed over reviewing the stock ticker when a soft voice punctuated his thoughts. "Mind if I sit down?"

Jason looked up to see Kate standing over his chair, as if he'd conjured her from his overheated thoughts, and he quickly sat up. "Of course. Please."

She took the seat opposite and set her large coffee mug down next to his. "You look very important sitting there."

"Just staying up on the news."

She raised her eyebrows in a move eerily reminiscent of Grier. "The *Wall Street Journal*'s a far cry from the *Anchorage Daily News*."

"It's all news. Here today, gone tomorrow."

"I'd have said the same for you, but you're still hanging around."

"I have some unfinished business."

"Is that what you're calling it?"

An unexpected annoyance broke his composure and he wondered at the reaction. "Do you think you know better?"

"All I know is that you came here presumably to win Grier back, yet you've steered clear of her. It makes me wonder why."

"She's been busy."

"Planning a trip with another man."

Jason had spent his life ensuring no one knew what he really thought about anything—not his father, not his friends and certainly not women. And he was damn good at it.

So he was more than a little surprised when Kate's eyes lit up like a slot machine.

"I can see from the expression on your face that you didn't know about that."

"I'm not blind." Jason quickly regrouped. "I know she's got a thing for the pilot. And it's more than clear he's got one for her."

"That's an interesting reaction from a man who's trying to win a woman back." Kate leaned forward, a light, sexy smile playing around the corners of her lips. "So tell me. What'd you do? To piss her off, I mean."

His stomach tightened as he remembered those dark moments in the office. He'd barely even looked twice at Charlotte, their temp, but she'd sought him out.

And once sought, he'd allowed himself to be caught.

The teasing smile dropped and Kate sat back. "That bad? What a shame."

As if finally finding his voice, he said, "What's a shame?"

"I thought you were a stand-up guy. A confused guy, but a decent one all the same. It looks like I was mistaken."

Kate stood and he wanted to ask her to stay. He was technically a free man and, to Kate's incredibly astute observations, the woman he was up here looking to win back was interested in spending her personal time elsewhere.

But something held him back.

The sad truth was, he hadn't been a stand-up guy. When it counted, he'd not only dropped the ball, but he'd betrayed the one person he'd selected to be his ally on the field.

If he couldn't make things work with a woman who came from within his social circle, it'd be a damn stupid idea to start playing with someone who came from outside of it. He couldn't go backward and make up his actions to Grier, but he didn't have to drag someone else into his mess.

Especially when that someone was Grier's sister.

Kate picked up her coffee and tapped him on the shoulder as she passed alongside his chair. "You don't seem all that hung up on Grier's social calendar. An odd reaction for a fiancé, if you ask me."

It was an odd reaction, but he *wasn't* all that hung up about it. He was man enough to admit it chafed his pride, but beyond that, all he felt was a glorious sense of freedom.

It was just too bad that the woman walking away from him was off-limits.

Something buried in the recesses of his heart began to beat—in that place where he'd hidden away all of his conflicted thoughts and emotions for as long as he could remember.

And as he watched Kate Winston walk away, Jason allowed his mind to wander to a place where things might be different. Where she wasn't off-limits.

To a place where Kate Winston might be his.

Chapter Fourteen

"Now Grier, that's not the way it happened and you know it!" Sloan's laughter carried through the kitchen and the other women were quick to come to her aid.

"I believe you, Sloan," Sophie added. "My grandson didn't pick a shy retiring wallflower; I just know it."

Grier enjoyed the way Sophie came to Sloan's aid and she knew her friend was in good hands with Walker's family. They'd been together only a short time, but it was clear they'd already accepted her.

"Fine," Sloan said on an exaggerated sigh. "I'll tell the story."

Grier settled in to hear the story the two of them had spent years recounting like a Laurel and Hardy routine and reveled in the soft, sweet glow that surrounded her. Dinner had long since ended and they'd moved back into the kitchen for coffee, dessert and more conversation.

God, did it feel good, Grier thought, to be standing here, spending time with these people.

Their hockey double-header over, the men had joined them after dinner and it hadn't escaped her notice how

Mick had hovered nearby, his glances and light touches full of promise.

She knew things would change on their trip. And she knew even more that she wanted them to.

But none of it could change the fact that after they took the trip to the North Slope, she'd have gotten what she'd come for.

Walker had already reviewed the letters and was preparing the paperwork to get Kate's arguments for contesting the will thrown out.

It was only a matter of time before she'd be leaving Indigo.

Mary patted her arm, drawing Grier's attention off her thoughts. "Would you help me? I want to get the coffee and begin slicing the dessert."

"Of course."

Grier followed her to a small butler's area off the main kitchen, still amazed by the extraordinary size of the house. Mary pointed toward a small refrigerator built into the wall. "The cake's in there. I just want to get the coffee started."

"Thank you for the invitation to dinner," Grier said as she set the cake on the counter. "This has been absolutely lovely."

"A fitting send-off before heading into the far reaches of Alaska."

Grier fumbled a bit as she pulled the plastic wrapper off the top of the cake. She wanted to make some reference to Fairbanks, but the omission of the real purpose of their trip felt like a lie if she voiced it.

"Barrow's a cold, hard place. But it's also a place of unique beauty if you peel back the layers."

Grier crumpled the plastic wrap and turned toward Mary. "You know where we're going?"

The older woman nodded but only smiled. "I've always thought Barrow was a metaphor for Alaska itself. It was built out of sheer will and determination. It's amazing what those two things—and a good old-fashioned dose of human spirit—can do."

"I'm not trying to lie to anyone about going up there." Grier reached for a large knife in a wooden holder to cut the cake. "I just haven't wanted to be very public about it. And this trip has become a surprisingly well-known secret."

"You should be able to keep a few thoughts as your own. That's one of the hardest things about living in such a small town. Sometimes people forget there are things they have no business knowing."

"I need to know my father."

"Of course you do." Mary scooped coffee into the open lid of the filter. "And you're entitled to that."

They both worked in companionable silence as Grier wondered at Mary's words.

Was she entitled to it?

It was the one thing she'd been unable to reconcile to herself since learning of her father. He'd clearly not wanted anything to do with her in life. While the packet of her mother's letters had shed some light on why he'd kept his distance, the reality was that she was no longer a child and hadn't been for some time.

And he'd still not made an outreach to her, long after her mother's influence was past.

"He'd be proud of you," Mary said as the coffeepot began to brew. She reached into the cabinets above the counter and pulled down a set of small dessert plates. "The woman you've become."

"Did you know him well?"

"Well enough. Everyone knows everyone in Indigo, but he and my husband were poker buddies. Sat in that kitchen more Wednesday nights than I can count, giving each other a hard time over cards."

Grier smiled at the thought. No matter how much she struggled with what never had a chance to develop between them, every little glimpse into Jonas Winston's life was an enticing puzzle piece. And if she gathered enough of them, Grier knew, she might have a picture to fill her memories.

"Grier."

She turned toward Mick's grandmother, the woman's vivid gaze—so like her grandson's—sharp and aware. "I see the way my grandson looks at you."

"Mrs. O'Shaughnessy—"

Mary held up a hand. "Please. Let me finish. I see how he looks at you and I know how much he cares for you. And there's nothing to be done if you don't feel the same way. But I want you to promise me you'll give it a chance."

"He and I come from very different worlds."

"And you also come from the same one." Her words were steel. "Don't forget that."

* * *

Mick mixed his grandmother a highball and listened with a small smile as Mary walked Grier around the living room. The rest of the dinner party had already left, but Mary had asked them to stay a little longer.

He set her drink on the coffee table and settled himself on the long sofa that dominated the far wall of the room. Something warm expanded in his chest as he watched his grandmother and Grier, their heads bent together over a small table full of pictures.

And it was only when he heard Grier's voice that the harshest of realities intruded on the moment.

"Who's that?"

"Mick's mother."

"She's beautiful." Grier picked up the photo and Mick already knew the image she saw—that of a bright, smiling woman with long black hair and dancing blue eyes, her arms spread out along the edges of a park bench.

The picture had been taken at his eighth birthday party, after the guests had departed. His father had snapped it and he'd boasted to anyone who would listen that his wife looked that gorgeous after spending the afternoon keeping up with fifteen eight-year-old boys.

"Mick, your mother is beautiful. Why haven't you mentioned her?"

He shrugged, careful to keep his voice neutral. "It just hasn't come up."

"She's passed, dear," Mary said as she gently took the frame. He saw Grier give the photo up willingly and move on to another and the knot in his gut began to loosen.

Fuck, how could he have not thought this through?

It wasn't a secret, exactly. Hell, the whole damn town knew. But it just wasn't something he discussed. Ever.

And he'd sure as hell be damned if he'd discuss it while she stood there looking all dewy and perfect and unspoiled.

Because his mother's death was none of those things.

It was in the past. And he was unwilling to allow the truth in to make its ugly mark in his present.

Mick walked around the front of the SUV after settling her in the passenger seat. Grier couldn't stop the flutter of nerves that whispered under her skin at the thoughtfulness of his gesture.

He was a consummate gentleman. Kind and thoughtful. A man who knew how to treat a woman like a lady.

And he'd been more than patient with her.

Maybe it was that knowledge, she thought to herself, that had finally made the decision so very, very easy.

"We've got an early morning tomorrow. I'll pick you up around six to head out to the airstrip." Mick eased away from the curb and headed down his grandmother's street, stopping at the light on Main.

"I think you make a right here." Grier pointed in the opposite direction of the hotel.

"The hotel's to the left."

She heard the distinctly puzzled tone of his response and smiled to herself. He was a gentleman to the core; her instructions hadn't even registered.

"I realize I've never been there, but I believe your home is to the right."

Mick put the SUV in park and turned toward her. "Grier."

"I'd like to see your home, Mick. I think it's time."

She saw the questions in the vivid blue of his gaze. "If you're sure?"

"Yes, I'm sure."

The drive to his cabin didn't take long and she didn't miss the sense of anticipation that arced between them as he drove down the small, narrow road that led out of Indigo. Within moments, they were pulling up to a small cabin with a warm light burning in the front window.

She took in the small frame of the house and realized that it suited him. It was both rugged as well as an oasis of calm in the middle of a harsh, unforgiving land.

Sort of like Mick.

He came around to help her out of the car and as his gloved hand covered hers, she knew she was making the right decision.

The front door of the cabin was unlocked and he opened the door, then gestured her through it.

"It's not much."

Grier looked around the warm, inviting room and saw Mick indelibly stamped in every bit of it. The space was sparsely furnished, with a large TV dominating one wall and a thick-cushioned, L-shaped leather couch filling the other side of the room.

She stamped her booted feet on a braided rug near the door before toeing off her heavy boots. An image teased her memories of the first time they were together—when her boots got stuck on her jeans—and she wasn't interested in repeating the experience.

Satisfied she wasn't at risk of falling flat on her face in a second display of grace and decorum, she turned to smile at him. "Your home is lovely and rather like what I imagined."

He pulled her coat from her shoulders, his breath warm at her ear as he spoke. "And what did you imagine?"

Grier turned into the heat. "Pretty much this. Although I did expect the TV to be bigger."

She reveled in the heavy bark of laughter he emitted as he moved to settle her coat on a rack by the door. "It's fifty-seven inches."

"Well." Grier shrugged. "You are a bachelor. Isn't your TV sacrosanct or something?"

"Grier," he mumbled as he moved back to wrap her in his arms. "I really don't want to talk about my TV."

She lifted her head back to nip a quick kiss on his chin. "I really don't want to talk about your TV, either."

With infinite tenderness, he laid a hand on either side of her face and tilted her head until their gazes locked. "I'm glad you're here."

"Me, too."

He lowered his head and pressed his lips to hers.

The delicious warmth that had filled her since Mick had whispered in her ear while removing her coat spread throughout her body. Her limbs filled with a combination of lazy ease and urgent need.

They stood in the living room for several long moments, the contact of their mouths reaffirming the want and longing that had danced between them for the last month.

"What changed your mind?"

Grier pulled back, breathless. "A lot of things, but you make it so easy just to be me. Other than my friendship with Sloan and now, Avery, I never feel comfortable in my own skin with anyone. But you give me that and I'm tired of making excuses to myself for why I should deny it."

He ran a finger down her cheek before cupping her face in his palm. "This is unchartered territory for me."

"For me, too."

At his skeptical look, she rushed on, not wanting a discussion of Jason to spoil the moment. "I've never wanted anyone like I want you. And no one's ever made me feel as disoriented as you. So when I say me, too, I mean it."

"I believe you."

"Then make love to me."

His eyes had gone a deep sapphire in the soft light of the room and his furrowed brow relaxed as his mouth spread into a broad smile. "I think I can die a happy man."

She smiled up at him. "Maybe you can wait about another hour before expiring on me?"

As laughter shook his shoulders, she wrapped her arms tight around him and held on as he scooped her up.

"I'll do my best."

Mick stared down at the woman in his arms, bone-deep satisfaction spreading through him with each step he took toward the bedroom. He knew they'd made progress—knew instinctively over the last week they were moving toward something deeper between the two of them—but he'd been willing to give her space.

Her announcement in the car that she wanted to come to his home had been as surprising as it was satisfying.

She'd come to him.

Mick knew it smacked of his caveman roots, but that satisfied on a level he could barely explain, even to himself.

When the moment did eventually arrive, he'd envisioned himself making love to her slowly, drawing out each and every moment until they were both mindless with wanting. Their first time together had been fun and unexpected, happening without any conscious act on the part of either of them.

This time would be different.

This time he was determined to brand her as his. He wanted the way he felt about her to leave something permanent between them.

He lowered her to the bed and followed her down, lost in the smoky gray of her eyes.

"The way you look at me—it's heady."

"How do I look at you?" Her hands settled at his hips as she stretched out alongside of him and his stomach muscles clenched at the contact.

"Like I'm precious."

"You have no idea." His hand skimmed the seam between her sweater and the sexy little skirt she wore, parting the material to find warm flesh underneath. He ran the pads of his fingers over that stretch of skin and felt her muscles bunch just as his had moments before.

Impatient, he took fistfuls of her sweater and pulled the soft material over her head, catching his breath as his gaze alighted on the lacy material of her bra, an enticing shade of baby blue he'd forever associate with her.

With aching slowness, he worked his way down her body, replacing his fingers with his mouth as he allowed his hands to roam. He ran his tongue along the small well of her belly button, satisfied at her gasp of pleasure, before shifting his attentions up over her rib cage until he reached the rim of her bra.

He felt the light touch of her fingers at his neck, threading through his hair. Light moans came from her throat in delicate gasps and the sound roused another set of Neanderthal applause from his caveman instincts.

And then he feasted.

The sight of her nipples, pebbled under the silk of her bra, drew his attention and he placed his mouth over one peak while he plied his fingers against the other. Grier's soft moans grew more urgent as her legs ran along his own and she moved her hands to grip his shoulders.

"Mick—"

His name on her lips drew him up and he shifted up onto his arms to stare down at her.

"If I make you feel precious, you make me feel like a conquering hero. As though I can literally pick up the world and twirl it on my finger."

"You *can* fly."

He leaned down and pressed his lips to hers. "Let's fly together."

Shifting, he moved to the edge of the bed and made quick work of his boots before standing to unbutton his shirt. His fingers felt too big as he fumbled with the buttons and he nearly forgot what he was doing as he caught sight of Grier.

She'd stepped before him, her hands at the back of her skirt working on the zipper. Her lush breasts thrust forward at the movement, nearly spilling from her bra.

Mindless, he reached for the hem of his shirt and dragged it over his shoulders, pulling the T-shirt underneath along in the process. He heard rending thread and the light tinkling of a button falling to the hardwood floor beneath the bed, but he ignored all of it.

Grabbing Grier in a tight hold, he fell back onto the bed, cushioning her with his body as they fell. "Mick!"

"I can't wait for you."

"My skirt's stuck around my knees."

He reached for the skirt with a foot, pushing it down even as his fingers reached for the hook of her bra. "I swore we'd take it slow, but there are too many clothes."

Loud, muffled giggles echoed off his chest and he

twisted his head to look at her as he still struggled to work the skirt down her legs. "Are you laughing at me?"

"I . . . I . . . am," she said, hiccupping through her laughter.

"What's so funny?"

"Didn't we get tangled up in our clothes the last time we did this?"

"We'll work on it," he muttered as her skirt came free of her legs while he pulled the bra down her arms.

"Practice makes perfect," she whispered as she took the bra from him and tossed it over the side of the bed.

"My thoughts exactly."

Grier wiggled up until she was straddling him, the thin silk of her panties the only thing that separated a full view of her body from his gaze. Her dark gray eyes bore into his as she ground her hips over the fly of his slacks. "You're still wearing pants."

Pleasure hit him so hard, Mick saw a wave of stars, and he groped for her hips to hold her still, even as his hips pressed mindlessly up toward her.

"I think we need to fix that." With slippery ease, she slid from his hands and crawled down his body, reaching for the fly of his slacks. He was so hard he ached, but he still had the presence of mind to stop her hands before she could lower the zipper.

"Allow me."

A knowing smile crossed her lips—full of feminine promise—as she moved off him. He shucked his pants and underwear as she made quick work of her silky panties. The sight of her—her heavy, full breasts, the triangle of hair at the apex of her thighs and her long slender legs—was nearly his undoing. His body, free of the binds of his clothing, grew even harder, painfully ready for her.

She lay back on the bed and he followed her down, settling himself over her as her hand closed over his cock. A hoarse shout rose up in his throat and she only smiled and applied more pressure, moving her hands with increasing speed.

"This is torture."

"I know." She reached up and bit his ear. "Which is why I can't understand why you won't put me out of my misery."

"Now? But I had all these grand plans." Although he wanted to drag this out, he was already reaching for a condom in his end table.

Her husky voice floated toward him. "Save those ideas for later, darling. I'm not going anywhere and I can't wait."

He stilled momentarily as her words registered.

"I'm not going anywhere."

Rationally, he knew she meant this evening, but the words were the equivalent of a sucker punch to the gut. Because the truth of it was, he didn't want her to go anywhere.

Ever.

"Mick?"

Pulled from the moment, he smiled down at her. "I'm just trying to decide."

"Decide what?" She filched the foil packet from his hands and made quick work of the wrapper.

"If I want you on top or bottom."

Grier reached between their bodies, fitting the condom over his long length. Once again, he nearly came off the bed at her touch.

And then the decision was made as she pushed on his shoulders before rising above him, straddling her legs at his waist and taking him deeply into her body. He leaned up and took one nipple in his mouth, gratified when she let out a long, sensual moan as her thighs tightened around his hips.

Reaching for her waist, he helped her set a rhythm that worked for both of them, then laid one hand behind her neck to pull her down for a kiss. Her small hands splayed across his chest as their tongues mimicked the give-and-take of their lovemaking.

And then he released her, allowing her to take over the rhythm as she rode him into a mindless oblivion with her head thrown back as she took her pleasure. The sensation of finally having her again—of watching her in such an intimate moment—was even better than the sheer bliss of their joined bodies.

He gazed up at her through heavy-lidded eyes, as pleasure swam through his system.

It was Grier.

And she was here.

And for tonight, at least, she was his.

Chapter Fifteen

The smell of coffee hit her first, followed by the low rumble of Mick's voice. "Wake up."

With her eyes still closed, she burrowed into the covers, seeking more warmth. "What time is it?"

"Five."

"We went to bed at three," she mumbled, even as the tantalizing aroma of caffeine had her eyelids drifting open.

"Why don't we stay here all day and we can go to Fairbanks tomorrow?"

Her lids fully snapped open at that. "We have to go today to stay on schedule."

Mick's dark hair was still wet from his shower and his piercing blue gaze crinkled at the corners. "Thought that might get you up."

"You don't fight fair," she grumbled. "And you're clean already."

"Let's just call it an act of self-preservation."

Grier sat up and took the mug he offered, taking a quick sip. "How so?"

"If I waited for you, there'd be no way I could keep my hands off your wet body in the shower."

Warmth suffused her at his words and she couldn't hold back the happy smile. "I'm glad I stayed the night."

He leaned in and pressed a coffee-flavored kiss against her lips. "I'm glad you're here."

A million thoughts floated through her head, but only one mattered. "I'm glad I'm here, too."

Grier buckled herself in, getting comfortable as she watched Mick start the plane's engine and begin a check of his instruments. Fascinated, she could practically see the way he ticked off each task in his mind, his gaze roving over the extensive panel of gauges and readouts.

As he buckled his own seat belt, she couldn't resist asking, "You do this every time you take off?"

"Every time."

"But didn't you fly yesterday?"

He shrugged as he flipped a few switches, the engine roaring to life in a heavy hum. "Doesn't matter. Something could have changed on landing. Or I could have missed something on my last check. Or the plane could have finally picked this moment to act up. I don't mess with my equipment."

Mick leaned down beside his seat to grab a small binder and jotted down a few notes. She watched the swift, efficient movements as he printed neatly in the log.

The moment was an incredibly enticing peek into a side of him she never would have expected. The casual flyboy with the two days of scruff on his cheeks was a thorough, careful pilot.

He's a thorough lover, too, her conscience picked that moment to remind her as images of the night before flooded her thoughts.

Incredibly thorough.

Mick handed her a headset, then pulled on one of his own as they taxied down the runway. The cold metal in her hands pulled her back to the present moment, even if the low hum that had settled in her stomach had nothing to do with the rumbling engine warming up beneath them.

She pulled the headphones on and could hear the sharp, tinny voice clearing Mick for takeoff. And then they were off, the small plane barreling down the runway before making a smooth rise into the dawn.

The dull hum of voices in the headset faded as Grier focused on the sky. "It's gorgeous."

"The sky is extra special up here. No matter how many times I make this trip, I never tire of it."

"I can see why."

A long, slow roll of need filled her belly as Grier turned to look at him. Arms outstretched, Mick's large, capable hands gripped the steering mechanism as he held the plane steady with an ease that belied the fact he maneuvered them twenty thousand feet above the earth.

Tamping down on the increasing distraction of desire, she focused instead on the voices in her headset. He'd set her headset to the same frequency as his and she could hear a steady stream of instructions that continued to come through to him. The voices from the tower fascinated her and the fact that he understood anything they were saying was an intriguing peek into his daily life.

An irresistibly intriguing peek, she thought as she glanced over at him; he was completely enmeshed in his task. His jaw was set in hard lines and the edge of his tongue poked out past his lips.

"You're quiet this morning." Mick's voice stole through her headphones, pulling her from her thoughts.

"I didn't want to interrupt." *Or miss the opportunity to observe you doing something you love.*

"We're well on our way. I thought I'd fly past Denali before heading up. Does that work?"

"I'd love to see the mountain."

The mention of the mountain refocused her and a question hovered on her tongue. She'd nearly put it to words before pulling back. Mick had brought some researchers off the mountain the night they'd been together in December. They hadn't spoken of it since that night and she'd wondered more than once how he was handling it.

She didn't have to wait long.

The mountain loomed before them, its broad peaks an awesome testament to what nature could create.

"It's absolutely beautiful."

"She is, isn't she?" Grier heard the pride in his voice—the sheer love for his home—and she smiled.

Whatever had happened with the researchers, he could clearly still see the beauty in something he loved so much.

"I want you to see the peak from the other side." They worked their way around the mountain, the plane moving in and out of cloud cover, and Grier had the sudden realization that she was in an airplane and he was flying it.

Which was about as absurd as suddenly realizing she had two legs, but it was her reaction all the same.

"What's that look for?" She heard the smile in his voice and turned toward it.

"You're really and truly flying this plane."

His eyebrows shot up. "You thought I had a pack of elves in the back?"

"I mean, this is all you. We're up here because of you."

A light blush crept up his neck and Grier only smiled more broadly. "It's awfully sexy. You know that, don't you?"

He shrugged. "That's the generally accepted wisdom."

"Oooh, and you're so modest, too." She couldn't resist poking him a bit.

"I'm a tough bush pilot. It's in my nature. The stoic and silent type." He extended a hand toward her and she reached out and took it, their fingers entwining together.

"You're the first woman I've brought up in a plane since I was nineteen."

"Is that a come-on?"

He shrugged. "It's a fact."

"And that gal at nineteen?"

"I was young, horny and misguided," he said on a wry grin. "What can I say?"

"I'm quite sure she was bowled over by your bush pilot prowess."

His grin grew even broader. "How'd you guess?"

"I was young, horny and misguided once, myself. And if I had known you then, I'd have been all those things over you."

"Don't break my heart and tell me you aren't all those things now."

As they soared over the peaks of Denali, Grier simply smiled.

Once they were on the ground in Fairbanks, Mick waited for the deliveries to finish up. He had several sights lined up for the day and was itching to get out and show Grier around.

To her credit, she seemed to be enjoying herself in the meantime. She chatted with the locals over coffee, making fast friends with the woman who managed the delivery area. In his trips back and forth to gather up paperwork, he'd overheard coos over baby photos, discussion of the merits of white rice versus brown rice in managing weight loss and the relative value of buying a treadmill.

When he finally collected her an hour later, he didn't miss the disappointed expression on Dana's face.

"We'll be at the Rooster later on for dinner. Bring your family and come join us."

Dana brightened immediately and Mick knew he'd made the right choice.

Within minutes, they were in the SUV he'd rented, the heater going full blast. "That was nice of you to invite Dana and her family to dinner."

"I hope you don't mind," he said.

"Of course not. She's lovely."

"I hear a 'but' in there."

"But—" Grier paused. "It's not what I expected."

"What did you expect?" He turned to look at her when they came to a stop at the next light.

"Most men don't invite families with small children on their dates."

"Yeah, well, most women have no interest in having a date in the nether-reaches of Alaska. We'll chalk it up to the two of us making a unique pair."

She gifted him with a smile that lifted him up and scared him shitless, all at the same time. "I'll give you that."

He'd spent half the day thinking about the night before and no matter how hard he tried, he couldn't shake the idea that something very significant had changed last night. And it wasn't just the sex, although that had been singularly spectacular.

It was the fact she'd come to him.

First for his help to take this trip and then to his bed.

The two were intertwined and both said a lot about her increasing trust of him and what they had between them.

This trip was as much about Jonas as it was about the two of them. Mick might not be able to keep her in Alaska, but he'd make damn sure she'd remember it—and him—when she left.

And if the thought of her leaving burned like acid in his gut, he'd just have to keep ignoring it.

Her voice broke into his musings. "I've thought a lot about what you said the other day. About Jason."

His veins ran cold at the man's name, but he was intrigued all the same. "And?"

"And I think you're right. I think he would have struggled with my friendship with Sloan after a while. I'd like to think I'd never have let it get to the point where I'd choose him and shut her out, but I'm also not naive enough not to think that it wouldn't have been hard."

"Now you won't have to make that choice."

"Thank God."

The light turned and Mick refocused on the road. He'd had several thoughts about Wall Street over the past week and not a single one of them had been favorable. Before he knew it, the question that had pounded with the most insistence spilled forth. "Are you sorry you're not still with him?"

"No."

"That's awfully definitive."

"I feel awfully definitive." She let out a small laugh. "No matter how screwed up my life has been the last several months, the one thing I've never regretted—not even once—was walking away."

"That's a bold statement."

"Or a very sad statement on the man I thought I was going to spend my life with."

"Life's detours are sometimes the most interesting part of the trip."

Her light laughter filled the car and Mick found himself caught up—in the moment and in her.

"You're quite the philosopher."

"Occupational hazard. I spend a lot of time in my head."

"I never thought about that, but I can see it's true. Yet another similarity between us." Grier must have seen the question in his face, because she continued to explain.

"Spending hours with spreadsheets requires a lot of tuning out the world around you. I'm always amazed at the problems I work through in the back of my mind as I'm adding columns of numbers."

"A sexy number cruncher," he crooned. "Tell me more."

"What do you know about if-then statements?"

Kate worked her way through a column of numbers and wanted to scream in frustration.

She'd been fighting with the insurance companies since her father's death and another round of bills had come in over the last week. She'd tried diligently to keep a spreadsheet of all the activity, but the sheer volume of statements had made it hard to keep up.

And every time she thought she had a handle on all the expenses, another bill came in to mess up her orderly figures.

She reached for her coffee, calming slightly as the warm brew hit her stomach. At least she was out. She'd been crawling the walls at home and couldn't get settled, so she'd walked over to the Indigo Café for a hot breakfast and some quiet time in different surroundings.

But even in new surroundings, she couldn't quite shake her restlessness.

Every time she had a spare moment—and of late

she had quite a few—her thoughts reverted to Jason Shriver.

Their conversation the previous evening at the coffee shop had shaken her up and as she'd lain there in bed, restlessly tossing and turning, she couldn't rid herself of the disappointment that the guy was an asshole.

She might have blocked Grier at every turn since her sister had arrived in Indigo, but she wasn't a fool and she didn't think Grier was one, either. A woman didn't walk away from the guy she was going to marry unless something pretty awful had happened.

And if she had to guess, that something awful had everything to do with sex.

Which was why she had to stop these foolish thoughts about a man she had no business being interested in.

On a sigh, Kate turned back to her computer screen.

Who'd have thought it would come to this? Too much time on her hands and nothing to do. As her father had gone downhill, she'd taken a leave of absence from teaching. She'd gone from never having a free moment to having so much free time, she was swimming in it.

She'd even gone over to the school and asked to revoke her leave of absence, but they'd hired someone on for the year to fill the vacancy. Although the position was hers when her LOA was finished, she couldn't go back now.

"You're never happy." Her mother's words floated through her mind. It had been Laurie Winston's favor-

ite accusation to fling at Jonas and as she'd gotten older, Kate had heard her fair share of it as well.

As if reaching for something more were a bad thing.

She'd known her parents didn't have the world's most ideal marriage, but her father had assured her in his last years that he had loved her mother.

He just hadn't known how to love her enough.

She hadn't quite known what to do with that information, so she'd filed it away and figured she'd take it out someday when she was strong enough to think about it. Or when she'd hit a point in her life at which she could accept that her parents had been flawed humans, just like she was.

In the meantime, she left it to lie there. Not like there was all that much to be done about it.

These bills, on the other hand . . .

On a sigh, she ran a hand through her hair and reached for the one on top of the stack.

"That looks like about as much fun as a root canal." She glanced up to see Jason sliding into the booth across from her.

"Good morning."

"Morning. You have a spreadsheet open and a stack of paper in front of you. Anything I can help you with?"

The urge to close up her laptop and hide the bills was strong, but she resisted, an image of Trina primping and fluffing for every man that passed her by roaring through her mind's eye.

She was who she was. No use in trying to hide it.

"Thanks for the offer, but I've got it."

His hand snaked out before she could register his intention and he snatched the first bill off the stack. "Hospice?"

Kate snatched it back and laid her hand over the stack. "It's from my father."

His eyes narrowed as he stared at her. "Does Grier know about these?"

"She doesn't need to know about these."

"Why not? It's her father, too."

"She doesn't need to know about them." Kate heard the screechy tone of her voice, echoing in her ears, and modulated her tone. "This isn't her problem."

"Come on, Kate. Grier would help you if you asked. I know she would."

"Do you really? Because you haven't spent a lot of time around Grier the last few months."

"I know her well enough to know she'd take responsibility for this. Would help you with them."

Jason turned his cup over as their waitress approached them and Kate kept her mouth clamped firmly shut. She had no interest in spreading this issue around town. Her bills were her business.

And why the hell did she think she could come here and do this, anyway? She should have stayed home. Fuck crawling the walls, at least she'd be away from prying eyes.

"Did your father have insurance?" Jason asked as Debbie headed back toward the kitchen with his order.

"Yes, he had excellent insurance. The pipeline took care of their own."

"So they'll pay these?"

"Almost all of them. It's just a matter of sorting them out and every time I think I've gotten through the last of them, more show up. Cancer's a vicious bitch and she's the gift that keeps on giving."

Kate hated the tears that tightened her throat, so she reached for her water glass and tried to swallow around them.

"I'm sorry."

The tears hardened into a knot in her stomach and before she could stop them, words were spilling forth. "Funny. Everyone loves to use that word. That they're sorry. Sorry for what? You didn't do anything."

His warm brown eyes widened in surprise and Kate knew she should pull back—knew this man didn't deserve to be the recipient of . . . *this*—but she didn't know how to stop it.

Didn't know how to hold back the grief now that she had an outlet.

"Kate—"

"Everyone's sorry. Everyone feels bad. But no one really wants to hear about all this." She slapped the stack of bills under her hand. "And then they all look at me like I'm the bitch of the universe because I've pushed back on Grier's claims."

If he missed the connection between a misguided offer of sympathy and what it had to do with her attitude toward her sister, he didn't show it. "I'm sure no one looks at you like that."

A harsh, brittle laugh wheezed through her lips. "You haven't been here long enough. Ask around."

Before he could answer, she barreled right on

through. "Grier waltzes in and tries to collect her in-heritance. She was never here. Hell, I didn't even know I had a sister until the damn will got read. How fair is that?"

"It's not."

"So I'm supposed to sit back and act like it's okay?"

Jason sat there in silence and Kate wondered why he hadn't run from the diner with his hair on fire.

After a few long, tense moments, he reached forward and laid a hand over hers. Immediately, warmth flowed over her and ran up her arm, and the taut knot of rage that had gripped her with tight claws loosened a bit.

Abstractedly, she allowed her gaze to run over his fingers. Long, with neatly sculpted nails at the end, they were surprisingly strong as they lay over hers.

"You asked me something last night."

She lifted her gaze to his as the fire and the fury passed completely, leaving as quickly as they came. "What was that?"

"You asked me if I was a stand-up guy."

She nodded, their conversation at the Jitters still vivid in her mind.

"I wasn't a stand-up guy. I've always thought I was, but I'm starting to wonder if that's a lie I've told my-self. Regardless"—he waved his other hand—"I wasn't a stand-up guy to Grier. I made an incredibly poor choice and I hurt her. And she didn't deserve it."

His grip tightened. "And you don't deserve what's happened to you. You didn't deserve to lose your father. And you deserved to know you had a sister, especially since your father had more than enough time to tell you about her if these bills are any indication. So yeah. You have a right to be mad and angry and so pissed off you can't see straight."

"Thank you," she said quietly as she continued to stare at their joined hands. "You're the first person who's agreed with me."

He lifted her hand and turned it over so that their palms pressed together. "You're welcome. Of course, that doesn't mean you still don't need to do the right thing."

She met his gaze and saw the compassion in those rich, mocha depths. In that instant, she started to wonder if maybe Jason Shriver was truly sorry for what he'd done.

And if maybe he deserved a second chance.

Chapter Sixteen

"Can I peek, please?" Grier felt the SUV come to a stop, but she still had her hands over her eyes.

"Keep 'em covered or it won't have the same impact." Mick's voice rolled over her and Grier noticed how he sounded even sexier than usual with her eyes closed.

How was that even possible?

"We're stopped. Why can't I look?"

"God, woman, you are impatient." He let out a long-suffering sigh before tapping her shoulder. "Okay. You can look now."

Her eyes widened on the sight before her as she looked through the front window of the SUV. "No way."

"Yep."

"Reindeer?" A giggle floated past her lips as she stared at the huge animals walking around behind a high fence. "Those are really reindeer?"

"They are."

She twisted in her seat to look for signs. All she saw were other cars, full of animated families as they looked at the animals. "Where are we?"

"The University of Alaska. They've got a large-animal research station."

"Can we go look at them?"

"The tours are only in the summer and I think the viewing platform's going to be too cold. But I couldn't let you get this close to them and not come out for a look."

She watched in awe as a mother walked with a few babies. "They're amazing. How'd you find out about this place?"

"Most anyone who comes up here knows about the research station. It's a pretty big draw. But Jack and I did some transporting for a few of the scientists a few years back."

"You had reindeer in your plane?" She turned away from the animals as she measured the antlers in her mind's eye. "In the plane we came up on?"

He shook his head. "No. We had to rent a DC-3 to do the job, but it was worth it. It was a rare treat. We also transported caribou and musk ox."

"That's wonderful. How far did you have to fly them?"

"We helped them pick the animals up in the wild. Although neither Jack nor I did much around the animals, we had to make sure they were safe in the cargo hold, especially since they were tranqued."

She turned to look at the reindeer again, their elegant necks holding racks of inordinate size. "I guess getting them settled and safe is quite a job."

A rather indelicate idea took hold, but Mick beat her to the punch. "And yes, the plane smelled to high heaven when we got done. Jack and I scrubbed that damn cargo hold down for two days before we were able to deliver it back to the company we rented it from. Maggie threatened at one point to walk around with clothespins on her nose."

Grier giggled at the image Mick painted of their intrepid air traffic controller.

"It's a dirty job, O'Shaughnessy."

"But a fun one. I'd do it again in a heartbeat."

They sat in companionable silence as the herd continued grazing and the two of them lapsed into casual conversation.

"Chooch offered me a puppy from their new litter."

"That's quite a compliment."

"A compliment?" Grier turned again from the view. "I figured it was a ploy to get me to waive my tax fees. She seemed pretty hurt when I declined."

"They don't sell those dogs to just anyone. She's really taken a shine to you."

"That's how the rumor started spreading I was headed back to New York."

"I knew Chooch was the source, but didn't know why." He grinned broadly. "What's the matter—you don't want to curb a husky in New York?"

"I'd give my eyeteeth for one, but it just doesn't seem fair."

"I'm sure lots of people have dogs in the city. Why can't you?"

"A lot of people make it work, but I'd begged for one growing up and my mother never relented, no matter how many times I asked. Once I was on my own, it just seemed too late. I mean, what would I do with a dog?"

"I don't know—love it? Enjoy it? Walk it in the park and take it to the vet? Lots of people find a way, Grier. You would, too."

His words struck a nerve she hadn't even realized was all that sensitive. "It just wouldn't suit my lifestyle."

"Is that you talking? Or your mother?"

She felt the jab clear down to her toes. "You want to try that one again, cowboy?"

"You want to come up with a different answer? Hell, if you'd just said you didn't want a dog, it'd be fine. But what are all the excuses for?"

"They're not excuses."

"Then what are they?"

She snapped her mouth shut, not sure why they'd even begun fighting. It wasn't how she'd envisioned her day and it certainly wasn't how she wanted to remember these wonderful moments with the reindeer.

"They're baggage. Now can we just shut up and watch Vixen and her babies?"

She thought for a moment he was going to continue arguing with her, but at the last minute he turned toward the window and pointed to the far side of the field. "See that one over there? With the heavy antlers? They call him the Tank."

And if visions of puppies still floated in the air between them, for the moment, Grier could pretend they were still simply enjoying the sights of Fairbanks.

* * *

Mick knew he'd been an asshole earlier and he hadn't figured out yet how to make it up to Grier. If she was angry with him over the dog comment, she didn't show it. In fact, she'd been incredibly pleasant in the face of his rather aggressive words.

Sometimes your honesty isn't wanted or needed, O'Shaughnessy, he cursed himself yet again. *Learn to keep your fucking thoughts to yourself now and again.*

They'd visited the El Dorado mine after the big-game preserve. Although the mine was closed to visitors, he knew the owners as he'd ferried more than a few tourists their way.

He and Grier got a private tour of what they could actually see that wasn't covered in snow. She'd even bought a mug and a T-shirt on their way out while promising the owner she'd e-mail the name of a jeweler she'd recommended in New York.

Mick turned toward her as he started the SUV up once again. "You truly have a gift."

She held up the plastic bag full of her purchases. "For shopping?"

"For meeting people. Dana this morning and now the name of the jeweler for Charlie. You talk to people."

"You do, too. It's one of your nicer traits." She paused for a moment before shooting him a saucy grin. "You know. When you're not ranting and railing about puppies."

"I deserved that."

"A little bit. And it's been a few hours. I'd rather laugh about it than leave it to linger."

The tire iron that had sat on his chest since they'd left the game preserve lifted and he took his first easy breath in three hours. "You ready for dinner?"

"Will there be wine there?"

"Yes."

"Then I'm ready for dinner. The Rooster, you said earlier?"

"Yep. I love it. The owner is from Georgia and the food is about as down-home as you can get."

"Then I'm definitely in."

Ten minutes later, he pulled into the parking lot and cut the engine, the welcoming lights of the Rooster beckoning them like a homing device.

He came around to Grier's side and helped her out of the car, pleased when she hung on to his arms as she slid out. "Watch your step."

"This place smells divine."

"Sarah's food is incredible. I usually get the fried chicken, but if she's got her potpie on the menu, I may have to drop you like a hot potato and ask the woman to be mine forever."

He held the door for her and Grier moved into the large hallway that bracketed an inner door from the outer cold. Mick didn't miss it when her gaze lasered onto the framed newspaper articles on the wall of the foyer.

"Is that large man there next to her Sarah's husband?" She leaned in and read the caption. "Big John?"

"That'd be him."

She glanced back over her shoulder, her gaze doing a saucy run from the top of his head to the tips of his boots. His body responded immediately, tightening as heat built between them in the enclosed space. "It must be some damn good potpie. That man could eat you for breakfast."

Grier forked up a bite of the most amazing coconut custard pie she'd ever eaten as she bounced an eight-month-old on her lap.

"Watch it, Grier." Dana smiled from across the table. "Betsy will have half your whipped cream before you can stop her."

Grier leaned in and nuzzled a warm cheek, satisfied when she got a baby belly laugh. "We're just giving Mommy a break tonight, aren't we, Betsy?"

She gave the baby another raspberry to the cheek and was rewarded with yet another giggle as she pushed the pie away from plump, waving fists.

Mick had his arm draped behind her on her chair and every few minutes his fingers ran a tantalizing dance along the edge of her back.

It didn't escape Grier's notice their evening had turned oddly domestic with the arrival of Dana, her husband, Will, and their three children. So how could it be that she was both enjoying herself tremendously and counting down the moments until they'd walk out the door?

With a long arm reach, she snatched another forkful of the pie and continued to bounce Betsy on her knee.

Conversation hummed all around them and it was easy to see Sarah and Big John had a thriving business. The town was out in full force and Grier couldn't help comparing it to Indigo. Although Fairbanks was definitely larger, the same overarching small-town welcome was in evidence.

"Mr. O'Shaughnessy." A gangly teenager moved up to their table and Grier didn't miss the look of hero worship in his dark brown eyes.

"Kevin. How are you?"

"I'm doing well. My mom said you were back in town for the day, making deliveries. I'm sure glad I got to see you again."

"Have a seat and join us for some pie." Mick extended a hand and the boy leaped into the seat with an eager mix of trepidation at the opportunity and pride at being asked.

"You've been keeping your grades up like we talked about?"

"Yes, Mr. O'Shaughnessy."

"And how's the physics?"

"I've aced every one of my tests. I had no idea physics was so important for flying."

Grier exchanged a quick glance with Dana and squeezed Mick's knee at the sweet exchange. She'd never insult the boy, but it was clear physics hadn't been very high on his list of priorities until Mick had made a few suggestions.

"And how are your other grades?"

"Other than a C in history, all As and Bs."

She didn't miss Mick's broad smile as their waitress set down another slice of dessert in front of Kevin. "That's great to hear. You keep that up. Now, how are your lessons going?"

The boy's eyes nearly rolled back into his head as he began to tell Mick about his flight lessons, and Grier settled back in her chair with the baby in her arms.

She wasn't sure how it kept happening, but every time she observed Mick, she saw something different. There was a casual confidence to him that just sort of brought everyone right along.

His patience with Kevin. His easy way with Dana and Will's children. Even his gentle way with his grandmother.

Not that she'd had any doubt, but Chooch had been on the money.

Mick O'Shaughnessy was a good man.

She leaned down and whispered in Betsy's ear. "You pay attention to this, sweetheart."

The baby waved her arms and let out another belly laugh.

Avery flipped through the newspaper, idly reading what caught her fancy. The hotel was quiet—January always was—and she'd finished up any outstanding paperwork a while ago.

The newspaper wasn't all that interesting, either, but if she played one more game of Sudoku, she'd go cross-eyed and she'd already blown through the latest Jayne Ann Krentz hardcover she'd gotten for Christmas.

As she opened the sports page, her boredom fled as she caught up on the expectations for the weekend's NFL play-offs. After a quick scan of the injury report, she made up her mind on how she was betting Chris for each of the games.

She'd beat his ass soundly for the last two weeks and had no intention of losing her mojo. Besides, he had no idea how to bet against the point spread, which she knew she should feel guilty about, but well . . . she didn't.

Satisfied with her picks, she flipped the page.

And lost her breath as Roman Forsyth stared back at her from a photo that dominated the top half of the page. Dark hair plastered itself to his head and a nasty red cut lined the corner of his eye.

He looked like an avenging warrior, home from battle and celebrating his victory.

She stared at the photo for a long time, as heat and need warred with the voice of common sense that was never quite able to break through the memories.

Why couldn't she get past this? Past him?

And why did looking at his picture only ignite the need that curled through her body like a flash fire at the knowledge he'd be in Indigo soon?

They'd been broken up a long time and still, these feelings for him had lingered far longer than was considered normal or healthy or even remotely sane. But try as she might, no one she dated ever quite measured up to her high school boyfriend.

And oh, how she'd tried.

She'd gone after smart guys, dumb guys, guys who wouldn't know a sports term if a dictionary was handed to them. She'd gone out of town and she'd tried online. Hell, a year ago she'd even agreed to a blind date on a weekend trip to Anchorage.

Nothing worked.

Nothing and no one had ever allowed her to give up the ghost.

She'd even considered a psychiatrist—would have gone if the cost simply hadn't been too exorbitant on top of the bills from her mother—so she'd bought Father Tom coffee a few times and chewed his ear off.

The priest had been helpful—and the one person in town she could trust not to repeat anything that came out of her mouth—but even after a year of cappuccinos she hadn't gotten any closer to healed.

Slamming the paper closed and tossing it in the trash can, she reached for the Sudoku book, resigned to another evening of eye strain, when the phone rang.

"Indigo Blue, how can I help you?"

The line crackled briefly before a lilting voice flowed through the end of the phone. "Is Avery Marks there?"

"Yes, this is she."

A nervous laugh echoed briefly in her ear before the voice spoke again. "This is Lena O'Mara. From Ireland. I wonder if you might have a moment to talk."

Mick smiled as Dana and Will's two-year-old lifted his arms for a hug.

"You look like the Michelin Man, buddy." Mick lifted the well-insulated boy onto his lap and gave him a big hug. "Don't forget what I told you."

"Don't hit girls, especially not my sister," Bryce grumbled.

"Exactly. And remember. You're going to like those girls someday."

He gave the small body one more hug before passing him across the table to Will.

Grier gave Betsy one more squeeze—the baby was also bundled up like a burrito—and then Dana, Will and their brood were off.

Mick dropped into his seat with a sigh. "Wow. I know my mom took on a lot, but I had no idea three kids were that much work. How'd you do that thing with the baby?"

"What thing with the baby?" Grier piled up some of their discarded plates into the center of the table.

"She was bound and determined to get your dessert and you held her back every time. The kid was like an octopus."

She gave him a small triumphant smile. "I was voted the best babysitter in our building, three years running."

"Wow." He leaned over and wrapped an arm around her neck. "You're a world champion."

"My personal record is four children at one time. A set of twins, their younger brother and an infant."

"How'd you do?" He leaned back to get a better look at her face and didn't miss the pride that shone in her eyes.

"All in bed by seven. And the baby slept through the night."

"Nice going."

"Of course, those same children ruined it the following weekend by letting the dog out of the back bedroom. A dog, I might add, who was in heat and who ripped off her doggie diaper within about two minutes of the parents' being gone. The twins subsequently painted each other with cake frosting, the toddler ate a crayon and the infant projectile vomited three times."

"And you lived to tell the tale."

She reached for her glass of wine. "And never got invited back to babysit, either."

The smile that suffused her face and lit up her gaze grew brighter, if that was possible. "You were good with him. Kevin."

"Our future pilot."

"He worships you."

"He just needs a role model. He's had a few tough breaks—his dad passed away about a year ago—but I think he's back on track. I helped his mother get a deal on his flying lessons to cut the cost a bit. He also works out at the airstrip, which adds to his ability to defray the costs of his lessons."

"No wonder he worships you." She leaned in and pressed a kiss against his lips. "I think you're pretty groovy, Mr. O'Shaughnessy."

He smiled against her mouth. "I have a way you can prove it to me."

Grier sat back, her mouth dropped in a mock *O* of surprise. "Are you suggesting I relive my young, horny and misguided days?"

"You read my mind."

"And here I thought I was going to go to bed lonely tonight, seeing as how you ordered the potpie and all."

Mick shot a glance toward the kitchen where Big

John kept up a steady stream of conversation with the customers while he worked the grill. "I'll let you in on a little secret. I'm afraid of Big John."

Her answering smile shot heat straight to his groin and Mick reached for his wallet, intent on settling the bill so they could get out of there.

"I'm sorry to interrupt."

The voice registered before he made the connection and Mick looked over to see a man he recognized but couldn't quite place.

"David Barnes. I'm a friend of Ken Cloud's."

Mick stood and extended his hand. "Of course, Dr. Barnes. Good to see you again." He made a quick introduction to Grier before sitting back down.

"I'm sorry to interrupt. I can see you've finished your dinner, but I wanted to share my condolences. Ken told me about your actions last month. When you picked up those researchers off Denali. It was quite heroic."

Ice coalesced in his veins as Mick kept a broad smile on his face. If it were up to him, he'd never discuss that night again. And he certainly didn't want to discuss it with Grier around.

Before he could stop them, images of that night played through his mind. The crackle of static in his headphones as he searched for the researchers who'd radioed in for help. The pools of blood that had congealed on the ice and snow, leading him straight to the two men who fought to save their friend's life.

The experience had been so eerily reminiscent of his mother's death that he still saw the blood when he closed his eyes. And he'd had a few long, sleepless nights as he worked through the memories again.

"Those are kind words, Dr. Barnes. But I did what had to be done."

"At great personal expense to yourself."

"Well, unfortunately, one of those researchers paid a far higher price."

Chapter Seventeen

*T*he short ride to the hotel was eerily quiet. Grier kept glancing at Mick, but his gaze never veered from the road.

Nor did his grip relax on the steering wheel.

The thoughts she'd had earlier on the plane ride up, when Mick had flown her over Denali, came back in full force. How silly of her to assume because he still loved the mountain, he didn't bear its scars.

Bright lights welcomed them to their hotel as Mick turned into the parking lot. He pulled up under the porte cochere and popped the trunk as a porter ran up to secure their bags. As was his custom, Mick came around to open her door and help her down.

She tried to catch his gaze—and get some sense of how he was doing—but he kept his eyes averted as he helped her from the car, pointing out various spots to avoid. He kept her hand in his as they walked into the hotel, but she felt the distance and knew his thoughts were somewhere else.

Check-in was quick—the hotel staff knew Mick well and had already prepared for their arrival. But it was the sight of two keys sitting on the counter that blasted a shot of cold through her, numbing her right down to her toes.

The quiet ride up the elevator with the porter grew heavy with unspoken words as they took the short trip to their rooms. Although Mick needed her compassion, she could barely hold back the rising fury that mixed with disappointment like thick, wet cement.

Nor did she make much effort to hide her disappointment.

The moment the porter crossed the threshold of her doorway, a large tip in his hands, she closed the door and crossed to the bed.

How had the evening gone so wrong, so fast?

She'd barely kicked off her boots when the light knock on the adjoining doorway between her room and his echoed moments later.

Grier crossed to the door. "What do you want?"

"Grier, please open the door."

Unwilling to stand on the other side and argue with him, she unlocked the heavy bolt and threw open the door.

And was cut down at the knees by the raw, abject misery that covered his face in harsh, craggy lines.

"Two rooms?"

"I was trying to be respectful. I didn't agree to take you on this trip just to sleep with you and I'd already booked the rooms before last night."

"I know you didn't take me on this trip to get into my pants. I also know you should have talked to me about it. All you said was you'd taken care of accommodations."

"I was trying to give you space."

"Fuck space. I want you, Mick." She reached out and grabbed a fistful of his shirt in her hands. The heavy cotton was soft to the touch, but it was the heat that pulsed underneath that set her senses on fire.

Mick wrapped his arms around her and Grier found her hands flattened against his chest, her upper body cocooned by his. His mouth devoured hers as he walked her slowly backward into the room and in the direction of the bed. Her body boiled over to flashpoint at the expert strokes of his tongue, the excitement that frayed her nerve endings leaping to life.

Her breasts ached for his touch and every movement—every step—had her jeans brushing against the swollen flesh at the apex of her thighs. She wanted to be mindless underneath this man, a slave to the passion that lived and breathed between them.

Even if he had pissed her off with their accommodations and the silent treatment in the car.

Need pulsed off him in hot waves, but it was the pain layered underneath that had her pulling back and had the memories of their car ride from the restaurant rising back up to the forefront of her mind.

"We're not doing this again until you talk to me."

"You're the one grabbing my shirt." He ran a trail of hot kisses along the column of her neck and she fought to remember her point as wickedly pleasurable sensations tripped gleefully along her spine in a searing rush.

"Mick," she said with a sigh. "Come on. Talk to me."

He pulled back and dropped his arms. "What do you want me to tell you, Grier?"

"I want you to tell me what happened that night."

"A guy died because he wasn't careful. I had to help his buddies get him back to town. A sad story, but that's it. That's all there is to it."

She knew the experience was anything but "it," but decided to shift her tact. "We had sex once so you could assuage the pain. We're not doing it again."

"For the record"—he leaned in, his breath ragged—"you came to me that night."

"And I came willingly. But it's clearly still there, causing you pain. I want you to tell me about it."

He flung out a hand. "Like you tell me things? Like you give me a chance?"

The barb hit its mark, but he didn't allow her a reply.

"You've made it more than clear that we're separate people with separate lives. Why the hell do you want me to take something so dirty and ugly and bring it in here? I don't have that much fucking time with you and I'm not spoiling it."

"I'm asking you to tell me about it only so it's not between us. It's clear Dr. Barnes upset you at dinner. I want you to get it out."

"I was going to. With hot, mindless sex."

Grier shook her head as confusion mingled with unbridled need. She wanted him so badly, she could barely stand. Her skin felt stretched too tight, her body sensitive to every movement.

The angry tension that corded his neck relaxed and she saw the change immediately. She saw how the blue of his eyes morphed from glittering anger to a desperate need for understanding. "Grier. Please don't ask me to go back there. Ask me to leave, but please don't bring that between us."

She wasn't sure if it was the look on his face or the husky tones of his voice that pleaded with her to understand, but she went willingly back into his arms.

Grier lay in the lazy circle of Mick's arms. He had one leg thrown over hers and his head was buried in the crook of her neck. She could tell he wasn't asleep, but his breath had grown even as they both returned from the edge of oblivion.

She couldn't stop touching him—couldn't stop herself from running her hands over the long length of his biceps or trailing a finger down the hard planes of his chest.

Why had she been running from this?

And even as she asked herself the question, the answer quickly poked its way into the soft, warm union of their bodies.

She was exposed to him. Emotionally naked in a way even bare skin couldn't convey.

Although she resisted allowing Jason inside her private moment with Mick, thoughts of her ex-fiancé found their way into her mind. He'd hurt her—doing damage she hadn't even realized he'd been capable of.

It wasn't the cheating, although that was the outward sign and hurtful in its own right.

It was the sense that she wasn't enough.

That she didn't deserve a true commitment from another person. She'd lived a life with parental abandonment and she'd never thought she'd find it in the man she was going to marry, too. She wasn't naive. She knew life was hard and marriage had its ups and downs. But she'd gone into her engagement willing to work through the ups and downs.

Willing to give it her all.

To be found less than worthy of that had cut deep. And it had opened a wound that dated back to childhood.

Mick shifted, pulling her closer. As his heart beat against hers, she felt that wound closing. And she knew it didn't have the power to hurt her any longer.

Because no matter what came next for the two of them, Mick made her feel that she was more than enough.

The real question was, could she give him the same?

Mick heard the steady hum of his alarm and buried more deeply into Grier's warm and deliciously naked body. He didn't want to move, let alone get into a cold car and drive to the cold airstrip, only to fly to one of the coldest places on Earth.

Serves you right for living in Alaska, his conscience taunted as the shrill ping of his cell phone alarm kept ringing.

"Mick," her sleepy voice whispered against him. "It's your alarm."

"I know," he groaned into her neck.

"Turn it off."

He released her and reached for the offending item, slapping down on the OFF button. With quick moves, he pinned her right back into the same place on the bed as his sleepy thoughts woke up and took a new direction.

He had an armful of warm, naked woman underneath him and the day was a-wasting.

With a grin against her neck, he shifted and ran a hand over the sweet curve of her breast and down her stomach before settling at the soft curls that framed the apex of her thighs.

"Mick!" Her sleepy voice hit a high-pitched squeak as his fingers probed through the curls and into the tight sheath of her body. Hot warmth flooded his palm as her thighs fell open to allow him better access.

"You were saying?"

Her gray eyes were fast losing the haze of sleep as passion moved in to electrify their depths, but she could only utter a heavy moan. Invigorated, he kept up a relentless pace, determined to drag a response from her.

He didn't have to wait long. The telltale signs of her arousal let him know she was close and as her hands gripped his arms, he felt her body react in kind, gripping his fingers as pleasure erupted from the deepest part of her.

Satisfaction that bordered on primeval rose up in his chest. Unwilling to waste such a warm wake-up call, he shifted and buried himself to the hilt as her thighs wrapped around him. Her already-sensitized body sheathed his in welcome and he nearly went cross-eyed as Grier turned the tables on him, pushing him to his back so she could rise up above him.

She set the pace now, forcing him at the same breakneck speed that he'd initiated. He felt her rise up, again and again, his avenging angel of pleasure.

Hot, wet heat surrounded him, drugged him and made him mindless to the insatiable needs of his body. It captured him so that the seducer became the seduced.

And it was the triumphant smile of the seducer that filled his vision when he gave up the fight and allowed her to take him over.

"You can just get that smug expression off your face, Mick O'Shaughnessy." Grier wagged a finger at him as she buckled herself in. "We're an hour late because of your little wake-up call."

"I didn't see you protesting."

She grinned broadly as she took a sip of coffee from an insulated mug. "Hell no. You're looking at one deeply satisfied woman who has a hot memory to keep her warm as she enters the Arctic Circle."

His preflight checks completed, Mick snapped his binder closed and leaned over to place a hard kiss on her coffee-flavored lips. "We could screw the Arctic Circle and I could give you more to remember."

"But then what would be your reward for bringing me back home again?" She batted her eyelashes before offering up a disgusted sigh. "Why does the whole eye-batting thing look so cute in cartoons and so dumb in real life? I probably look like I've got an eye condition."

Mick was still hung up on her use of the word "home," and he mumbled a quick, "Beats me," as he tapped his headphones. After giving his flight authorization number, he got his clearance and began the short taxi to the runway.

The word still stuck in his gut ten minutes later as he watched Grier lean over in her seat, her head pressed to the glass. "That's just incredible."

"We're going to follow the pipeline up to the North Slope, then head west to Barrow."

She turned toward him. "You're allowed to do that?"

"I already cleared the flight plan and other than staying out of the way of a few other maintenance flights, it's a light morning."

"I guess that would be all that's out right now. I can't see this being the first place people would think to go sightseeing in January."

"Exactly. June and July, on the other hand. There's a parade of planes in the sky."

They sat in companionable silence for several minutes, the heavy piping visible beneath them, then snaking through the snow as far as the eye could see north.

His thoughts continued to churn as they flew away from Fairbanks, the last few weeks playing on a loop in his mind. He thought about the strange push-pull of their relationship as they both tried to figure the other out, and the impending sense that they were on the verge of something . . . big. Important.

He'd wanted her from the first moment he'd laid eyes on her, in early November when she'd first arrived in Indigo. She had been walking out of Walker's office as he had been walking in, and it had been all he could do to keep from following her right back out.

The long, artful waves of hair and the petite frame

had captivated him in an instant, but what had really done him in were her eyes. That subtle gray was so unusual and so incredibly enticing.

Her eyes held dark secrets and whispered promises. And with one look from her he'd been gone.

It hadn't been one-sided, either. They shared an easy flirtation and quiet looks. The entire town hadn't just decided on a whim that the two of them should be together. All of Indigo had seen what blazed to life every time they got within a hundred yards of each other.

Even if he could put all of that aside—and he wasn't one to take good old-fashioned attraction lightly—he enjoyed her company more than that of anyone he'd ever been with. He was a man who counted himself lucky. He had family he loved and friends who were like family, and he valued each and every one of those relationships.

But with Grier, it was all that and more. Moments with her were easier than he could have imagined.

And in that easiness came something so special, he couldn't imagine his life without it.

How could she think of walking away from that? And more to the point, how was he going to let her go when she did?

"To think people built this." Her reverent voice broke the quiet. "The heartiness and sheer determination to come up here and conquer the winter like this. It's fascinating."

"It's a pretty spectacular feat."

"And my father was a part of it."

Mick pointed out a pump station as they flew over

it, grateful for something to pull him from his thoughts. Focused on the ground below them, he described what he knew of the pipeline's mechanics. As a kid, lessons on the pipeline had been all the rage and he'd spent many hours listening to stories from the men who'd worked the line.

He smiled as he remembered the story that had been his personal favorite and began to tell her.

Moments later her eyebrows shot up, her skepticism clear as he took her through his story. "They actually call it pigging?"

"Yes. They have these mechanical devices—called pigs—that are sent through the pipe to clean it out. Of course, I didn't understand that as a kid."

"You thought they were real pigs?"

"Absolutely. Cried my eyes out one night until my sister told me I was being a moron and there weren't real pigs in the pipes."

"She knew better?"

"Only because she'd made the same mistake herself until my father sat her down and explained it."

"The poor, sweet O'Shaughnessy children." Grier reached over and patted his arm. "Such sensitive souls."

He couldn't hold back a smile at the memory of what had come next. "As I recall, that night actually ended in a grounding since I punched her for the moron comment."

"Hence your sage advice to Bryce last night in the restaurant."

"Exactly. Don't hit girls. It was as true then as it is now."

"Where does your sister live?"

"She got married to a guy from the Lower Forty-eight she met in college. They lived up here for a while and then moved to Minneapolis about ten years ago."

"You see her much?"

"Couple times a year. And we talk every week on webcam so I get the added benefit of seeing my nephews."

"And your dad? Where's he?"

The question had his mouth going dry, a stupid reminder that this was what casual family conversations usually involved. Actual conversation. And questions. "He travels a lot."

"Oh? Does he still live in Alaska?"

"No, he's been a wanderer since my mom passed."

He heard the inevitable next question and went on preemptive strike. "What about your mother? You talk about her without saying all that much. What does she think about all this?"

The question had its desired effect—it was a curiosity he'd been meaning to ask about *and* it got her off the subject of his family.

"Oh, how does one begin to describe my mother?" She glanced up at the ceiling as if seeking guidance from the heavens. "Patrice Thompson is the most well-bred woman on the planet. Seriously, she makes Miss Manners and the Queen of England look like slackers."

"I bet there's a wild side underneath."

"Presumably, since I was actually conceived. Add in it happened up here in what was apparently a wild fit of uncontrolled lust."

"If I ever meet her, I'll have to thank her for passing on that personality trait."

"Yes, well, no offense to you and your fellow states-men, but if given her druthers, I think she'd be happy if Alaska broke off and sank to the depths of the ocean."

"Now that's just mean."

"That's Patty-cakes. If it can be ignored, it's not a problem."

He shot Grier a sideways glance as he reached for his coffee. "Patty-cakes?"

"Her nickname. Used by those nearest and dearest." At his raised eyebrows, Grier added, "It's okay if you sort of throw up in your mouth when you hear it."

"Good to know."

"But," Grier added on a soft sigh, "she's my mother. And no matter how crazy she makes me or how much I want to shake her sometimes and tell her to throw off those manners and go get her freak on, I love her."

Mick nearly choked on the mouthful of coffee he'd just taken. "Get her freak on?"

"Well, yeah. Sure. I mean, don't you ever think about that?"

"Think about what?"

"Your parents having sex."

"Not really."

She sighed loudly and the sound echoed around his headset. "Sloan gets all freaked out when I bring this up, too. Maybe it's the side product of growing up with only one parent, but I like the idea of thinking my parents were healthy, vibrant people who enjoyed each other's company."

"And got their freak on?"

"Well, yeah. I mean, if they did, well—"

She broke off and he didn't miss the fact there was something more there.

"If they did, what?"

"Never mind. It's dumb."

He turned toward her and waited until she met his gaze. "Try me anyway."

"If they enjoyed it, it makes me feel like I wasn't quite so big a mistake."

Mary O'Shaughnessy cracked the third egg into the bowl and flipped on her fire engine red KitchenAid Artisan stand mixer. She watched her pound cake batter swirl under the large beater and thought again about what she planned to do.

She'd made it a policy not to interfere where she wasn't wanted. After more than seven decades of sticking to that policy, she wasn't all that keen on changing direction now. However, interfering and gently nudging things in the right direction were two completely different activities.

One suggested you believed your own ideas had more merit than the recipient of your meddling.

And the second said you were in possession of some information that—if another person knew you knew— might make that person act differently.

"Oh, spin it any way you want to, Mary O.," she muttered to herself as she flipped off the mixer and used her spatula to scrape the edges of the bowl. "You're thinking of interfering."

The temptation to invite Julia and Sophie over to discuss it was strong, but she knew this was something she couldn't share, not even with her two closest friends. Because if she did, that thin veneer of "not meddling" would be shot to hell in a handbasket.

They might be the sisters of her heart, but they had big mouths and a vested interest in aiding and abetting her crimes.

Which meant she didn't fully trust either of them to play this close to the vest.

Satisfied the batter was well mixed, she disengaged the arm and lifted the bowl over her greased Bundt pan. As the pretty yellow batter filled the pan, she thought about the conversation she had had late one night with Jonas Winston in this very kitchen.

She'd seldom seen the man drink—not even beer with his poker—and she'd always had a liter of Coke ready for him when he came over to play cards with the guys. So she'd been more than a little surprised when her husband had come to bed one night and told her Jonas was sleeping a drunk off on their living room couch.

While she loved her Charlie to distraction, the man wasn't known for thinking through a problem, so she'd gone downstairs to make sure Jonas had pillows, blankets and a cup of coffee if he wanted one.

And heard the light weeping as soon as she'd cleared the bottom step.

She had very nearly turned around right there, but something kept her moving forward. She'd never backed down from awkward situations and a friend in need was a friend in need.

Period.

"Jonas? Is everything all right?"

"Mary!" He'd turned from where he stood before a row of photos on their mantel and brushed quickly at his eyes. "I'm sorry to be so much trouble."

"Nonsense. I wanted to make sure you were comfortable." She held up the blanket and pillows in her arms. "And to see that you didn't freeze down here."

He slashed at his eyes once more before reaching out to take the pillows and she wondered how hard to push. And then she mentally said to hell with it and pointed to the couch. "I'm going to go make coffee. Sit there and wait for me."

Jonas was still there ten minutes later when she walked back in with two steaming mugs. He'd stopped crying, but she didn't miss the fact his eyes never met hers as he thanked her for the coffee.

"You want to talk about it?"

"Not really."

"Do you want me to go back upstairs?"

"Not really."

So she'd sat there with him awhile and wondered what could have possibly made such a kind, sweet man so incredibly upset.

"I have a daughter."

She knew immediately he wasn't talking about his little one, Kate, so she just nodded.

"She lives in New York. With her mother who doesn't want me to have anything to do with her."

"Are you okay with that?"

"I have to be."

"Why?"

"She's only ten. She doesn't need a man with another life and another family, flitting in and out and telling her he's her daddy."

"Is that what you really think or is that her mother talking?"

"Hell, Mary, I don't know." He ran his fingers through his hair, then tugged on the ends. "It's this endless loop of questions. And because I didn't go after Patrice when I should have, now I have a family, too. What'll Laurie say?"

"This is your child, Jonas. I'd hope she'd support you."

His lack of comment was all the answer she needed about just how supportive Laurie Winston would be.

He pulled a photo out of his wallet and passed it over. Mary didn't miss the pride in his eyes. "She's got my mother's eyes. And the sweetest smile."

"What's her name?"

"Grier."

The buzzer pulled her from her thoughts. Mary picked up the heavy Bundt pan and settled it in the oven. She set the timer for an hour and headed off to her office.

She'd filed Patrice's name away years go in the event she'd ever need to use it and it looked like the time had come.

She had some inquiries to make in New York.

Grier looked out her window and found it hard to believe it was only eleven o'clock in the morning. The sky had gotten progressively darker as they neared the Arctic Circle and now that they were inside it, the sky was a deep, indigo blue.

"Are you going to fly me over one of the White Alice sites?"

A wry smile ghosted his lips as he slowly turned the plane west. "How do you know about those?"

"I've done my research."

"You're not going to be able to see anything because it's already dark."

"Is it as creepy as they say?"

"Define creepy."

"Are there bodies of virgins strewn about the base and a carpet of zombies who lie in wait for whoever comes next?"

Laughter shook his shoulders. "Nah. It's an old communications system, Grier. It was set up before satellites so they could get some sort of reliable communications in the state."

"I know."

"And old antenna systems attract both zombies and virgins? Clearly I hung out in the wrong places as a teenage boy."

"When I read about them, it sounded like something cool to see. Especially from the safety of the air. Zombies can't get at you from the air."

"I'll keep that important tidbit in mind. That said, don't lose any sleep over it. A good number of them have been demolished and most of the ones that are left are considered disaster sites."

Grier had read the same and she couldn't help but

think that was the truly scary part of it all. The sites might not be infected with literal zombies, but the mess left behind wasn't easy to clean up. "I'd actually say that's scarier."

"Fair point. It's taken a lot of nasty stuff to civilize us up here."

She didn't miss the disgust in his voice. "Does that bother you?"

"I wish it could be different. Don't get me wrong—I'm not against progress. Not at all. But maybe not everything's meant to be conquered. Part of what makes it beautiful up here is that it is so barren. Wild and untouched."

"I'm sure spending your day in the air gives you an even better perspective on that. You can see it on the ground, but up here"—she couldn't resist a look out her window again, even if all she could see was black sky—"it's vast and awesome."

"And there are days when the only thing I can think is that we've spoiled it."

"I do believe you have the soul of a poet, Mr. O'Shaughnessy."

He actually blushed at that and she enjoyed the slight sputter as he looked for something to say. "I'm no poet. Just a guy who spends way too much time living in his head."

The thought struck without warning and was out of her mouth before she even thought to censor herself. "Have you ever been to Manhattan?"

"A few times to visit Roman."

"Well, that's not a real visit."

"Why not?"

"You went to visit Roman Forsyth, the hockey god. I bet you spent the entire time you were there with a gaggle of virgins, just lined up and waiting for you to deflower them."

"What the hell is it with you and virgins today? And for the record, Roman has a very nice penthouse overlooking Central Park, which has been virgin-free each and every time I've visited."

She couldn't resist poking him a bit more. "I'll ask Walker. He'll give me the real dirt."

"The brotherhood sticks together."

"What happens in New York—," she said.

"Stays in New York," he finished for her.

"Did you like it?" Subtlety had never been one of her stronger suits and now that the question was out there, she was anxious for his response.

"Is this a quiz?"

"Consider it a curiosity."

"It's nice enough. Big and crowded, but invigorating, too. The food's great. And it was fun to get lost in the people for a few days. No one knows your name, which means no one knows what you did the night before or who you did it with. You certainly don't get that in a small town."

Grier heard the tinny voice in her ear, alerting Mick through the headset that he was in the proper flight pattern and could begin his landing into Barrow.

"I'll let you focus on the landing."

"It's all right. I can talk and fly at the same time. Anything else you want to know?"

Did you like it enough to consider living there? burned the edges of her lips, but she held back.

In the same way humanity's march toward progress had spoiled parts of Alaska, Grier knew in her heart of hearts New York would do the exact same thing to Mick O'Shaughnessy.

So what was the point of even asking?

Chapter Eighteen

*I*n a move that had become pleasantly familiar, Mick helped her out of the car. He'd made arrangements with a guy he knew at the airport to borrow his SUV for the afternoon in exchange for a discount on a run of goods back down to Anchorage.

Grier thought there was a lovely sort of practicality to life in Alaska. People helped one another out. Maybe it was something that naturally happened when so few people lived under such isolated conditions or maybe they were just nicer than she was used to people being.

Would Brett Crane be nice?

She glanced up at the bright lights blazing in the windows of his small house and hoped so. He'd been nice enough over the phone the other day. A little caught off guard, but he warmed up quickly.

"What time is it? Do the clocks change this far north?"

Mick held her arm as they walked down a snowy sidewalk toward a small row of clapboard houses. "It's three minutes after the last time you asked me and no, the time's fine. Alaska's all on one time zone except for the Aleutians."

"The darkness throws me off. And I thought it was dark in Indigo."

"It's because we're inside the Arctic Circle and technically still within polar night. They'll come out of it in another week or so and be on the upswing toward the midnight sun."

"What must that be like?" Grier asked, as a stab of regret struck her square in the stomach at the knowledge she'd not be here to see it. "To see the sun at midnight?"

He squeezed her hand where their gloved fingers were intertwined. "It's pretty incredible."

She wanted to ask him to bring her back—in the summer—but they were at Brett Crane's front door. The small stocky man had a kind smile and he had his door wide-open, welcoming them in.

"You must be Grier."

She dragged off her glove to shake his hand, not surprised when he quickly embraced it in a firm grip.

"I'm Brett Crane. Come on in and get out of the cold. You picked a tough day to head up here."

Grier was confused at the comment. "There's no snow?"

"But it's about thirty below," Mick added for her benefit before extending his hand to Brett's.

Brett ushered them into his small living room and Grier was immediately captivated by the warm, cozy feel. A fire crackled in the fireplace and thick throws layered the surfaces of a couch and two overstuffed chairs. "How'd your plane do in this?"

"She's used to it." Mick shrugged out of his coat. "But no one will be sorry to see spring roll around."

"No one ever is," Brett added with a wink.

The two men exchanged a few war stories about frozen transportation equipment before the three of them settled into chairs.

"First things first." Brett rubbed his hands. "Maeve gave me a heads-up you were going to call. I didn't expect it would happen so quick, but there's no time like the present."

"You know my aunt?"

Grier had a momentary twinge at the question, seeing as how *she* didn't actually *know* her aunt, but it didn't seem like the time to try to explain that.

And then any sense of worry vanished as she took in the blush that suffused Brett from his ruddy cheeks straight down his neck and on down past the neck of his frayed sweatshirt.

Maybe her aunt wasn't so reclusive after all.

"I take it you and Maeve know each other pretty well?"

"Well enough." He coughed. "Anyway, she told me what she was going to do. It ate at her a bit, seeing as how it feels a little disloyal to Kate and all."

"Mr. Crane—"

His dark eyes crinkled and his smile was warm when he interrupted her. "Don't get all mister-mister with me, hon. It's not a judgment; it's a fact."

Grier sighed and knew he was only being honest. She had a right to her father's things, but her sister had the relationships. And to assume people would simply go against that was asking a lot.

But she didn't have to like it.

As if on cue, Mick reached for her hand, lacing their fingers in a tight squeeze.

"But because I knew, I've had a chance to pull a few things together. So first, I need to thank you. I hadn't expected to enjoy a trip down memory lane quite so much."

Brett pointed to an album on the coffee table and a small box of photos that sat alongside it. "I've known your father since the first day I started up here. His family was from Montana, but he wanted to see Alaska, he said."

The startling revelation that her father wasn't actually from Indigo was yet another tidbit to file away. Were there other family members out there somewhere?

Would Kate tell her about them if she asked? Maybe other aunts or uncles. Nieces or nephews.

Family she never knew she had. People related to her, yet as distant as strangers.

Because they *were* strangers.

Mick squeezed her fingers again and it was enough to bring her out of her thoughts. Brett held the album out to her. "Go on and take a look. I think you'll like what you see."

Grier opened the book and was immediately struck by the bright smiling faces that stared back at her. Two men bookended the photo. Brett, stocky even then, was on the left and a taller, thinner man stood on the right. Both had women under their arms and all four of them laughed with carefree abandon.

"That's my father?"

"Yep. He was about twenty-six years old in that pic-

ture. Cocky as a rooster and as sure of himself as a grizzly bear. I swear, that man was a pistol. Nothing scared
him."

"Who are these women?"

"The one with me was my late wife." His tone grew
quiet—speculative—as he tapped the plastic cover.
"You don't recognize the other woman?"

Grier leaned in and studied the grainy photo.

And nearly dropped the book off her lap when the
image registered.

"That's my mother?"

Patrice Thompson tapped the Montblanc pen on her
blotter in a hard, staccato rhythm. She was torn between the horrifying feeling that she'd just been visited
by a ghost and the exhilarating acknowledgment that
things were going to change.

She was headed back to Alaska.

The summons had been more than clear. In fact, she
had to admire the tone with which it was delivered as
it was one she'd employed on more than one occasion
herself.

Harsh. Implacable. And layered with the honeyed
sweetness of well-bred manners and a spine of steel.

The trip would be different this time. Jonas wouldn't
be at the other end of it.

But their daughter was.

A stab of regret arrowed through her as she thought
about what Grier had endured for the last few months.
It had nearly broken her to watch her daughter struggle to deal with her father's inheritance, but a cold,

slithery fear had kept her from saying or doing anything that would possibly bring Jonas—even his ghost—back into her life.

And look where it had gotten her, she thought on a rueful laugh.

He was back anyway.

She'd lost him once and the thought of going through that agony once again sliced at her heart with deadly precision. But it wasn't to be helped.

Her daughter needed her.

And it was about damn time she proved she was up to the task.

With one final, indulgent sigh, she stood up from the desk and moved to the walk-in closet in her bedroom. She did a quick scan of her clothes and acknowledged she needed to do some shopping to prepare for the trip.

And in exactly one week, she'd take all those new clothes, board a plane and head back to the one place on Earth to which she'd sworn she would never return.

Avery folded and refolded the brochure in her lap and waited for Julia Forsyth to arrive. She'd selected the most remote section of the Jitters and dropped her purse on one of the overstuffed chairs to ensure no one took the seat.

Would Julia really do it? Would she run interference for her with Susan?

Avery hoped she would, but thinking and doing were vastly different things.

She should know.

She'd *thought* about the exchange opportunity for a year. When she'd first heard about it, she'd researched it and asked some questions of other travel and tourism professionals she knew. They'd all raved about the program and promised not only a well-run experience, but the chance of a lifetime.

So she'd applied on the sly, never thinking her application would be accepted. Or that she'd be chosen.

And here she was eleven months later with the proverbial golden ticket in her hands.

Julia swept into the coffee bar and headed straight to the back. "Hello, my dear. It's good to see you."

Avery kissed her cheeks and gestured to the chair. "I got your favorite. A full-fat mocha."

"Oooh." Julia's eyes closed on an expression of ecstasy. "Don't let Dr. Cloud know I'm drinking this cup of sin."

Avery had often thought Roman's grandmother and Dr. Cloud should actually get up to a little sinning together, but she'd kept it to herself. For one thing, you just didn't say that to an older woman.

And second, well, it was Roman's grandmother for God's sake. Talking to her about getting it on with the town doctor—no matter how appealing he still was well into his seventies—just wasn't done.

Brushing off the odd notions, she took her seat and lifted her own steaming mug of coffee. "Thanks for coming to meet me."

"Is everything all right?"

Julia had been one of the few people she'd confided in over the years about her mother, and the woman had an uncanny ability to read her. "Fine. Good, actually. Really good."

"You look excited. Has Ronnie finally gotten up the gumption to ask you out?"

"Ronnie?"

"That hunky hunk at Maguire's. He's always had a thing for you. I thought this would be the winter he'd finally do something about it."

"No, no he hasn't. And that's probably a good thing."

"Why?"

"Grier and Jess asked me the same question," she muttered before she caught herself.

"What, dear?"

"Well, for starters he's like a decade younger. And I babysat him as a kid."

"He's not a kid any longer."

"No, I can see that."

Okay, time to get *off* Ronnie. Literally *and* metaphorically.

"So, what I wanted to talk to you about was something a bit different."

"What is it?"

She handed Julia the brochure before she could chicken out.

The older woman looked at it before glancing back up. "Exchange program?"

"A nationally accredited exchange program. The hospitality industry is one hundred percent behind it and all the candidates are fully vetted so that you don't get a serial killer in your hotel."

"Honey." Julia reached out and grabbed one of her hands. Avery looked down to realize she'd been flinging it wildly as she talked.

"Yes?"

"Why don't you start from the beginning?"

So Avery filled her in on her research into the hotel exchange program and the woman named Lena who'd called her the other day and introduced herself and asked if she wanted to change places for three months.

"So it's in County Clare. In a town called Ennis. That's where Lena's from and her family owns a B and B there."

Julia nodded and it was impossible to miss the snap of interest that lit up her dark brown eyes.

"And I need your help in convincing Susan that I should go do this and she should accept a stranger from Ireland to work in her hotel for three months."

"Is that all?"

A heavy breath escaped her throat, one Avery hadn't even realized she'd been holding. "All? Well, yeah."

Julia leaned forward and Avery felt the warm press of her thin hand against her cheek. "Yes, dear, is that all? Because I suggest we finish these sinful coffees and march straight over to the hotel. You and I need to make plans."

"Plans for what?"

"We're headed to Anchorage. You've got a trip to plan for and I absolutely will not let you get on a plane without brand-new luggage."

It was long minutes later—long after Julia had pulled her in for a tight hug and long after Avery had brushed away the silly tears she hadn't been able to hold back—that she finally relaxed enough to smile.

And once she started, she couldn't stop.

Grier flipped through the photo album once more, her gaze drawn yet again to the picture of the happy, smiling couples on the first page.

Was that really her mother?

Once it had been pointed out to her, it was evident that it was Patrice Thompson, but she struggled with reconciling the laughing, carefree woman in the photo with the reserved person who'd raised her.

Brett laid a tray on the table, laden with cups of tomato soup and a stack of grilled cheese sandwiches.

"Oh, you didn't need to go to all this trouble."

"It's not trouble. And I'm glad you're here. You've given me a reason to go through those old photos and I've enjoyed the reminiscing."

Mick laid a stack of photos next to the album and reached for his coffee mug to get it out of the way. "Did you and Jonas keep in touch?"

"We lost touch after he moved to Indigo. My Wendy and I got married and traveled a lot." Brett patted one of the afghans that lay under his elbow and Grier didn't miss the wistful expression that flitted across his face before he continued. "The pipeline was hard work, but it was good work. Good-paying work. We never had kids, so we traveled and enjoyed ourselves."

"When did Wendy pass away?"

"A few years back. She wanted me to move away

from here, but it's my home. And it was our home. And hell, I make a mean casserole. As long as a man can cook himself a casserole, he can eat, you know?"

Grier laughed and found herself once again enamored of the hearty spirit of the Alaskan locals. They grieved and missed their loved ones, but they had a pragmatism about life that was refreshing and engaging.

"So anyway. You didn't come here to get my recipe for tuna casserole. Jonas and I lost track of each other and then I got on Facebook a few years back."

"An endless resource for friendships, old relationships and friendly stalking," Mick said with a broad smile.

Brett slapped his knee. "You're right about that. I found Jonas and shortly thereafter hooked up with Maeve."

"Are you, um"—Grier reached for a square of grilled cheese and deliberately kept her tone casual—"with my aunt?"

"We're special friends."

Her gaze collided with Mick as the words "special friends" lit the air above both their heads, but they both kept their thoughts to themselves.

"I'd like more, but she's been resistant. If you could put in a good word for me, though, I'd sure appreciate it."

Grier looked into Brett's hopeful face and couldn't resist leaning over and planting a quick kiss on his cheek. "I'd be happy to."

"So. Let's get back to your mom and dad. Your mother was up here making a documentary."

"My mother?" The sensation she'd walked into a different dimension seized her and the slightly panicky feeling that maybe zombies really did lurk around every corner sent a shiver through her. "My mother was a filmmaker?"

"She wasn't the director, but she was part of it." Brett snapped his fingers. "She was the producer."

"On a documentary?"

"About the pipeline." Brett nodded as he reached for a sandwich. "She sure was. Your mother was quite the looker and Jonas took a shine to her immediately and she fell just as hard. The film crew was up here for about four months and the two of them were inseparable. When they weren't working, they were—" Brett broke off, another one of those sweet blushes suffusing his skin.

"Freaking?" Mick added helpfully as he reached for a helping of grilled cheese.

Grier swatted at his knee as Brett gave them a slightly puzzled frown, but he picked up on the subtext quick enough, the frown morphing into a smile. "That's about right."

"I'm not asking you to give anything away that makes you uncomfortable, but I just don't understand how they went from being this happy, lovey-dovey couple to living an entire continent apart. Did something happen?"

Brett reached for a sandwich. His gaze was sharp

with memories and his shoulders tensed in a straight line. She could see he struggled with what to say.

"None of us ever really understood what happened. I don't say this to speak ill of your mother, Grier, but my Wendy wasn't all that fond of her. Kept telling me there was something off that she couldn't quite put her finger on."

Grier knew that sense. It was the same one she'd lived with her entire life. Her mother had an odd, unsettling way about her that kept people at a distance. Even when you thought she was with you and in the moment, there was a gap.

A chasm that simply couldn't be crossed.

"It's all right, Brett. My mother has her eccentricities."

He nodded, then continued. "Even when things were going perfectly with Jonas and Patty, Wendy kept at me that something wasn't right. Said every time she tried to pull your mom into conversation, she held back."

"A person's entitled to his own thoughts," Mick said, pushing his point. "Is it possible Grier's mom is shy? The small-town nosiness isn't for everyone."

"That's more than fair and I said that to Wendy plenty, but she kept at it. And I was a skeptic until the last story she told me. Right before your mom left Alaska."

"What was it?"

"She and the woman she was making the documentary with invited Wendy to see a preview. She was bored off her ass up here and leaped at the chance to do something while us guys were off on the site."

Grier didn't even realize she was holding her breath

until Mick reached for her hand and gave her fingers a tight squeeze.

"Patty was laughing with the film's director, and they were drinking some champagne they'd managed to dig up on a trip to Fairbanks and that they'd saved for the occasion. The director was pretty far into the bottle when Wendy arrived, and Patty just kept waving this full glass that never went down. Wendy said it was funny at first, their laughing and celebrating that the movie had come out and all."

Brett stopped and once again, Grier could see how discomfort stamped itself across his kind face. "It really is all right. You can't hurt my feelings."

He wiped his brow and nodded. "I never have liked speaking ill of others. Gossip's an unfair business as it doesn't give a person a chance to defend himself."

"I'll tell you the truth. My mother hasn't been all that supportive of my trips up here and she hasn't gone out of her way to help me with learning about my father. Because of that, as far as I'm concerned, she's abdicated her right to have a say in it."

"That's fair." Brett laid down his sandwich and wiped his hands on a napkin. "So Wendy said she had a few minutes with your mom and before she knew it, Patty was crying. Big huge tears, the sort you get when you can't even catch your breath. And she tells my Wendy she's pregnant and that she doesn't know what to do. That she can't live up here and what would people think. This was supposed to be a fling—a fun thing after college—and here she was pregnant with a pipeline worker's baby."

Even if Brett felt it was gossip, Grier knew otherwise. She'd just learned the truth her mother had refused to share.

Not only had she been unwanted from the first, but Patrice Thompson had thought Jonas Winston beneath her.

Chapter Nineteen

Mick had glanced intermittently at Grier since they'd left Barrow, but the sight never changed. She hadn't looked away from the window once since they'd taken off.

"We don't have to stay in Fairbanks tonight. I can pick up our stuff and take you back to Indigo."

"There's no need to cut the trip short."

"Grier—" He broke off, at a loss for words. She'd kept up a bright smile for Brett and a steady stream of questions for the duration of their stay, but he knew better.

She was devastated.

And he had no idea how to help her.

"If you're sure?"

"I'm sure. It's been a long day and there's no reason to head home tonight."

"Do you want to call Sloan or Avery? I can patch them in from here if you want to talk."

"No, thanks."

"Do you want to talk to me?"

That finally got her turning from the window. "What is there to say? I went on a fact-finding mission and I got the facts. Brett corroborated what was in the letter."

"He also told you how much your father loved you."

"They were just words, Mick. Nothing he did in life supported that."

And that was something he couldn't argue with, no matter how he looked at her situation. He believed Jonas cared for her, but the man hadn't backed up those feelings when it counted.

The tower in Fairbanks alerted him he was cleared to land and he began their descent, leaving her once again to her thoughts.

His relationship with his own father wasn't the model example of a strong family bond, but at least he knew him. He had been given the opportunity to look the man in the eye and know he was his son. It was something he'd taken for granted, but faced with Grier's circumstances, he saw the basic comfort that knowledge imparted.

To know where you came from and that you mattered *meant* something.

Mick landed and taxied them to the hangar, working his way through the postflight paperwork as quickly as he could.

"You hungry?" Mick signed off on the last of the paperwork and reached for the small flight bag he carried with him. "We can go back to the Rooster."

"No, not really."

"Room service?"

"Sure."

The drive back to the hotel was quick and Mick settled his hand on her lower back as they walked into the lobby. They were nearly to the elevators when a familiar voice called to him from across the small space.

"Mick!"

He turned to see Petey Stone, the grocer from Talkeetna he'd seen recently. "What are you doing here?"

"My wife wanted to come up and get some shopping done and we also wanted to visit with our daughter who's at the university."

Mick made quick introductions and Grier smiled broadly, taking an interest in the man's daughter. He inwardly shook his head at the transformation as her words from the day before came back to him.

She could *be* with him.

The evidence of that—and the knowledge that she didn't put on airs or act for him—was strangely heady.

Mick keyed back into Petey's comments as the man turned his focus on him. "So it's funny I'm seeing you. I was going to call you after I got home. I meant it last week about that gun for your father. Do you think he'd like it?"

The memories of that conversation hit him square in the chest and whatever joy had filled him at the thought of Grier's trust of him evaporated under the reminder of his father's great love and passion.

"I don't think he's going to want it."

"Oh, so you talked to him?"

"Nah, but I know he's full up right now. I don't think he needs another rifle."

Confusion briefly flitted across Petey's face before

an embarrassed flush crept up his neck. "Sure, sure. Sorry to pester you about it."

"Nah, not at all, Petey. Look. We've had a long day running up to Barrow. We're going to call it a night."

"Sure thing. I'll see you in a few weeks for the February delivery."

"You bet."

Mick returned his hand to the small of Grier's back and continued their walk to the elevators. He didn't miss the sharp interest that lit up her gaze, but she said nothing until they were in the elevator.

"He seems like a nice guy."

"Sure is. He's a client of mine and Jack's."

"A good one, from the sounds of it."

"The best."

A sense of relief flooded him as they stepped off the elevator and Grier didn't say anything further. She followed him down the hall to their rooms and waited while he unlocked the door.

He allowed Grier to pass in front of him, watching as she walked and dropped the bag she'd filled with memorabilia from Brett onto the bed.

As the door clicked closed behind him, she turned tired eyes on him. "It seems I'm not the only one keeping my thoughts to myself. You want to tell me what that was all about?"

He saw the confusion stamped across her face, from the questions in her gray gaze to the firm set of her lips. Whatever he thought he'd managed to avoid in the lobby had been all in his head.

Grier had missed nothing.

And he simply couldn't bear to let the ugliness of his past touch what was between them.

Mick shrugged as a fifteen-year-old memory rose up to swamp him. "Not particularly."

The heavy tones of the doorbell echoed through Julia's kitchen. Avery glanced up from where she and Julia had their heads bent over a sleek laptop, trying to identify the best flights to Ireland and back.

"I'll get it."

The smile she couldn't stop spread across her face as she thought about the flights she'd take and the clothes she'd pack and the adventure she was going to have.

And it fell sharply as she opened the door and stared at Roman, standing on the porch.

"Can I come in?"

"Sure." She shook her head, suddenly realizing how cold it was standing there with the door open.

"Avery!" Julia's voice echoed from the kitchen in the back of the house. "Who is it?"

Roman bellowed into the house again. "It's me, Grandma!"

He closed the door behind him and she risked a glance at him as his attention stayed focused on Julia as she came down the hallway. God, but it was so unfair a person should look that good. Even after traveling what was probably the last twelve hours, he looked as if he had walked off a photo shoot.

His six-foot-four frame ate up all the space in the foyer and he looked like a giant as he enveloped his grandmother in his arms.

Julia's voice was a study in delighted surprise. "I thought you weren't getting in until tomorrow."

"I wanted to keep it a secret. I made the gals out at the airstrip swear to keep it to themselves."

"Not an easy feat," Avery interjected. She heard the dry, dusty notes of her voice and willed herself to calm down. Her evening with Julia had been fun and she'd be the worst sort of guest if she treated Roman like a piece of old gum she'd just peeled off her shoe.

Add to it Sloan had given her a dressing-down for her behavior the last time Roman was in town and she knew she needed to pull it together.

She had a new life and a new adventure coming up and she needed to let go of this stupid, petty attitude toward Roman. If she ever wanted more out of her life, she needed to start by letting go of the things that no longer mattered.

"What are you two up to?" Roman pulled out of the hug and positioned himself to look at them both.

"Avery got some wonderful news yesterday and we're celebrating." Julia beamed. "Come on into the kitchen and we'll tell you all about it."

Avery followed that large imposing frame down the hallway and did her level best not to look at his ass. She lost the battle about three steps into it, but at least she tried.

It was all part of her brand-new "put the past behind her" attitude adjustment.

"Come on, Ave. What's going on?"

Her heart constricted at the nickname, but she planted a broad smile and refused to lose ground to her memories. "I'm going to Ireland."

"What?" Those vibrant green orbs widened and his mouth slackened. "I mean, how did this come about?"

"She's doing an exchange." Julia beamed proudly as she puttered across the kitchen to grab a crystal tumbler out of a cabinet.

"Three months working in a B and B over there and then I'm going to travel for another month."

"That's incredible."

"Isn't it?" Julia set the glass in front of Roman. "I'm so proud of her. And to think we're going to get an Irish woman here in Indigo for three months. It'll be so much fun."

"Sophie must be rubbing her hands at the tourism opportunities," Roman said with a false lightness Avery didn't miss.

"I need to go get the scotch out of the front room."

"I'll get it, Grandma."

Julia waved a hand. "Nonsense. Let Avery tell you more."

Avery smiled at Julia as she left the room and began counting in her head.

Three . . .

Two . . .

"What the hell are you thinking, Avery?" Roman's harsh whisper echoed around the kitchen but was low enough not to carry down the hall.

"I was thinking about expanding my horizons."

"To go to another country and work as a slave for someone you don't even know?"

"And how is that different from what I do for your mother?"

"You're not a slave."

"No, Roman, I'm not. I'm an employee. And I'm taking advantage of a career opportunity by spending three months in Ireland."

He frowned at how she'd twisted his words, but it didn't keep him silent for long. "What does my mother think of it? You're leaving her at her busiest season."

"She's been quite encouraging."

Anger practically pulsed off him like blinking neon and Avery fought hard to hold back her smile. She hadn't looked into this opportunity to spite Roman—in fact, she'd done it in spite of him.

But his reaction was a pleasant surprise.

"What has you so worked up?"

"You're going to be a stranger in another country."

"I'm not going into a war zone. It's a bed-and-breakfast in Ireland. You know, big fluffy quilts on beds and tea towels and scones and clotted cream."

"It's too far."

"It's not the fucking moon, Roman. It's Europe."

"It doesn't matter. You can't do this."

Whatever humor had filled her fled on swift wings. "You don't have a say in it."

"I'm only thinking of you."

"Now that's a funny thing. You haven't thought of me in a very long time. And you have no right to think of me now."

"That's not true. I think of you often."

The words pricked holes in her carefully constructed armor and she fought the rising pleasure at his words. *Focus, Marks. Focus.*

Summoning up the biggest smile she could, she thought of her future. "Well, now you can think of me in Ireland. I'll be sure to e-mail you plenty of pictures."

Grier fought to hold on to her composure as she stared at Mick where he still stood in the small foyer of his hotel room.

"So you won't talk about it?"

"There's nothing to talk about."

"Right. Because the subtext of that conversation downstairs was about as subtle as a moose walking in that door over there. What are you hiding?"

His shoulders jerked as if she'd slapped him and she wondered all the more at the reaction. "I'm not hiding anything."

"Mick. What is it?"

"Nothing." He slammed across the room and dragged off his coat, throwing it over the room's lone chair. He pulled his cell from his back pocket and started fiddling with the screen.

"If you're trying to convince me nothing's wrong, you're doing a piss-poor job of it, Mr. Honesty Is the Best Policy."

"So now you're going to play the hypocrite, Grier?"

She shrank back from the anger in his gaze. "I'm the hypocrite? You've been the one telling me for the last two weeks I need to address things head-on."

"You just spent the last three hours sulking in my plane, refusing to talk to me. I'd hardly call that head-on."

The urge to move closer and touch him gripped her, but she stood still and held her ground. "So this is some sort of quid pro quo? I had a few bad moments trying to digest what happened at Brett's and you're going to shut me out?"

"Damn it! I'm not going to sit here and talk about my feelings like this is some session with a shrink. Save that for your New York friends."

Another layer of shock came flooding in over the initial surprise of his reaction to her probing. Something was very, very wrong. The man standing across the room from her was as feral as a cornered bear.

Where was the Mick she knew? And what had possibly happened to him to make him act like this?

"Please don't make me ask you again. What is going on? It all happened when Petey mentioned that gun for your father."

"My father doesn't need a fucking gun."

"Okay."

When Mick didn't say anything else, she tried a different angle. "What did he say that was so upsetting? It was clear he was only trying to be nice."

His mouth twisted before settling into a harsh line. "You don't give guns to someone who doesn't know how to use them."

"I got the sense from the conversation that your father was a collector of some sort."

"My father's a hunter and he had an accident."

No matter how many ways she tried to work through his words, Grier couldn't see what had him so upset. "Mick. Please. Enough with the riddles." She moved slowly toward him until she stood before him and laid her hands on his chest. "Please tell me what's wrong."

"Fifteen years ago my father shot and killed my mother."

The words echoed around the room like a gunshot. Mick mentally berated himself for the shitty comparison, but nothing else quite fit.

"Oh God, Mick, I'm sorry. So, so sorry."

He planted his gaze on the top of her head and avoided meeting hers as she stared up at him. "It was a long time ago and it rarely comes up. And it was an accident. He was going after something that had wandered into their backyard. I don't even remember what it was, he's mumbled so many different animals in his grief. He was a six-pack into the evening and she'd followed him outside to holler at him to put on a coat. The bullet ricocheted off an old snowmobile he kept back there."

"Why didn't you tell me?"

"It's better left in the past."

"It's a part of your life."

"A part of my life that I've gotten past."

Which was a nice story to tell, but it was a sizable load of bullshit. The vision of his mother, lying in the snow, blood streaming from her temple, was one he'd learned to compartmentalize in the back of his mind, but it had come back with a vengeance since that night with the researchers.

And had continued coming back ever since.

Grier lifted her hands to cup his jaw. "It's a horrible thing to have to live with."

"It's an even more horrible thing to have happen to you. I wasn't the one who was shot, Grier." He slipped from the comfort of her arms, surprised by just how cold he felt moving away from her.

"Is this the real reason you were in the sauna that night after you pulled the men off the mountain?"

He thought about that first night they were together. The researchers he'd pulled off Denali had left him in a bad state and Avery had sent him into the sauna to warm up with a bottle of Jack.

"So Avery sent you in there?"

Grier hadn't moved from her spot and instead stood there, rubbing her hands up and down her arms. "She told me where you were. I went of my own accord. Important distinction."

"So it is."

"Do you have nightmares about it?"

"Occasionally."

"Have you talked to a professional about it?"

The urge to lash out at her once more was strong, but he held it back. "I've spoken to Father Tom about it several times as well as Doc Cloud. I'm fine, Grier."

"And the incident on Denali hasn't brought it all up again?"

"You're like a dog with a bone."

"And you don't appreciate the concern?"

The snow outside had left a heavy wet splotch on the top of his boot and he traced it with his eyes as he stared down at his feet. "I'm lashing out and it's the last thing I want to do to you. But this is something I simply don't talk about."

"I thought things had changed over the last few days."

He glanced up from his shoe. "What's that supposed to mean?"

"It means you've had no problem digging around in my past, but the moment I ask the same of you, I get silence."

"I didn't realize it was a competition."

Grier let out a small frustrated moan as she dropped into a sitting position on the bed. "That's a fucking cop-out."

"It's the only answer I've got."

Grier lay in bed and heard the sink run as Mick finished up in the bathroom. The urge to cry threatened in the back of her throat, but she refused to let the tears fall.

How had she never known any of this about his parents?

A big part of her wanted to be mad at Avery or even at Walker since they had to know about Mick's mother, but she quickly squelched it. Friends didn't randomly stir up issues and it was unfair to ask them to be the ones to deliver this news.

Mick needed to tell her himself.

And he hadn't felt the need to do so.

Just like you avoided telling him you'd been engaged, that extraordinarily reasonable voice in her head whispered. It was the same voice that told her to eat broccoli and carrots instead of cake and as far as she was concerned, the prissy bitch could just suck it.

Even if she happened to be a one hundred percent *right* prissy bitch.

She heard the bathroom door open and moments later Mick's heavy tread as he walked toward the bed. "Are you asleep?"

"No."

"Why not?"

"Because I'm arguing with my sensible inner voice." Grier moved to the far side of the bed to give him room to crawl in next to her.

"Do you want me to join you?"

"First you get two rooms after we sleep together. Now you want to sleep somewhere else. Are you trying to piss me off, O'Shaughnessy?"

He climbed in without saying anything else and pulled her against his side once he was settled in. "That's better," he grumbled against her temple before pressing a kiss there.

A flutter of warmth floated through the middle of her chest and she took her first calm breath since their fight started.

"So you're having an argument?"

"Yes. With that über-reasonable voice that tells me when I'm being unreasonable or making poor food choices. I call her the prissy bitch."

"Oh."

She rose up on an elbow to look into his eyes. "Before you go convincing yourself I'm hearing things and/or crazy, I can guarantee you every woman has a prissy bitch in her head. Most just aren't as vocal as I am about mentioning it."

"I'll keep that in mind."

"See that you do."

She lay back down against his side and ran a hand over his stomach. He still wore a T-shirt and she enjoyed the feel of the soft cotton, warmed by his body heat, under her fingertips.

The stress of the last few days faded in the comfort of Mick's body and Grier felt herself begin to relax. She knew she and Mick still had a lot to work out, but she'd muster the energy to discuss it tomorrow.

As the lure of sleep overtook her, Grier gave in and let it come.

Chapter Twenty

"What did you find out in Barrow?" Sloan demanded the following night as they settled themselves into Avery's suite.

Grier looked at her two friends and marveled again at the easy camaraderie among the three of them. Her trip with Mick had been exhilarating on one hand and confusing as hell on another and she was deeply grateful for the company of friends as she tried to puzzle through it.

She'd gone to the North Slope hoping for answers and she'd gotten them.

They just hadn't filled her with the warm, fuzzy feelings she'd hoped for. Add to it the horrifyingly sad story from Mick's past and the last two days had been an emotional roller coaster.

"First I want to know what's going on with Avery and Roman. It was all anyone could talk about out at the airstrip."

Avery groaned as she finished pouring mugs of hot chocolate all around. "Don't think asking me about this morning's train wreck is going to get you out of telling us about your trip with Mick."

"You expect me to kiss and tell?" Grier asked as she reached for a mug.

"Yes." The uniform—and immediate—reply came from the two of them.

"I want to know what happened here. Mick and I are old news. Roman being a jerk is new news."

"Well, when you put it that way."

"Actually, it's sort of refreshing. I figured Mick and I'd get a grilling upon our return and instead Maggie started in about Roman the moment Mick and I got within three feet of her."

"What did she say?"

"That he acted like a major ass at the hotel this morning."

"That's an understatement," Avery mumbled as she blew on her hot chocolate. "But where he made his tactical error was being an asshole in front of Chooch."

"What was Chooch doing at the hotel this morning?" Sloan frowned. "Clearly, living at Walker's, just across the square, I might add, is hell on my gossip meter. This is the first I'm hearing of it."

"Roman's in town with the network people so they can film a piece on him. Which is why Chooch was at the hotel this morning, parked in the lobby dressed to the nines and hoping she'll get some airtime."

"Was Myrtle with her?" Sloan asked suspiciously.

Avery rolled her eyes. "She arrived about a half hour later, pissed Chooch showed her up."

"That explains her mood today. Walker came home at lunch, so mad he was spitting nails. He swore he was going to fire her."

Avery set her mug down on her small coffee table and reached for one of the cookies she'd set out. "Just so you know, he's been saying that he was going to fire Myrtle since the day he hired her. You'll learn to ignore that one."

"Come on, come on." Grier pushed Avery. "I want the rest of the story. Why was Roman an asshole?"

"He's mad I'm going to Ireland."

"You're what!" Sloan screamed, and Grier couldn't hold back the smile.

"I'm going on an exchange." Grier waited while Avery caught Sloan up on the program she'd applied for and made a mental note to pick up something green for her.

Even if it was petty, Grier couldn't say she was all that sorry Roman was suffering at Avery's expense. "So, let me see if I've put the pieces together. Roman's decided that's just too far away for you to go on a trip, out in the big bad world all on your own."

"Bingo."

"And he's decided that it's up to him to tell you about this and warn you off going," Sloan added.

"Right again."

"I hope you told him to fuck off." Grier knew it wasn't a very kind sentiment, but Roman had walked away from Avery and their relationship. The idea that he felt he had a say as she made such a positive step forward just wasn't fair.

"In not so many words. And I have to tell you, I'm having way more fun than I ever expected telling him it's none of his business."

Grier smiled and raised her mug. "You should. He has no say in your choices."

Sloan leaned forward, her blue eyes bright with excitement. "But the fact he seems to think he does have a say is rather interesting, don't you think?"

"He wouldn't even know about it if he weren't here for the TV piece."

"But he is here and he does know about it," Sloan persisted. "And his reaction *is* interesting."

"Interesting, maybe, but totally misplaced. He and I have had no relationship since he left for New York other than the occasional sighting at the hotel."

"He does send you the wine." Grier felt the need to point that out. "That glorious Rothschild that you've neglected to share in the new year, even though I know for a fact you received a brand-new shipment before the holidays."

"Smooth," Sloan whispered.

"I'm not trying to be smooth; I'm trying to be obvious." Grier continued to press her point. "It's especially interesting as I've yet to even see Susan pick up a drink. Despite his teetotaler mother, that glorious, phenomenal vintage shows up like clockwork, addressed to the woman running the Indigo's bar."

Avery shrugged, but Grier didn't miss the slight tilt of her head as she considered the curiosity of the wine.

"Not that I want to stir up old wounds, but I have to agree with Sloan on this one. His behavior doesn't match the situation."

"Well, it still doesn't change anything." Avery

reached for another cookie, a broad smile riding her mouth. "And I'm still going to Ireland."

Grier held her mug up and waited for the others to do the same. "Hear, hear. To new adventures."

Mick made the motion for another round to their waitress before turning back to his friends. He and Grier had gotten back before lunch and he'd spent the afternoon catching up on the dreaded paperwork that never seemed to end.

When Walker had called inviting him out for a few beers, he'd jumped at the opportunity like a drowning man reaching for a life preserver.

"Maguire's is hopping." Roman looked around. "When did this place get so popular?"

"When everyone found out your camera crew might show up to get a few shots of the locals," Walker added dryly.

Mick took a drag on his longneck. "To be fair, they do a decent business on the weekends, but random Wednesdays don't usually see this much action."

"How'd the trip to the North Slope go?" Walker dug into the beer nuts on the table.

"I think Grier got answers, just not the ones she was hoping for."

"It's a bad situation all the way around," Walker muttered.

"Well, it'll be over soon now that Grier's got the letters."

"A few more days. I've already filed the motions and

we should have this resolved by the end of the week," Walker said.

"She found out about my mom."

Mick didn't miss the glance that crossed between Roman and Walker before Walker asked, "How?"

"We ran into one of my customers in Fairbanks. He mentioned a gun for sale for my dad and she saw the temperature drop about thirty degrees between us before it all got as awkward as hell."

"She figured it out on just that?" Roman asked before taking a large swig on his beer. "A bit of body language?"

"Yep."

The same melancholy that had ridden him on the flight home settled once again in his bones. While he didn't want to talk about his mother—had no interest in ever talking again about what had happened to her—Grier hadn't been completely off base. He had been riding her pretty hard to open up and take a chance.

And then he went and fucked it up by clamming up and refusing to talk.

Their waitress interrupted his thoughts as she laid another round on the table. As he glanced up at her to offer her a smile, his gaze caught on the front door and Jason Shriver as he walked through it.

Poetic, Mick thought. Another subject he and Grier refused to discuss at any level of depth.

Roman caught his gaze. "Who's that?"

"Grier's ex-fiancé."

"Ex?" Roman's eyebrows shot up. "What the hell have I missed?"

"More than you know."

Something itched at Mick as he watched the guy take a lone seat at the bar and give his order. He also didn't miss the glance Jason had given Kate as his eyes found her at a table across the bar when he walked in.

Curious.

Ronnie laid a glass in front of him and Mick saw the unmistakable shape of a bottle of Patrón as it was lifted off the back shelf. "Excuse me."

He crossed the crowded expanse of tables and a series of not-so-subtle scattered glances followed his progress as he approached the bar. "Make it two, Ronnie."

"Sure thing, Mick."

"And put them on my tab as well as whatever else Mr. Shriver wants."

Jason's gaze was inscrutable, but he shifted in welcome and pointed to the empty seat next to him. "Feel free to join me."

"I believe I will."

Ronnie laid out the shots and Mick avoided all the fuss of the salt and lime, preferring the smooth perfection of the liquor as it slid down his throat. Warmth filled his chest as he drank it down and he was reminded of an old saying his grandfather used to use with gusto: *"Candy is dandy, but liquor is quicker."*

"How was your trip?"

"Eventful." Mick reached for the fresh beer he'd carried over to the bar.

"I understand Grier went up there to find out more about her father. Did she get it?"

"In a manner of speaking." He saw the question in Jason's raised eyebrows and clarified. "She learned more about both of her parents on this trip."

"Her mother's a piece of work," Jason snorted as he reached for the glass of bourbon Ronnie had poured him. "Between Patrice Thompson and my father, I'm not sure who grew up with more dysfunction, but I'd likely give her the edge."

"I'd say Grier turned out well in spite of all that."

"I couldn't agree more." Jason stared into his glass. "They're the reason I'm up here. My father and her mother. Both suggested it would be a good idea to correct my past mistakes and grovel."

"Did either of them consider Grier's wishes? Or yours for that matter?"

"Nope."

"Have you?"

"Funny thing is"—Jason took a sip—"I've finally started to. Grier did me a favor walking away."

"Maybe you both did each other a favor."

"I suspect you're right." Jason turned toward him and for the first time Mick saw something underneath the smooth, polished veneer. "Grier's a good woman. The best. She didn't deserve what I did to her, but she does deserve a future. A good one. I won't stand in your way."

"I appreciate that."

"I'm leaving."

Mick turned toward the tables behind them, his gaze

alighting on Kate where she sat with Trina and a few other local women. "Maybe you can make good use of the time you've got left."

Jason's gaze followed his and Mick saw the man's fingers tighten on his glass. "Maybe so."

Mick slapped him on the back. "Enjoy the rest of your stay."

Chapter Twenty-one

Grier refolded her aunt's note and tucked it in her pocket. Maeve's words in the letter had held a deliberate order and Grier knew she couldn't resist following it any longer.

One final suggestion. Go visit your father's grave. I know you haven't been out there and while I don't think he deserves much from you, he does deserve that.

She knew she needed to go visit the small cemetery on the edge of town but had found excuse after excuse to avoid making the trip. A big part of her wanted to visit the grave by herself, yet every time she prepared to go, something held her back.

The knowledge that she really didn't want to go all by herself.

Sloan or Avery would go along if she'd just ask, but it didn't seem right, somehow.

And she and Mick hadn't spoken since they'd returned home the morning before.

Maybe that was for the best, she acknowledged as she layered up for the walk across town. Things had gotten awfully intense their last night in Fairbanks and she couldn't quite shake the underlying hurt that he hadn't told her about his mother.

The morning was crisp and clear, and hardened snow crunched under her boots as she walked across the town square. She allowed her gaze to range across the buildings that made up the businesses on Main Street.

The Jitters and the diner and Tasty's store. A small knitting store that had become quite the center of the town grapevine from what she'd been told. The grocery store that stood on the opposite side of the street from the diner. Grier smiled at someone's sense of humor as she read the specials posted in the large windows.

Advanced Blizzard Planning—
Ground Chuck for $1.59 a pound.

Get 'Em Before Spring—
Canned Corn and Peas $0.49 each.

And her favorite:

The Snowpocalypse Special—
Ice Cream Pints $3.19 each.

She passed the stores and the large monument that stood at the far end of town drew her gaze next. Conceived years before by the grandmothers, the monument was erected as a dedication to love and loss. Julia's husband had died when she was a young woman and the monument had been one of the ways Julia, Mary and Sophie had coped with the grief.

As Grier walked toward the large piece, the arches of the granite captivated her. She stopped for a moment and allowed her thoughts to roam as she filled her gaze with the graceful curves and hard lines that abstractly suggested a man and woman embracing.

An enduring testament to the power and strength of love.

Her thoughts drifted to Mick, the only place they ever seemed able to land these days. She loved him. The acknowledgment was so simple, really, as she finally admitted it in her heart.

She loved him.

The feeling should have lifted her up; instead, all it left her with was questions.

Did she even have the ability to make something work for a lifetime? Her mother hadn't set the best example and no matter what the reports from others regarding his feelings for her, her father's misguided approach hadn't set the best example, either.

And even if she could get past all that and allow herself to let go and really love Mick, could she make a life here? She knew with absolute clarity he'd never be happy in New York. And for all its charm, Indigo was a far cry from the life she'd grown up with.

Could they make a real go of it? A successful go? For as much as it pained her to think of leaving him in Indigo, it hurt even more to think of how desolate she'd be if they did try to have a relationship and it didn't work out.

And her own track record of success in that area didn't exactly sit in her favor.

She stared up at the monument once more. The piece stood for real, enduring love that would withstand the test of time, a love that formed a bedrock between two lives.

She believed that she and Mick had the foundation. But was it enough?

So many questions without answers. Rationally, she knew there were no guarantees and you simply did the best with what you had. But what if the cards were stacked against you from the first?

On a sigh, she stamped her feet to warm them and moved on. She could ask herself questions all day and it didn't mean she was any closer to the answers she sought.

The cemetery lay about a hundred yards from the monument and she could see the wrought-iron gates that surrounded the edge of the grounds. She walked toward them, surprised by the sheer trepidation that filled her with each step closer to her father.

It wasn't until she passed through the gates that she saw the lone figure, his large frame standing vigil over a grave, his head bowed.

Mick.

Mick heard the crunch of snow and turned away from his mother's headstone. A hard fist lodged in his throat as he registered Grier's small form, wrapped head to toe in wool.

He thought to say something to her—knew he

should—but all he could do was reach for her and pull her up into his arms, burying his face in the curve of her neck and breathing in.

Deeply.

Grier.

And in that moment, he knew what he needed to do. Stepping back, he kept her hand firmly in his. "I'd like you to meet my mother."

Her gray eyes glistened with tears and she nodded. "I'd like that."

The moments passed quietly and he filled in some of the gaps he'd been unwilling to discuss in Fairbanks. He was still living in his parents' house at the time, saving up enough money for the business he and Jack were working on. He was supposed to be out on a run, but it had been canceled at the last minute due to a change in the customer's order.

He recounted the sheer terror of that moment when his father had called for him and he had known something was wrong. And the even more terrifying moment when he rushed downstairs and outside, only to see his mother lying, motionless.

Her hand tightened on his. "I'm so sorry, Mick."

"So am I."

She squeezed once more. "Tell me something about her. Something wonderful."

The question caught him off guard for a moment as he fought to push aside those last images. To dig deeper to find something else.

"She loved cookie dough. With a passion."

"Smart woman."

He laughed at that. "She'd make a batch of cookies and we'd be lucky to get half of them baked. She'd give herself a stomachache, she loved the batter so much, but she'd keep on eating it anyway. Would keep on, all the while saying how bad it was for her."

Grier's laughter joined his, bright music that tinkled in the wind swirling around them. He couldn't help but feel lighter at the memory.

"Did she have a favorite kind?"

"Not really, so long as it was raw. Chocolate chip, peanut butter, sugar—she loved them all."

"I can see the photo of her, with her smiling face. The one in your grandmother's house. And now I can picture that warm smile as she laughed in the middle of her kitchen. It's a lovely image."

Yes, it was, Mick thought. "Thank you."

"For what?"

"For making me remember something other than the end. I haven't meant to, but somehow I've let that horrible image of her, lying in the snow, crowd out all the wonderful images that came before."

He'd robbed himself of something by not focusing on the good and it was time to start getting it back. As the memory of cookies faded, others came up to swamp him. Christmas mornings and birthdays and random Tuesdays when she helped him puzzle through his algebra or quizzed him and his sister on spelling words.

Those and so many other images that made up their life and formed his childhood.

With one last squeeze of their hands, he knew it was time to help her. Mick pointed toward a row of markers about three lanes past his mother's. "Jonas's grave is over there. Would you like me to go with you?"

Something like relief swam in her eyes and he could see the transformation come over her face. The small lines that bracketed her eyes faded and a slight furrow above her eyebrow relaxed. "Yes."

"Let's go."

He held her hand until they got to Jonas's row, then shifted to walk behind her, his hand on her shoulder as he helped her navigate through the snow.

And he felt those slim shoulders shudder as they neared the granite marker.

Kate stood outside Jason's hotel room door, shifting from foot to foot. It was early enough that she'd avoided any real notice in the lobby. Chris was on duty and his sleepy hello hadn't suggested he was about to burn up the phone lines with gossip.

And it wasn't as if she needed to explain herself.

She was a grown woman and she could come and go as she pleased. Could do as she pleased. Could risk making an absolute fool of herself if she pleased.

It was that last part, really, that had her hesitating.

What if he wasn't interested?

What if he brushed her off?

What if . . .

On a quick rush of courage, Kate made a fist and rapped on the door of his room.

There was no going back now.

She heard sounds on the other side and then nearly melted at the sight when Jason opened the door. His normally straight hair stuck up in odd angles at the back of his head. The look would have been little-boy cute if it hadn't been counterbalanced by his very naked—and broad—shoulders and chest that tapered to a narrow waist covered in navy blue sweatpants.

Her stomach clenched in a wash of need and she fought to pull her gaze up toward his eyes.

Sleep-glazed eyes that were rapidly clearing.

"Kate. Good morning."

"Hi."

As if catching himself, he pulled on the door and gestured her in. She stepped past him and a wave of raw desire washed over her at the heavy scent of him. He smelled of sleep—that warm, dry heat that was still unspoiled by the day—and she wanted to wrap herself up in him.

Drawing on pure courage and the small, flickering flame that had come to life since Grier's arrival, she took a seat on the desk chair that flanked the edge of the bed. That flame had lit up inside her, reminding her she wanted more out of her life and she wasn't going to get it if she didn't start taking some risks.

"So, I know you're leaving soon and I wanted a chance to talk to you."

"Sure. Good."

"I wanted to say something last night, but you looked occupied with Mick and, well, Trina's a bad audience."

He smiled at that and she took the small encouragement to mean he was still interested in hearing what she had to say.

"So I thought it might be better to talk to you alone, away from prying eyes."

"The bane of small towns."

"Our observations are our greatest strength and our biggest sticking point."

"Sort of like anonymity in New York. It's great and it sucks."

That made a poetic sort of sense, Kate thought. The things that defined us often were our biggest Achilles' heel. She'd learned that lesson well enough from her parents.

"I've been rather unwelcoming to Grier since this whole thing with my father started. And I've felt pretty ashamed of it, too."

He said nothing, but his gaze never wavered, so she continued.

"After I got past the initial shock of my father's secret, I think the person I've been most upset with has been me."

"Why's that?"

Kate marveled at how quickly the tears welled up, clogging in her throat in a tight, painful ball. "I always thought I'd be braver. With a life far more interesting than the one I have."

Up until now, he hadn't moved from the doorway of the hotel room. Fascinated, Kate watched as he walked toward her, the tight sinew of his shoulders shifting in tantalizing motion at the slight swing of his arms. He came to a stop in front of her and planted his hands on the rails of the chair before leaning down to press a kiss at the base of her neck.

"I think you're very interesting."

Heat lit up a path from the point on her neck where his lips pressed in a powerful wave to her very center. His breath was hot as he trailed a kiss up to her jaw.

"And quite brave."

He continued moving until his lips pressed to hers. "And you're someone I'd like very much to get to know better."

Kate heard the words but couldn't quite believe them. She knew the interest arcing between them hadn't been one-sided, but the evidence of his attraction to her was heady. And sexy. And so very, very life affirming.

Before she could say anything in response, his hands grasped her arms and pulled her up so they stood face-to-face. With infinitely gentle movements, he placed his hands at the base of her throat, the pad of his thumb playing over the sensitive flesh there.

"I want you. But I don't want to sell you a bad bill of goods. I don't live here and I can't live here."

The hope that had flared to life dimmed. She knew her face telegraphed her emotions and it took all she had to reach up and lay her hands over his, ready to pull them away.

She suspected she'd follow Jason anywhere, but one simply didn't say that to a man she'd known a week and hadn't even kissed.

Or had *just* kissed.

As she was about to step away, Jason tightened his hold. "But I'd like to get to know you better. And if you wanted to come visit, maybe we could find out just how much you liked New York, too."

Hope returned on swift feet and Kate nodded. "I'd like that. A lot."

"I'm so glad." Jason leaned in and pressed his lips to hers.

As she wrapped her arms around his neck, accepting his kiss and the promise of so much more, Kate knew she had made a move toward her future.

After several long minutes, he lifted his head. "Maybe we could go grab some breakfast?"

"I'd like that."

As he smiled down at her, Kate knew life would never be the same again.

Grier's vision blurred as she stared at the name on the grave marker.

WINSTON

Grier read two names underneath, in neat chiseled rows: JONAS SHANE and LAURIE MARIE and a series of dates.

From the dates listed, she saw her father's birthday would have been in two days. She'd known he was born in January—she had seen it on some initial paperwork that had come to her at the start of the inheritance process—but the reminder struck a chord.

For the first time in sixty-one years, he'd not be here to celebrate the day.

That thought morphed into another. She knew her father had married someone else—Kate's existence was the proof of that—but seeing it etched in granite felt so real.

Finite.

And offered indelible proof that the woman he chose to spend his life with was not her mother.

"Are you all right?" Mick's voice was gentle and he kept his hand at her lower back. The gesture was warm and supportive, and she hadn't realized just how badly she needed it until she leaned into him and soaked up his quiet strength.

"I've avoided coming here." Her voice sounded foreign to her own ears—the husky tones thick with emotion. "I expected to be sad, maybe even angry I never had a chance to know him. But I never expected I'd be jealous of Kate for having her parents lying side by side, six feet under the ground."

"If it makes you feel any better, they never seemed, at least on the surface, to be a love match."

Others had made similar comments, whether in hopes of making her feel better or simply passing on what little they'd observed. None of it assuaged the searing sadness that she couldn't shake.

A piece of her life had been taken away years ago by the actions and decisions of others, and now she could never hope to get any of it back.

"I used to imagine what my father would be like."

"Your mother never talked about him?"

A harsh laugh choked her as she thought about her mother's stubborn refusal to engage in discussion on this subject. "She didn't even have him named on my birth certificate."

When Mick's only response was to tighten his grip on her waist, she let the rest of her thoughts spill out.

"She married my stepfather when I was an infant, so I didn't know until I was a teenager that I even had a father other than William Thompson. When he left my mother, the truth came out."

"He abandoned you?"

"No, but the divorce proceedings and custody hearing took into account I wasn't his biological child. I begged my mother to tell me who my real father was, but she wouldn't tell me. And through the subsequent years, I'd painted him into some sort of mythical figure."

"Who could leap tall buildings?"

"Something like that." Grier laid her head on his upper arm, just below his shoulder, and took comfort in the solid feel of him. "He was a lot of things in my mind, but the one thing I never imagined was a man who couldn't be bothered to have anything to do with me."

Grier stepped away from Mick's solid strength and moved up to stand at the foot of the grave plot. A small bouquet of roses sat at the base of the marker and the pink ribbon that wrapped them up said *Loving Daughter* in gold script.

Kate had been here.

The flowers struck her on a level she couldn't describe, and whatever anger she'd harbored for her sister fled on the harsh January wind.

Kate had been deceived as well. She'd spent a life never knowing she had a sister, either. Yet she'd still come to honor her parents.

The words of Maeve's letter once again filled her thoughts and Grier puzzled through the mixed emotions of guilt and anger. Jonas deserved her visit to his grave.

Did he?

He'd never visited her. He had never found a way past his own grief or pain or fear. Grier knew it made her a small person. She knew her inability to see past this would only continue to hurt her, for the dead had already been laid to rest.

But damn it, she'd deserved better.

And staring down at her father's grave, she couldn't find it in her heart to feel anything. The nameless, faceless father Patrice had always refused to talk about hadn't been worth a single fantasy she'd spun about him.

And all that was left in her heart was a gaping, empty hole.

Her gaze caught on the flowers once more and Grier thought again about Kate. There was a relationship that possibly she could still fix along with a person she could get to know better and see if they had anything in common.

A small spark flared in her heart, lighting up that dark, gaping hole. Maybe all wasn't lost.

Turning to face Mick, she reached up and placed a hand on his chest. "Please, take me away from here."

"Where do you want to go?"

"Your place."

"Grier, are you sure?"

Whatever doubts she'd harbored since arriving fled on the renewed hope that beat in her chest. Despite his absence, her father had led her here.

To her family.

And to Mick.

What she had with him was real—the sort of heart-pounding, blood-pumping real that made her feel alive. With a soft smile, she nodded. "Yes. I'm sure."

Chapter Twenty-two

Heavy twilight lit the sky outside his bedroom window as Mick ran his hand over Grier's bare shoulder. Her arrival at the cemetery had been a balm to his battered senses, and even now, hours later, he marveled at how simply and succinctly she made him remember the good times.

The violence of his mother's death had rattled him, but it wasn't until the trip up to Denali to rescue the researchers that he realized just how fresh the scars still were. How had she managed with one request—to tell her something wonderful about his mother—to begin a healing fifteen years in the making?

It was with that sense of awe and gratitude that he struggled to make sense of her pain. And he wished like hell he could find some way to help her.

Although he couldn't see much of her face as they'd stood over Jonas's grave, both of them staring in the same direction, he didn't miss the weight of her grief that lay so heavy over her shoulders.

She was so compassionate and vibrant. He'd watched her over the last weeks—hell, he'd been watching her since she arrived—and Grier always took great care and consideration of the people she was with.

Sloan and Avery were the recipients of her fiercest support and loyalty. She was warm and respectful of everyone in town, completely ignoring how unfriendly and unwelcoming they'd originally been and putting it behind her as if it had never happened. And despite the temporary debacle with the offered puppy, Chooch and Hooch—harsh critics on their best day—sang her praises up one side of Main Street and back down the other.

In a matter of months, Grier Thompson was universally loved by everyone. Even more important, the entire town *liked* her.

She stirred next to him and he shifted to press a kiss to her hair.

And he realized one powerful truth.

He loved her.

Over the years, he'd come to believe he'd feel some pain, or maybe disgust at being an easy mark if he ever fell in love. Instead, all he felt was a deep joy.

Bone deep.

As if he'd finally found a missing part of his soul.

In the same way flying was more for him than just a job, Grier Thompson was his more.

She was his everything.

And as he lay in the dark, holding her against his chest, Mick began to fear. Because he had no idea what he was going to do when she went away.

Avery lined up a row of margarita glasses and poured out the batch of frozen cocktails she'd whipped up in the blender. She'd never understood anyone's interest in drinking one when the temperature was twenty below, but who was she to judge.

She made the drinks; she didn't have to drink them herself.

The lobby bar was in full swing as the denizens of Indigo put on their best smiles and hoped they'd be captured on film for Roman's big TV interview.

A glance toward the open office doorway indicated they hadn't started the latest round of filming yet and Susan paced nervously outside the door. She was up first for the interview and Avery saw the photo she had clutched in her hand.

Avery knew that picture. It was one of Roman, at seventeen, dressed in his full hockey gear and holding a trophy high. He'd set a record in the state league that year for the most goals and had been given the trophy after their last game of the season. It had been her sixteenth birthday and she'd lost her virginity to him the same night.

That picture had sat on Susan's desk for years and every time she looked at it, a small knot settled just underneath her heart.

That was what no one understood.

The reminder of Roman Forsyth was so ever-present— so tangible and real in the town of Indigo—that there really was no escape. No time to heal.

There were many things she looked forward to experiencing on the trip to Ireland, but that one sat at the top of her list. Four glorious months where no one knew her. No one knew about that night she had too much to drink and puked in Mrs. Waters's bushes. And they had no idea she'd lost her first serious boyfriend to the NHL. And they most certainly wouldn't look at her in pity for having given up her twenties taking care of her alcoholic mother.

No one in Ireland knew her and she couldn't wait to get there.

"Those margaritas ready?" Mindy Trexler smiled at her across the bar before turning her attention toward the office. "It sure does take a long time to put together a TV shoot."

"You should have seen all the setup they had to do earlier. It's an endless process."

Mindy had agreed to pick up an extra shift tonight and Avery was grateful for the help. She handed off the margaritas and pointed toward a door at the end of the bar that led to the storeroom. "I have to get that Cab you wanted from the stockroom. I'll be right back with it."

Mindy nodded and headed off to Margaritaville, and Avery made a beeline for the stockroom. She couldn't hold back her curious gaze as the camera people continued to putter around the office door. Susan wasn't standing outside any longer, so things must have started moving forward.

About time, she almost muttered out loud, catching herself at the last minute.

All the fuss was starting to wear on her. The camera crew had stayed up extra late the night before, drinking in the lobby until two. She'd then gotten up early to help deal with the breakfast rush. Images of her bed flashed through her mind and she slapped lightly at her cheeks, willing away the walking dead image she had to be projecting.

A few more hours and it'd be over.

And Ireland awaited, she reminded herself once more, the idea glowing like a beacon in her mind as she opened the door to the stockroom.

"You're Avery Marks?"

Avery turned from where she balanced on a small step stool, attempting to pull the desired bottle of wine from a top shelf. The voice was familiar, but it wasn't until she turned that she recognized its owner, Priscilla Davies, the woman interviewing Roman.

"Yes, can I help you with something? Is there something you need for the shoot?"

The woman waved a hand in the direction of the lobby. "My crew's still setting up."

"All right. Do you need something to drink, then? I can get you some bottled water or a soda if you'd prefer."

"Actually, I'd like to talk to you."

The slight confusion that had her asking Priscilla hospitality questions faded as a small frisson of awareness skated down her spine. Avery snagged the bottle she wanted and stepped down off the stool.

The polite proprietor's smile she'd put on evaporated in the calculating gleam of Priscilla's narrowed blue gaze. "About?"

"You and Roman Forsyth."

"I don't think I'm on your interview schedule." Avery held still, even though the urge to rush past her through the storeroom doorway was strong.

"I'd consider you a last-minute addition. The town's

awfully friendly and people have been very quick to point out your history with Roman."

The woman practically purred Roman's name and Avery bit back her annoyance. "I'm sorry, but as you can tell by the crowd in the lobby, we're very busy tonight."

Avery did push forward this time, moving steadily toward the door so Priscilla was forced to step outside of it. With a hard snap, Avery pulled the storeroom door closed behind her.

"You can tell your story. I'm more than willing to be fair and present your side."

Panic swam in her stomach in hard, stifling waves and it felt as if hot clammy fingers gripped the base of Avery's neck. "There's nothing to present, Ms. Davies. Nor do I have anything to tell."

Priscilla's voice had her turning back despite her best efforts to keep moving toward the familiar comfort of the bar. "But you *are* the one Roman left behind to pursue his goal of the NHL. Love's collateral damage."

"It was a long time ago."

"And yet here you are, still single from what I hear. And working in Roman's mother's hotel, too."

Despite her efforts to remain calm, Avery heard the slight quaver in her own voice. "As are several women in this town."

"I'm simply looking to paint a full picture of Roman's life. Tell his story, as it were."

"Well, clearly you're looking in the wrong place." Roman's voice rang out behind her and Avery turned to find him striding forward, murder in his gaze.

She'd seen that look before—he usually wore it just before he got into a wicked fight with an opponent on the ice. The image had often reminded her of a warrior headed into battle.

"I'm just talking to an old friend of yours, Roman." Priscilla's voice was smooth, but Avery didn't miss the dark light that filled her eyes with calculating menace.

"You've got that right. Avery is an old friend. And as I told you before we began this process, I wasn't going to burden my friends with an intrusive peek into their lives."

"I didn't think someone you'd known as well as Ms. Marks here was included."

Roman extended an arm to her. "Well, she is. Now, if you'll join me, the camera crew is ready and you've kept my mother waiting long enough."

"I'm sorry to bother you, Ms. Marks." Priscilla took Roman's arm and allowed him to turn her back toward the lobby.

Anger lit the depths of Roman's eyes, coloring them a bright shade of green. He gave her one last, long look before turning toward the lobby and marching the errant reporter back to the staging area.

Avery took a deep breath as they walked away. Her hands shook and her legs had a decidedly rubbery feel, but she was safe.

Roman had come to her rescue.

And if she wasn't mistaken, the apology in his eyes was about far more than a nosy reporter.

*   *   *

Grier smiled to herself as she rooted through Mick's refrigerator for the ingredients to make breakfast. And she wasn't surprised when she came out with bacon, eggs and a packet of hash browns.

Everything about the man screamed hale and hearty. The fact his pantry wasn't a bachelor wasteland of Pop-Tarts and Froot Loops only reinforced that.

She ran her hands over the large long-sleeved T-shirt that covered her to her knees and rolled up the sleeves to start preparing breakfast. She'd found the shirt folded on a chair in his bedroom and reveled in how his scent surrounded her.

Twenty minutes later when he came out of the bedroom, freshly showered, his hair still wet and curling around his neck, she had the eggs scrambled and waiting to cook last as the bacon and hash browns merrily hissed in skillets on the stove.

"That smells good. Usually I have to do this myself."

"I'm impressed you cook at all. And I'm even more impressed I've seen nary a Pop-Tart in your kitchen."

He smiled as he pressed a kiss to her lips, then moved to the coffeepot to pour himself a cup and refill hers. "Oh, I've been known to ride the morning sugar rush on occasion, but I prefer something a bit more substantial."

"Very self-sufficient of you. Sadly, I fall all too often in the bachelorette camp of 'grab it and go.'"

"Strawberry or chocolate Pop-Tarts?" He looked over the rim of his mug.

"Granola bars. And forget the fruity ones. I want chocolate with my breakfast."

"Sustenance from a box and no hidden nutrients like dried fruit for you."

"In short, yes." Grier turned back to the stove to flip the bacon strips.

"You're a woman on the go. I'm sure an hour making breakfast isn't doable."

She hesitated briefly at his words, not sure why they caught her up short. There wasn't any censure or criticism in his tone, but the sentiment chafed all the same.

Shaking it off, Grier transferred the bacon onto a plate and did a fresh whisking to the eggs. The temptation to drop them into the skillet was great, but she grabbed a new pan. No matter how often she worked out or how much she enjoyed a hearty breakfast, there was no way she was frying her eggs in bacon grease.

A gal had to draw the line somewhere.

"Go ahead and grab some plates and I'll get the eggs going."

His footfalls were heavy behind her back as he padded around the kitchen and she couldn't deny the sweet coziness of the moment, especially when it came on the heels of a night spent wrapped up together.

"Thank you for yesterday."

He stepped up behind her and pressed his lips to her neck. "For what?"

"Everything. You helped me through my first trip to the cemetery. I didn't want to go alone but knew I had to. And then you were there."

Grier thought about the trepidation she had felt walking toward the cemetery and the incredible rush of reassurance when she saw him standing there.

He shifted behind her, lifting his lips and resting his chin on her head. Even in that simple gesture, he understood her. Their sexy moment had shifted into one more akin to comfort, and she marveled at how easily he read her and changed to fit her needs.

"You doing okay?"

She briefly laid a hand over his before returning it to the pan. "I am. And my aunt Maeve was right. I owed my father the respect of going. Even if I had a few resentful moments."

"Healing's a process, Grier. You're not expected to figure it out in a day. And when you layer on Jonas's choices, well, you're only human."

"I'll do better next time."

As she said the words, she knew they were true. The anger she'd struggled with had calmed overnight. Although she still felt raw, the bleakness had faded, and in its place was the resolve to move forward.

For herself and for the relationship she wanted with her sister. She couldn't change what had come before, Grier knew, but she could eventually put her feelings to rest.

"I think the eggs are about done."

Grier saw that moment when their excessive runniness turned over into scrambled eggs. "I never cease to be amazed at that."

"At what?"

"That singular moment when a bunch of runny eggs becomes breakfast. It's magic."

"It's transformative. Sort of like the first time I saw you."

His arms tightened around her and Grier wondered that she didn't melt right there. Although she'd never have imagined being compared to a pan of scrambled eggs was sexy, she couldn't imagine a better compliment.

He shifted behind her and she didn't miss the sexy proof of his arousal pressed into her backside. Heat licked at her spine and she toyed briefly with the notion of shutting off the stove and turning into him. "You're going to make me forget breakfast."

She felt his smile against her skin as his lips returned to her neck. "I didn't think anything kept you from breakfast."

"That's not entirely true. Nothing keeps me from pancakes." She arched into his touch, all the while trying to keep her attention on finishing the eggs. "Bacon and eggs are a distant second."

His fingers skimmed along her rib cage. The touch was featherlight, but it had the impact of a cyclone. Sensations swirled in her stomach as need built at the apex of her thighs. They'd made love three times the night before and still she wanted him.

With a desperation that bordered on madness.

She was rapidly losing her focus on breakfast and turned the knob off on the gas. "Just let me get these off the stove."

"Here. Let me."

He took the heavy pan from her and slid the eggs onto a platter she'd pulled down. After setting the empty pan back on the stove, he turned off the heat under the hash browns, then pulled her close.

"Forget breakfast for the moment. I've got something far more delicious to nibble on."

"I couldn't agree more."

His arms wrapped around her and she tilted her head up for his kiss. His breath was warm and she could taste the light hints of his toothpaste underneath the heavier tones of coffee.

She opened for him, and a light moan rose up in her throat as his tongue stole into her mouth. Sexy and intimate, they stood there for long moments as desire built into a raging inferno.

"I want you, Grier. Always, always," he whispered against her mouth.

"Take me." She arched against him with the sinewy grace of a cat. "Please."

Mick obliged, pulling her up into his arms and quickly crossing the short distance from the kitchen to the couch. As he laid her on the couch, then followed her down, she gladly took his weight over her and encouraged the proof of his arousal as he pressed his lower body into hers by cradling him between her thighs.

Arousal pumped through her, vibrant and life affirming. Mick made her feel *necessary*. As if his next breath depended on her.

She ran her hands over the long, rangy muscles of his arms, enjoying how they bunched and tightened under her fingers. The lazy moments grew increasingly urgent and she shifted her legs restlessly against his. The oversized T-shirt she wore bunched at her waist and her panties were heated and damp where he pressed against her.

"While I love the way you look in my shirt, let's get you out of it." Mick shifted and sat up, pulling her with him.

She grinned at him. "I will if you will."

Mick laughed as his oversized T-shirt hit him in the chest. Leave it to Grier to manage a combination of sexy and funny all at the same time. "I have to say, I like you without pants."

He dragged his own T-shirt off and reached down to slip off his shorts.

"I'm just glad for once I'm not stuck in my clothes as I attempt to strip for you."

Mick reached for her and pulled her close. "Baby, never apologize for stripping for me."

"Let's just say clumsy and oafish doesn't scream sexy."

He nuzzled her throat. God, what was it about that wonderful spot where her shoulder arched gracefully into her neck that drew him again and again? "You always scream sexy to me."

He pulled them both back to the couch, settling so she straddled him in a seated position. He bent down and took one peaked nipple in his mouth, satisfied as it grew harder against his tongue. She tasted so fresh and sweet, the light tang of her skin the headiest aphrodisiac.

He felt her back muscles bunch under his hands as she arched into him, and he drank his fill as his body clamored for satisfaction. Unwilling to satiate his needs before hers, he kept one hand firmly on her back to hold her upright while the other reached down between their bodies.

Mick found her ready for him, her hot core slick with moisture as his fingers wove through the light tangle of curls at the juncture of her thighs. Grier writhed against him, her breath growing shallow with heavy pants as he pushed her higher, driving her to take all she could.

A desperate hunger consumed him as he watched her pleasure grow. His cock was painfully stiff; yet he pushed her on, the erotic image of her in the throes of pleasure emblazoned on his mind in vivid detail.

The heated flush that covered her chest. The lush swell of her lips, ripe from their kisses. The stormy gray haze of passion that darkened her gaze.

He drank it in—drank her in—and reveled in that moment when she went over. Her tight sheath clenched around his fingers as her hands tightened at his shoulders as she rode him.

"Now, Mick. I want you now."

Unable to deny the needs of his own body any longer, he shifted her on his lap, embedding his aching cock to the hilt. She wrapped around him, the internal aftershocks of her orgasm nearly dragging on his own right then, but he maintained his tight grip on control.

Grier's arms wrapped around his neck and her head pressed to the side of his head. He felt her fingers thread through his hair as she pressed her lips against his ear.

"It's your turn, cowboy."

And then she began to move.

In moments, his own release was upon him. On a

hard, heavy thrust he rose up to meet her as she drove her body over his. And then his world went blank in a wash of pleasure so powerful he wondered if he'd ever recover.

The next few days passed in a pleasant blur of activity. Word had gotten around that she'd put together Chooch and Hooch's taxes and, to Jess's original observation, many others had soon followed suit.

Grier found she liked the work, the time she spent with various townsfolk an enjoyable and productive way to pass the day. Walker had offered a small conference room he kept in his office, but she found the quiet of the hotel's conference room a suitable fit.

If her days were the height of productivity, her nights were the height of ecstasy. She and Mick hadn't spent a night apart since the day she found him in the cemetery, and she knew every moment they spent together drew them closer and closer.

A big part of her had been fearful at first, but over the last couple of days she'd begun to relax. She wasn't ready to give up life in New York, but she was in no rush to leave Indigo, either.

And why did she have to decide yet? Or choose?

The thought flitted through her mind as she double-checked a column of numbers and then jotted it down on a piece of scrap paper. A light knock on the open door pulled her from her task and she looked up to see Kate standing in the doorway. "Grier? Do you have a minute?"

"Of course."

When Kate didn't move from her spot in the doorway, Grier waved her in. "Don't be afraid of the receipts. Just push them out of the way and grab a seat wherever."

As if pulled out of a trance, Kate nodded and stepped into the room. She moved around the edge of the heavy leather chairs that ringed the table, choosing the one directly opposite from Grier's.

Kate took her seat, the chair dwarfing her small frame. On a half smile, Grier leaned her head back and realized they must look like bookends. While they were by no means identical in their appearances, based on their different mothers, their physical size and shape were similar.

And then there were the eyes.

She'd yet to meet anyone who didn't remark on the fact that they both had the same gray eyes as Jonas.

"Is something wrong?"

"I'm not sure."

The honest answer caught Grier up short. "Why don't you tell me what's going on?"

"I think I'm in love with Jason. And I had sex with him."

"That's fantastic." The words were out before Grier even thought about them. Kate's head shot up and a smile brightened her face before she spoke. "Really?"

"Ever since I saw the two of you sitting together in the lobby, something seemed to click. I think it's a great idea."

"It doesn't upset you?"

"It did at first, but not for the reasons you think."

Kate nodded as she picked up a lone rubber band and began stretching it. "So what are your reasons?"

"I think the two of you as a couple is an inspired idea. You can see it, looking at you both together." Grier leaned forward and waited until Kate lifted her gaze from where she played with the rubber band. "And I support it completely."

"Oh."

"But I'd be a bad sister if I didn't worry a bit that he'd do to you what he did to me."

Kate nodded. "Yeah."

Grier knew she was on dangerous ground. She couldn't predict Jason's behavior—or anyone's for that matter—and he *had* made a major mistake. But no matter how she spun it in her mind, she couldn't separate his behavior with his desire to get out of their relationship as opposed to a chronic character defect.

"For what it's worth, I really don't think Jason's going to make the same mistake if he's with the right woman."

"I didn't purposely go after him."

"I know."

"Do you?" Kate's expression changed, the light blush of love vanishing as something darker covered her face. "Because I've done other things to you. Purposeful things you didn't deserve."

Grier sensed the immediate change in the conversation and knew they weren't talking about Jason any longer. And while her usual approach to conflict was to be polite and wait for it to pass, she found she wasn't quite able to let Kate off the hook.

"Yes, you have."

"I'm sorry, Grier. I'm so sorry. You didn't deserve it and I don't have any excuse for my behavior. And I'm not just telling you this because you're okay with Jason and me."

"I know that. And you were sad." Grier was willing to give her that. "Any loss is hard, but you had to watch him suffer, too."

"And you never got to know the wonderful person that he was at all, so we both got a shitty deal."

"Did he really have a big Christmas light display every year?"

Kate smiled, the memories bringing a warm smile to her face. "Yes, he did. Lights covered the house. You would have loved it."

"I know I would have."

Grier paused as her thoughts from the cemetery floated back through her mind. "I want to have a relationship with you. I'd like to know my sister."

"I want to know my sister, too." Kate reached forward and took her hand. "And maybe if it's not too intrusive, I could join you and Avery and Sloan for wine sometime?"

Warm heat suffused her as Grier felt the subtle winds of change in her relationship with Kate. "I'd like that and I think my friends would, too."

The moment was broken by the ringing of her phone, Walker's name covering the display. As she answered it, a strange premonition came over her. It shot small sparks down her spine and she sat straighter as her skin prickled with awareness.

If he called with the information she believed, there couldn't have been a more perfect time for the news to arrive.

She was with her sister.

And they should hear it together.

Mick rapped two hard knocks on his grandmother's front door and inhaled the warm scents from the box in his hands. He couldn't shake the restless anxiety that crawled under his skin and knew a visit to his grandmother would help settle him.

He'd grabbed a pizza for them and ordered it loaded up just like his grandmother liked—sausage, mushrooms and a double order of anchovies. And he smiled when he realized he'd flown the anchovies in himself.

A broad smile appeared on Mary's face when she opened the door. "Darling. Come in."

The moment he crossed the threshold and pressed a kiss to her warm cheek, Mick knew he'd made the right choice. He followed her down the hall toward the kitchen.

"Your timing is perfect. I was just deciding between a salad and some leftover tuna casserole. A hot pizza— shared with my grandson, no less—sounds a million times better."

Within minutes he had them settled at her kitchen table, slices laid out on plates and cold Cokes fizzing in tall glasses. Mary took a bite of her pizza and closed her eyes in ecstasy. "Perfection."

"They order the anchovies for you."

"And well they should. I've been ordering them for forty years."

He smiled at that. "Forty years. A long time."

"Are you reminding me of my age, young man?"

"No, ma'am. Just thinking about how you've made a life here."

"I've made it here a lot longer than forty years."

"So you have."

Her blue eyes, so like his own, turned misty. "I'm a second-generation Alaskan. I can't imagine life anywhere else, even if people in the Lower Forty-eight think we're insane."

Mick lifted his glass and waited until she did the same, then clinked them together. "To insanity."

"Absolutely." She took a sip, her gaze growing thoughtful. "While I'll never turn down a pleasant lunch with my grandson, you're not here for fun. What's wrong, sweetheart?"

Her ease in reading him stung a bit, but Mick also knew that was why he'd come here. She understood him. And she'd always loved him just as he was. "You already know the answer to that."

"Grier?"

"Of course."

Mary gave him her full attention, laying her half-eaten slice on her plate and sitting back in her chair. "Tell me about it."

"She's the one. On some level I knew it from the first moment I looked at her, but the last few weeks have confirmed it."

"I believe she feels the same way about you." Mary

hesitated for a moment before adding, "I think you do, too."

"Yes. Unequivocally yes. Which is what makes all of this so damn difficult. She's going to leave. The information her aunt gave her about Jonas was the last bit of proof Kate couldn't block the inheritance any longer. She's got what she's come here for and she's going to leave."

"Do you want to go with her when she does?"

The question ate at Mick's gut. He'd go and he'd go willingly, but he knew the depths of what he'd be giving up. "I'd go in a heartbeat and leave my life here for her. I'd miss it, but I'd go."

"So what's the problem?"

"She hasn't asked me to."

Mary took a deep breath. "There's something I need to tell you."

He heard the immediate change in tone and knew something was wrong. "Are you okay?"

"Of course, darling." She patted his hand. "But I did something. And you may not be very happy with me."

"What is it?" Mick searched his mind, unable to come up with anything she could possibly have done that would upset him.

"I called Grier's mother. Told her—well, actually, I ordered her—to come to Indigo."

The words hovered in his mind, yet he was unable to make sense of them. "Grier's mother?"

"I heard her name years ago. From Jonas. And I kept track of it."

"You called Grier's mother?" Mick knew the question was inane, but he couldn't make sense of it.

On a soft sigh, Mary nodded. "Let me start at the beginning."

Kate handed Grier the key as they stood before the front door of the small house on Spruce Street. "You should do it."

Grier glanced down where Kate held the key to their father's house between her gloved fingers. Before taking the key, she turned and opened her arms, pulling Kate into them.

And was gratified when her sister held on as tightly as she did. Tears filled her eyes and Grier let them fall, happy she and Kate had finally come to an understanding.

On a final squeeze, Grier pulled back and wiped at her cheeks. Tears ran twin tracks down Kate's face as well. "To new beginnings."

Kate held up the key once more and smiled through her tears. "To new beginnings."

The key turned easily in the lock and moments later, Grier walked into her father's house. The small foyer was dark and she heard Kate move up behind her. "Let me get the lights on and some heat going."

Grier nodded as Kate walked off down the hall and continued to stand in place. The hallway led to a kitchen straight in front of her. A small living room lay to her left and a dining room to her right. She didn't know where to look first.

So she moved into the living room and looked around.

She was finally *here*.

In her father's house.

A floor-to-ceiling bookcase ran along one of the walls of the living room and she crossed to it. Neat, even rows of books filled the wall, all alphabetized and organized by genre, and another wave of hot tears blurred her vision.

"The heat should be up in a second," Kate's voice echoed behind her.

Grier turned and Kate's smile fell. "Are you okay?"

She swallowed around the hard knot in her throat. "He alphabetized them. The books."

Kate nodded and Grier didn't miss her puzzled smile. "Always."

"Just like me," Grier whispered. "I do that."

"Do you get twitchy if someone takes one out and puts it back wrong?"

"Yes."

"So did Dad." Kate extended a hand. "Come on. Let me show you around."

Chapter Twenty-three

Mick picked up his coffee and let the strong brew slide down his throat. The Indigo Blue's lobby was quieter than it had been in days. The town's interest had clearly waned now that the TV crew had headed back to New York.

"Have you heard from her yet?" Walker probed.

"She texted me as I was finishing up lunch and told me she and Kate were headed to Jonas's house. Said she'd fill me in when she got back."

"Sloan hasn't heard from her yet, either." Walker nodded to where she stood at the bar, talking to Avery.

Mick took another sip of his coffee and tried cracking his neck. Tension had his shoulders stiff; even his visit to his grandmother hadn't loosened it. In fact, it had only made it worse at her revelation that Patrice Thompson was headed their way.

Today.

Add to it that damn text message, and he couldn't shake the anger that lay beneath the tension.

He didn't even rate a phone call? Grier had been in Indigo for two fucking months, waiting for news of her father's home, and she couldn't be bothered to call him?

"You doing okay?" Walker's sharp gaze washed over him.

"I'm fine."

"Because you look like shit. And the coffee's a dead giveaway you're pissed."

"I drink coffee every day."

"It's the fact you're not drinking alcohol. You never drink when you're pissed off."

Mick shook his head and amended his earlier observation. Walker's gaze wasn't sharp—it was bug-under-a-microscope sharp. And he had no interest in being dissected.

"I didn't want a beer."

Walker held up his hands. "Fine by me."

His oldest friend was delivered from a smart-ass reply by Grier's arrival in the lobby. A broad smile filled her face as she walked toward them. Desire—sharp and insistent—spiked through him.

God, how could one woman affect him like this? He was growing madder by the moment and he still wanted her.

Still *needed* her.

And it was that realization that had him reaching for his coffee and an attempt to rein in his thoughts.

He'd gone to his grandmother's to get perspective because he knew he had very little when it came to Grier Thompson. And then that damn text message came through, and whatever perspective he *thought* he had was shot to hell.

They loved each other, or so he thought. And still, he didn't even rate a phone call?

After all they'd been through.

"Hi there." Her smile never wavered as she leaned over his chair and pressed her lips to his cheek. "How was your day?"

"Good."

Confusion flittered briefly in her eyes, but the bright smile remained. "Mine was outstanding. I made up with my sister and learned about my father."

"Great. Good."

Real confusion now clouded her eyes as Grier took the seat next to him. With a bright smile for Walker, she added, "Things went really well today. Thank you for all your help."

"It was my pleasure." Walker reached for his beer and stood. "I'm going to give you two a few minutes to talk about it and keep Sloan's and Avery's curiosity at bay. They're anxious to talk to you."

"I'll come over in a minute."

Mick kept his gaze on his coffee cup.

"Did everything go okay this morning? I know you were waiting on that big order to arrive."

"Yep. Everything arrived on schedule."

He saw Grier reach for him from the corner of his eye. "Mick, what's wrong? Did something happen?"

"Your message, for one."

"What message? The text?"

"That's all I rate, Grier? A fucking text?"

"I was excited. And it was a whirlwind. I was working on some tax returns when I got the call. Then Kate and I had to get to Walker's to sign papers and I wanted to get there as fast as I could."

"And there was no time to make a call?"

"Mick, why are you making such a big deal about this?"

"You're the one who's made a big deal out of it. Hell, you tried breaking into the house a month ago." He laid his empty cup on the small table in front of his chair and turned to her. "I'd have liked to hear about it from you."

"You did hear about it from me."

"Fine. I heard about it." He knew it was pissy and unkind, but to hell with it all; he was done with being understanding.

"Can we go talk somewhere else?" She looked around the bar.

"It's not that crowded. No one can hear us. And you're going to go tell Avery and Sloan the moment I'm gone, anyway."

"Gone where?" Her tone was sharp and whatever merriment had ridden her shoulders when she walked in was long gone.

"Home. I've got a big day tomorrow."

"You're not leaving until we talk about this."

A harsh laugh welled up in his chest. "Why does it matter? You've got what you came here for. Your father's estate is well on its way toward being settled. When are you booking your flight home to New York?"

"Mick, what's wrong?"

"Everything, Grier. Every fucking thing."

"Well, I'm not going to sit here and discuss it with you out in the open. I think I deserve more than that. I think we both do."

He nodded, her point well made. "Let's go back to the conference room. We can talk there."

She stood and he followed her. As they crossed the lobby, the heavy front doors of the hotel swung open. Grier stopped so suddenly, he nearly ran into her and he immediately reached for her shoulders to balance himself.

And felt her body go rigid under his fingers.

A woman stepped through the door. She wore a fur coat that surrounded her from head to toe, and a matched hat covered her familiar, sable-colored hair. She stopped before them and Mick could only imagine what the three of them looked like to anyone watching, all of them frozen in place.

Grier moved first, stepping backward into his chest. "Mom?"

If Jason's sudden arrival in Indigo the few weeks prior had filled her with shocked surprise, her mother's was like an asteroid striking outside the door.

What the hell was she doing here? How'd she get here?

And *why*?

"Hello, darling." Her mother ignored the chilly reception and moved forward. Grier felt her hands lifted as she was pulled forward, away from the warmth of Mick's solid chest. "I've missed you."

"As I could no doubt tell from all your phone calls

since New Year's." The dig rose up with surprising swiftness.

"It's been a busy time."

"Yes, it has. To that end, could you excuse us? We were just finishing something up. I'm sure Avery can get you settled in."

She reached for Mick's hand before her mother could protest and took off down the hall toward the conference room.

"I don't believe you left her standing there."

"Yeah, well, if you think you're pissed you didn't get a phone call, I'm mad as hell. First she springs Jason on me and now herself."

"My grandmother invited her."

Grier whirled on that, just as they cleared the threshold of the large conference room. "She what?"

"She told me earlier that she called your mother and insisted she come."

"How does your grandmother know my mother?"

"Your father let her name slip at some point in the past and my grandmother hung on to the information."

Although she'd been prepared to apologize, disbelief clouded out any feelings of contrition. "Why didn't you tell me?"

The anger she'd sensed in him as they sat in the lobby came roaring back in full force. "I only found out at lunch and I didn't talk to you today—remember?"

"You could have called me."

"I'm not getting into a pissing contest over this."

"To hell with a pissing match. I didn't call you about the house, so you didn't call me about this."

"Grier, it's not like that."

"So what's it like, Mick?"

The barely leashed tension she'd seen in the lobby broke through. "What's going to happen to us?"

"When I walked into the lobby, I didn't think anything was going to happen to us. I'm still not convinced it won't, but I don't understand you."

"You got what you came for. The inheritance is settled. It's time for you to go home."

The disjointed conversation began to make sense as she dug underneath his words. "Do you want me to go home?"

"You don't seem to want me to go with you."

"We haven't talked about it. And the few times we danced around the subject, you weren't jumping up and down, telling me how much you want to live in New York."

Grier felt the weight of all the words they didn't say begin undermining the ground beneath her, as if a chasm were opening up between them. "And you've never told me your feelings, so why should I put myself out there and ask what you want to do with the rest of your life?"

"It hasn't seemed like the right time."

"Funny, you and I've managed to do a lot of that. It wasn't the right time for me to tell you about Jason. And it wasn't the right time for you to tell me about your mother. And we haven't talked about our living arrangements and we haven't talked about my leaving."

He nodded. "No, we haven't."

"And you'd think we could find a way since we've spent a hell of a lot of time together over the last few weeks."

"I told you once I live in my head."

Grier smiled and knew there was nothing more to say. Moving forward, she reached for his hands. "Yes, Mick. But we're talking about us living together. And I don't think either of us knows how."

"So that's it? That's how it ends?"

"Can you give me any reason why it shouldn't?"

"It's too good between us. We're great partners, Grier. We *work* together." Before she could respond, he pulled her forward, crushing his lips to hers. She reacted immediately, the heat and the passion that flared between them so easy.

So why was the rest so very, very hard?

She loved him. But he never once said anything about love. And she'd be damned if she was going to ask.

Pulling back, she took a few steps to give herself distance.

"We work together." Mick's husky voice washed over her and she nearly walked back into his arms. And it was that knowledge—the realization that she would walk straight back to him, wrap herself in his arms and put aside her need to be told she was loved— that had her standing her ground.

"It's not enough. Not for me."

She moved around him and walked toward the door. And felt her heart break when he didn't follow her.

* * *

Grier rolled over in bed, the insistent pinging of her cell phone dragging her from the first few moments of sleep she'd gotten since the night before.

A quick glance at the face showed eight messages had piled up—three from Sloan, two from Avery, two from Kate and one from her mother.

Damn it, why couldn't they leave her alone to wallow?

And even as she thought it, she knew she'd do the same in their position.

With swift fingers, she sent a universal text to all four of them letting them know she'd talk later; then she turned off the phone. A glance at the clock showed it was eleven and despite her lack of interest in eating, her stomach growled in protest.

Hell, even miserable, she couldn't beat back the urge to eat.

Fifteen minutes later, after a shower that had her feeling only marginally better, she walked into the hotel dining room.

And saw her mother, fresh and pressed as she sipped coffee and paged through an architecture magazine. Patrice looked up and removed the elegant cheaters she wore. "Good morning."

"Hi."

"Get some breakfast and then let's talk."

Grateful for the reprieve, Grier walked to the sideboard and loaded up on the blessed pancakes that seemed so plentiful in Indigo. Adding sausage and hash browns, she crossed the room and took the seat opposite her mother.

"Your visit is rather unexpected."

"Yes, I know."

Grier spread the large pat of butter she'd selected at the counter and kept her attention on the preparation of her breakfast. "You really didn't think to call and give me a heads-up?"

"No."

"That figures."

"Grier!"

"No, Mom. It does. You've given me no support throughout this entire process. Hell, you wouldn't even acknowledge Jonas was my father. And now you expect me to sit here and indulge you and tell you everything's okay?" She slammed her fork down. "It's not fucking okay."

"I know."

Her mother's acknowledgment took the wind out of her sails and Grier picked up her fork again. She scraped off a small bite of pancake, barely tasting it. And then she laid down her fork again and faced her mother.

"I have your letters. The ones you wrote to my father."

"Those were private."

"And apparently were kept private until he passed away."

"Did you read them?"

"Yes."

"I see."

Grier didn't miss the pain in her mother's eyes, or the light blush.

"If it makes you feel any better, I skimmed over the private sexy parts."

"I suppose that's something."

"In fact, the love letters didn't hold all that much interest. The letters you sent him after I was born are another story."

"He kept those?"

"Yes."

"I don't expect you to understand why I did what I did."

Grier wanted to lash out, but she had a bit more insight into her mother's actions after her fight with Mick. "I don't understand it. Can you explain it to me?"

On a soft sigh, Patrice nodded, her eyes filling with tears. "I can try."

Grier tried to harden her heart—wanted to keep a tight leash on her emotions—but the harsh lines that marred her mother's face wouldn't allow it.

In each and every one of those lines, she saw the truth.

Her mother suffered. She suffered for her choices and she suffered for her inability to grieve.

"When I came up to Alaska, I was a spoiled rich girl. Before you say anything"—Patrice held up a hand—"I know I'm still a spoiled rich girl. But I was different."

Grier nodded unwilling to say anything that would stop her mother from telling the story she'd waited a lifetime to hear.

"I was part of this documentary crew and, frankly, I'd only joined it because I was bored and it was something to do. And then I got up here and something about this place spoke to me."

"It has a way of doing that."

"Barren and cold and so incredibly beautiful. I was captivated not only by the place itself, but by how different it was from anything I'd ever seen."

"It's a special place."

"Full of special people. I knew that when I met Jonas. And then I went and fell in love with him." Patrice reached down to play with her coffee cup, rotating it around its saucer by the handle.

"You did love him?"

"Oh God, yes. I loved him hard." Her mother looked up from her cup, her gaze inscrutable. "I suspect you now know what that means?"

Grier turned the words over in her mind and knew they fit. Knew they were the perfect description for the complex, crazy, incredible feelings she had for Mick.

"I do."

Patrice leaned across the table and reached for her hand. Her mother had always limited her attention and affection to simple pats and light kisses, so it was disconcerting to feel her tight grip.

"Then, darling, don't make the same mistake I did."

"Why?"

"Because Mick cares for you."

"I don't mean Mick. I mean why did you do it? All these years, why have you hidden the truth of my father from me? I can maybe understand it when I was young, but I'm a grown woman and have been for a while."

Patrice's gaze drifted to a small run in the tablecloth. With one manicured nail, she picked at the small loop. "I was so afraid."

"Of what? That he wasn't good enough?"

Her mother did look up at that. "No. Not that. Never that."

"But your letters." She thought about telling her mother about the conversation with Brett, but she held back. The revelation she'd read the love letters felt intrusive enough.

"I never once thought your father was beneath me. Quite the opposite, in fact. He was a brave adventurer, willing to see the world. What had I done? Nothing."

She said nothing in response, the reality of Patrice's side of the story another piece of information to take in and synthesize through all her assumptions.

"I was afraid of what I felt for him. Afraid I didn't have it in me to give that back. And," her mother continued, her laugh hard and brittle, "the truth of the matter is, I didn't."

"You don't know that."

"It doesn't matter what I think, Grier. Or who I thought I could be. I wasn't that person. I didn't make the choice when it counted. In the end, neither your father nor I did, and you paid the price. That's why I don't want to see you make the same mistake."

Grier laid her free hand over her mother's. "What if Mick doesn't love me back? He hasn't said anything along the lines of love."

"The man I saw in the lobby last night loves you fiercely."

"You saw us for two minutes."

"Grier," Patrice said, tightening her hand, "I only needed two seconds. I know I came in on something uncomfortable between the two of you, but the moment he saw me, he protected you. And you took comfort in that."

"He hasn't told me he loves me."

"Then you tell him."

"And if I'm wrong that we have what it takes?"

"Then you've done the brave thing and told him how you feel. And if he's a stubborn idiot who doesn't love you back, it's his loss."

Patrice reached for her hand again and Grier waited, curious to see something other than blatant self-assurance on her mother's face. "I've wronged you in so many ways and that was my own poor judgment. But know, I love you. I've loved you from the very first moment I knew about you. You come from the very best part of me. And you come from the only man I've ever loved."

Her mother's hand tightened reflexively as tears coursed down her cheeks. "Don't make the same mistake I did. Don't let the one you love walk away without a fight."

"But what if I don't have the words?"

"Just tell him what's in your heart."

Mary watched her grandson carry a stack of red filmy fabric, wrapped in bolts, into the town's community center. They always made sure the Valentine's decorations were done prior to the town hall meeting and she was anxious to get everything set up.

"Put them on the stage, darling." Mary pointed toward the small raised dais on the edge of the oversized meeting room.

"I'll get the rest of the decorations from the car. Be right back."

"Wait a minute, young man."

She saw the wary light hit his bright blue eyes at the command and smiled inwardly to herself.

This was going to be fun.

"You've been awfully quiet today."

"I've got a lot on my mind."

"The fight you had with Grier, no doubt."

"How'd you hear about that?"

Mary raised one lone eyebrow at him and stared down her nose. Despite the foot he had on her, she could still manage a dressing-down when she needed to. "It's hardly a secret. Especially when you start laying into the girl in the middle of a public place."

Mick shook his head and she saw the pain in the depths of his eyes.

"I am sorry my actions contributed to it. I understand Grier was shocked to see her mother."

"She laid into me pretty quick on that one."

"Did you not tell her I invited Patrice to be spiteful?"

"Hell no." Mick looked up sharply. "I wanted to tell her in person and I expected I'd have the time to do that. That's all."

"Did you tell Grier that?"

"I never got to it. We were focused on other things."

"Such as?"

"Like how we don't talk about things. The real things."

"Is that true?"

The miserable set of his shoulders and bleak coldness that filled his eyes had her heart breaking and all she really wanted to do was pull him close, but she kept her distance.

"Not intentionally, but yes, I suppose it is true."

"You've asked that girl to lay her soul bare to you, Michael Patrick O'Shaughnessy. And you didn't think you had to do the same?"

"I didn't want to spoil her with the shit that's come before. All the stuff with Mom. The piss-poor relationship with Dad. He and I are finally in a decent place, but it took us a long time to get there."

"All the more reason that she had a right to know. And has a right to know if you intend to make a life with her. Which," Mary said, keeping her gaze firm, "I presume you do since she's been sleeping out at your house every night."

"All that stuff is ancient history."

"No, it's your present and future if you keep giving it power over you."

Mary pulled him toward the rows of chairs set up for the night's meeting. She took a seat next to him and wrapped her arm around his broad shoulders. No matter how old he got—hell, no matter how old she got—it never ceased to amaze her that she'd once held him in her arms.

His blue eyes had blazed even then and his fist had wrapped so tightly around her finger.

Funny how in thirty-five years not much had changed. His eyes still blazed as he took in the world around him and he still locked down and didn't want to let go of the things he believed in.

"Do you love her?"

"Yes."

She pulled tight on his shoulders. "So what's so hard about saying it?"

"She hasn't said it. Hasn't even indicated she feels that way about me."

"She hasn't had it said to her all that often, from what I can tell. You have."

Mary could see the emotions flash across his face, but it was the final one—hope—that had her spirits lifting.

"Come on. Help me decorate. And you can work on how you're going to go find that woman and tell her how you feel about her."

Chapter Twenty-four

Grier glanced down at the three plastic bags in her hand and took a deep breath.

It was now or never.

"You ready?" Sloan smiled at her, her blue gaze bright with love and support.

"I think so."

Avery pulled her close for a hug. "I know so."

Grier handed a bag to each of them, keeping the third for herself. "Okay. Let's do it."

The town had to walk past the hotel before reaching the meeting center and people began trickling into the lobby as it grew closer to seven.

Chooch and Hooch were the first to arrive, quickly followed by Jess and Jack and Kate.

"I love what you're doing." Kate pulled her in for a hard hug.

"Thank you."

"Jason approves, too." Kate smiled as she stepped back from the embrace. "He sends his wholehearted support from New York."

"When do you leave?"

"I'll be there next weekend."

Grier was distracted as more people piled into the lobby and Kate gave her a warm grin before turning to help. "We'll talk more before I go."

Ten minutes later, Avery held out her coat. "I swear, there's nothing this town loves more than a juicy secret."

"That went fast." Grier glanced at her empty bag and the matched empties that dangled from Sloan's and Avery's fingertips.

From behind her back, Sloan produced the fourth bag. "And here's yours. Come on. Let's go."

Grier shrugged into her coat and then linked arms with her friends. "Thanks for your help. Now we just have to hope I don't crash and burn in horrible flames."

"Let's not tell her about our bet," Avery said in a loud, deliberate whisper as they walked toward the door.

"Okay," Sloan agreed, equally loudly.

"Bet?" Grier screeched, then winced at her own voice. "You bet on me?"

"Damn straight we bet on you." Sloan moved them determinedly toward the door. "And I'm quite confident in the outcome."

Mick knew it was small of him, but he was perfectly content to hide out in the meeting center's kitchenette with a cup of coffee as all of Indigo filed in for their monthly town hall meeting.

As mayor, Walker's grandmother, Sophie, ran the meetings on a tight schedule, and the pre-meeting rumbling had hit a fever pitch. He threw his cup away and walked back into the hall. Of its own accord, his gaze scanned the room for Grier and his stomach tightened when a full sweep produced no sign of her.

Maybe it was for the best.

He had no interest in laying his feelings bare for the entire town. What he had to say to her needed to be said in private. He snagged his usual seat in the middle of the room, next to Walker, and hoped the agenda was a short one.

Sloan sat to Walker's left and Avery was next to her. They both smiled at him, their bright grins far more supportive than he'd have expected after the fight he'd had with Grier.

Not that it mattered all that much. It was Grier's support he had to win.

As Sophie rapped the gavel to order, his thoughts drifted to what he was going to say and how.

A man had to work his way up to "I love you," after all. The words didn't just come pouring out of their own accord.

Sophie opened the meeting with an update on some proposed town improvements and then shifted gears into the upcoming Valentine's dinner dance. In a town drunk on love, the grandmothers supported that event with almost as much gusto as their annual bachelor competition.

"Does anyone have anything to add to the motion?"

Mick tuned back into the meeting when Kate Winston, who sat across the aisle from him, raised her hand and stood. Kate was notoriously quiet, so the fact she had even raised her hand was a surprise. He turned to stare at her, more than curious as to what she was going to say, when something hit him in the shoulder.

As he turned to see what it was, something hit him from behind as well. A white paper floated toward the ground from where it ricocheted off his shoulder and he reached for it.

A paper airplane?

As he pulled it closer, he could see writing on the wing.

OPEN ME.

Kate was forgotten as he opened the piece of paper. And his heart stopped as he read the words.

I'M SORRY.

On a heavy thud, his heart started up again, triple its usual speed. Walker handed over the second airplane and Mick saw writing on its wing as well. Opening the paper, he read more printed words.

CAN YOU FORGIVE ME?

A light noise started to rumble through the hall as more paper headed his way, the folded airplanes coming at him from all directions. Mick stood and turned in a circle, taking in the town assembled around him.

And then he couldn't see anything else as Grier stood at the back of the hall and walked down the center aisle toward him. Her face held a solemn expression he couldn't read as the urge to touch her nearly overwhelmed him.

She stopped a few rows away and produced a pink airplane from behind her back. With swift, efficient movements, she sent it sailing straight toward him where it landed in the middle of his chest.

Mick caught it before it could hit the ground, and Grier smiled for the first time.

"Open it."

As he unraveled the neatly folded paper, he saw more words printed inside.

I LOVE YOU.

The words swelled in his chest and came out before he could even think to hold them back. There was nothing to work up to because the words were simply there.

"I love you, too."

Grier moved forward then and he opened his arms to pull her close.

"I love you, Mick."

"Kiss her!" Hooch's unmistakable shout came from his perch in the front row.

"We have a lot to work out," he whispered softly.

"Do you want to work it out?"

"God yes."

"Then kiss me before Sophie has to rap her gavel for order."

Mick smiled, the pain and anxiety that had filled him for days evaporating. She'd beaten him to the punch, declaring her love first, but he didn't mind.

Grier was here. She was in his arms. And she loved him.

If she asked him to, he could fly.

Epilogue

Mary let out a small sigh at the satisfying sound of a popped cork. "How'd you swipe that out of the hotel?"

"I swiped nothing," Julia said in mock horror as she puttered around her kitchen, grabbing glasses and small appetizer plates as she went. "Avery's a good girl who's willing to share her stash of Rothschild."

Julia carried the bottle and glasses over to the table and lined up her wedding crystal. She diligently pulled it out each and every week for their girls' night in. Mary could never stop the small twinge that had her wishing Julia would toast someone other than her girlfriends with the glasses.

"So, I want to go first." Sophie picked up her glass as soon as Julia had finished pouring.

Mary and Julia lifted their glasses.

"Two down and one to go."

"Sophie!" Julia hushed her. "Don't jinx it."

"It's not a jinx if it's true." Sophie's retort was quick and absolute.

"Oh, don't put on your mayor voice," Mary admonished her. "Julia's right. Avery and Roman need all the good mojo they can get."

"If it's even supposed to be the two of them." Julia stared into her wine. "She is going to Ireland."

"She's meant for Roman." Sophie's voice remained resolutely stubborn. "She can't end up with anyone else."

Julia shrugged, but Mary understood the concern. She'd had more than a few tense moments worrying about Mick and Grier. These things weren't guaranteed, no matter how right you thought something was.

"When it's meant to be, it's meant to be," Sophie persisted. "Like Mick and Grier. I kept one of the paper airplanes, by the way."

"I did, too," Julia said.

"Me, too." Mary giggled. "And aren't we a bunch of hopeless romantics?"

"Hopeful, Mary," Julia said quickly. "Hopeful."

"To hopeful." Mary raised her glass.

"Speaking of hopeful . . ." Sophie clinked her glass before turning thoughtful. "Has Grier heard from Kate? I'm glad to see something good happen for that girl."

Mary related all she knew. "A few days ago. She's enjoying New York and having fun getting to know Jason."

"Do we see another wedding on the horizon?"

"Grier said they're taking it slow. Kate's staying in her apartment as she and Jason get to know each other." Before Julia could say anything, Mary added, "The milk's still free, but the girl's got enough sense to learn how to be by herself, too."

"Oh, Mary, get off your high horse." Julia poked her in the ribs. "You didn't exactly close down the dairy when you and Charlie were dating."

Mary poked her back. "Of course I didn't. This is Alaska. You have to find some way to stay warm."

"So, how are Grier and Mick?"

"He's helping her get Jonas's house fixed up now that she's moved in with him. Mick and Jack have been interviewing pilots and they've found someone. And Grier's tax business seems to be thriving. Everyone's delighted they don't have to leave Indigo to get the help of an accountant."

"So the new pilot's going to rent the house when he gets here?" Julia took a sip of her wine. "That's great."

"*She's* going to rent the house."

"Mick and Jack are hiring a woman pilot?"

"Yep."

"Maggie must be beside herself."

"She doesn't know yet."

Sophie practically rubbed her hands together with glee. "So we know first."

"Yep." Mary nodded proudly. "I say we keep it a secret until she arrives. Have a little fun with it."

The three of them clinked glasses again. "Hear, hear." Sophie nodded firmly. "It'll give us a head start."

"Head start?" Julia said. "Head start on what?"

"We need to find her a bachelor."

Continue reading for a preview of the next
Alaskan Nights romance,

Just in Time

Coming from Signet Eclipse
in August 2013

$\mathcal{A}$very watched Sloan walk down the aisle of the small A-frame nondenominational church that dominated one end of Main Street and thought she'd never seen a more radiant bride. But it was Walker's incandescent smile as the bride's and groom's gazes met that would have caused any woman to sigh in ecstasy.

Grier reached over and squeezed her hand, a bright smile shining through her tears. Avery squeezed back, the sappy feelings that had filled her back in her room winging through her chest again in a heady rush.

So why the hell—in the middle of a moment of sweet, glorious perfection—did she clamp her eyes on her ex-boyfriend?

Roman stared back at her, his green gaze as compelling as it was when she was sixteen. Add in the fact that all six feet, four inches of him was decked out in a custom-fit tuxedo, and her traitorous body gave a leap of appreciation that wasn't quite appropriate for church.

One dark eyebrow lifted over those emerald green eyes in silent challenge, and Avery fought the urge to stick out her tongue.

Damn the man—he'd make a stripper blush, with those bedroom eyes and the thick, luscious hair that just begged to be mussed.

And wasn't that the problem?

Everything was way too easy for Roman and it always had been.

It had just taken her too long to understand that fact.

Dragging her gaze away, Avery focused on the bride. Grier took her flowers as Sloan stood beside Walker, and Avery quickly refluffed the train so it lay evenly on the aisle.

Jobs completed, she and Grier met the groomsmen, Mick and Roman, and they escorted them the few brief steps to their front-pew seats. Roman grasped her arm and it took everything inside her to keep her gaze straight and her smile firmly fixed as the entire town of Indigo looked on with interest.

"You look beautiful."

Avery swallowed hard at the warm breath in her ear, those inconvenient feelings rising once more in her clenched belly.

"Thank you."

She took her seat, the words playing over and over in her mind.

So many images stood out in her memories of the two of them, but the one at the top of the list was the year they began to notice each other as more than friends. Roman had whispered in her ear in the middle of a soccer match on the town square. He'd told her where to line up a shot and she'd nearly melted into a puddle as his words skittered down her spine, light as feathers and as powerful as an avalanche.

The sensation had taken her so off guard—because of a mixture of inexperience and the sudden change in a relationship she'd had since grade school—that she'd pushed him away with a smart-ass retort. But she'd thought about his words long into the night as she lay wrapped up in her tiny bed in the back room of her mother's house.

Clearly not much had changed in eighteen years.

"You ready?"

Avery felt Grier's quick poke to her thigh and realized she'd nearly missed her cue. She and Grier returned to the altar to help Sloan with her dress, then moved to the side as Mick and Roman stepped forward to flank Walker.

Mick produced two shining platinum bands from his vest pocket and laid them on the reverend's open Bible.

Avery watched with rapt fascination as Walker slid the band effortlessly onto Sloan's finger, and moments later when her friend returned the gesture. And when the couple kissed for the first time as husband and wife, the entire church let out a communal cheer.

Walker and Sloan began their walk back down the aisle and Mick and Grier followed. It was only when Roman took her arm once more to begin their procession through church that a thin layer of panic seized her throat.

Broad smiles greeted them as they moved down the

aisle, their progress slow as many guests stopped Walker and Sloan with hugs. Hooch even threw Avery an over-sized wink that his wife, Chooch, responded to with an equally oversized elbow to his stomach.

Roman seemed oblivious as they walked, his arm locked steadily with hers. She snuck a glance at his chiseled profile and—miracle of miracles—it looked as though he'd missed Chooch and Hooch's antics. As if sensing her attention, he turned with a smile.

"I haven't felt this on display since I did a calendar shoot for charity."

Avery involuntary sucked in a breath. She'd seen that calendar when someone had bought a copy for Su-san, her boss at the hotel. She'd even given herself per-mission to go look at it late one night when she was manning the front desk by herself.

Long ropes of muscles accentuated his arms from shoulder to wrist, and thick ridges sculpted his abdo-men. He'd always been well built, but the man that stared back at her from the photograph, wearing noth-ing but a strategically placed towel, took her breath away.

He was magnificent.

A warrior.

And he had been as foreign to her as if a stranger had stared back from the page.

Pulling herself from the heated memory, Avery just shrugged as those inconvenient flutters once again filled her stomach. "Small towns."

A slight smile grooved his cheeks as he leaned in. "So why don't we really give them something to talk about?"

"What's that supposed to mean?" Her hiss was low enough not to be heard by anyone else, but no one in the remaining pews between them and the door would miss the fury in her eyes.

"If you're so worried about what everyone thinks, let's make it worth their while. Have a little fun."

"I'm not worried about what people think."

Fresh air greeted them as they finally made their way through the doors of the church, and Avery dragged her arm from his.

"Could have fooled me."

Avery flung a hand in the direction of the church, even as she stomped across the small front lawn to give them some privacy. "Did you not miss how on display we were in there? The exuberant winks and broad grins, everyone so delighted we were walking down that aisle together? Like *we* were the ones getting married."

Roman couldn't resist poking at her a bit more. "Cupids in their eyes and all that shit."

"Exactly!"

"Which was all I was really pointing out." He kept his tone reasonable, but no matter how hard he tried, he couldn't hold back a grin.

"You were talking about sex and that's something else entirely."

"You've got a dirty mind."

"And you weren't talking about sex, Mr. Big Shot Hockey Player?"

"While I never turn down sex with a beautiful woman, no, that's not what I was talking about." He'd turned down plenty of sex, but Roman decided he didn't quite need to share that tidbit. Instead, he moved closer to Avery, intrigued when she held her ground. "I was actually talking about a little slow dancing. A few whispers in corners. Maybe even a well-placed kiss or two. You know, all the things people expect from the single members of the wedding party."

"This dress is not a neon sign for sex, despite what conventional wisdom—and *Cosmo* magazine—suggests."

"And there you go, right back into the gutter again."

As if suddenly realizing how close they stood, she moved back, but he didn't miss the light flush that suffused her chest and face.

"We're going to behave like civilized adults. Just because we have a past the entire town knows about doesn't mean we have a present. We can be nice and cordial to each other."

"I agree."

"You do?"

"Sure." He shrugged, deliberately casual, even as a flash of something very much like a flaming sword to his guts ripped through him. "You've got a new boyfriend you're all excited about. I'm big enough to wish you well and want what's best for you."

Whatever smart-ass remark was about to come out of her mouth—and he knew Avery Marks well enough to know there was going to be one—floated away on a light stammer. "You . . . do?"

"Of course."

The urge to rip something apart—preferably the Irishman he pictured in his mind—gripped him, but

Roman refused to show it. He'd spent far too long in the spotlight, hiding what he really thought about things in favor of what was politically expedient. He'd be damned if he didn't put the skill to good use now.

"Well, good, then."

Her wide-eyed stare didn't waver and Roman saw the effort she was making to shift gears, but he kept the stupid, fucking *understanding* smile pasted on his face.

A loud shout from the direction of the receiving line broke the moment between them, and Avery turned back toward the church. "I'd better go see if Sloan needs anything."

"You do that."

"I'll see you at the reception."

"Count on it."

Roman watched her go, her long, lean frame filling out the dark red silk to perfection.

And only then did he let his smile drop.

Also available from
Addison Fox

Baby It's Cold Outside
An Alaskan Nights Novel

When Grier Thompson is called to Indigo, Alaska, to
deal with the estate of her late, estranged father, she
meets pilot Mick O'Shaughnessy, a rugged dream
guy. But then an unexpected visitor from Grier's past
unsettles the entire town. By the time Mick comes
out of the clouds to realize he's fallen head over heels
in love, it might be just too late to win Grier's heart.

**"I cannot wait to return to the
wonderful town of Indigo, Alaska."
—Romance Junkies**

New York Times bestselling author

JoAnn Ross

SEA GLASS WINTER
A Shelter Bay Novel

As an Explosive Ordnance Disposal Specialist, Dillon Slater had one of the most dangerous jobs in the military. Now, he's enjoying the pace of life in Shelter Bay, where he teaches high school physics. He still gets to blow things up, but as the school basketball coach he also gets to impart leadership skills. His latest minefield: fifteen-year-old Matt Templeton—and Matt's irresistible mother…

Available wherever books are sold or at
penguin.com

facebook.com/LoveAlwaysBooks

LuAnn McLane

PITCH PERFECT
The Cricket Creek Series

Mia Monroe is done being Daddy's little rich girl. Buying an old car with the last of her money, she sets out for who knows where—until her clunker clunks out in Cricket Creek. With no plan and no credit cards, Mia has to find more resilience than she's ever needed before. And a little help from an attractive new acquaintance wouldn't hurt…

As first baseman for the Cricket Creek Cougars, Cameron Patrick has two jobs: win games and stay out of trouble. If he can do both, he might just make it back to the minor leagues. He knows Mia is trouble from the moment she catches his eye—but he can't stop looking. And maybe her kind of trouble is exactly what he needs.

"No one does Southern love like LuAnn McLane."
—Romance Dish